Isaac's Gun – An American Tale
By: Dan Strawn
ISBN: 978-1-927134-56-6

Bluewood Publishing Ltd
Christchurch, 8441, New Zealand
www.bluewoodpublishing.com

D1521697

Isaac's Gun –
An American Tale

by

Dan Strawn

Acknowledgments

Thanks to my writing friends: John and Louise Beckman, Fred Benton, Linda Odenborg, Herb Stokes, Iola Trautmann, and Helen Whitworth. They provided invaluable input and critical support in the writing of *Isaac's Gun – An American Tale.*

Thanks to my Clark College writing mentor, Debbie Guyol. She helped me bridge the gap between a lifetime of business writing and the nuances of the creative writing process.

Thanks to Bluewood Publishing. Their willingness to take on *Isaac's Gun* gives me a venue for reaching my audience—every writer's dream.

Thanks to friend and editor, Kristina Chilian. In addition to providing the panache that makes my work professional, she added breadth to the story of *Isaac's Gun – An American Tale,* and she taught me critical lessons about the writing craft and storytelling.

Thanks to unmentioned family and friends for their obvious enthusiasm and support.

Mostly, thanks to the women in my life: my wife, Sandi—she knows why, the cadre of aunts who populated my shelf with books on every childhood birthday or Christmas, my Grandmother Higgins, at whose knee I learned the nuances of good storytelling, and my mother—whose legacy rests in the creative efforts of her three sons.

For Beth

Enjoy!

(Don Strause

PROLOGUE
October 5, 2006

Megan stopped in front of the door with the frosted glass window. The serif letters on the glass confirmed she was at the appointed office: Thomas, Mathews, & Thomas, Attorneys At Law. She opened the door and entered.

The décor was as she expected: old family. The paintings on the walls were oils and watercolors, all originals. The only exception was on the wall behind the receptionist, a well framed Ansel Adams print of Yosemite Falls. The office furniture was of solid oak; the settee and divan covered in brownish-red leather. Even the receptionist fit in, with her well-appointed business suit, her classy yet somehow conservative platinum-to-hide-the-gray hairdo, and her age – late forties to early fifties. The interior decorator must have provided her as part of the furnishings.

Megan introduced herself. The receptionist picked up the phone and buzzed a back office.

"Miss Holcomb is here. She has a one-thirty appointment."

Megan looked at her watch: 1:18. Oh well, better early than late.

The receptionist hung up, looked at her and smiled. "Won't you have a seat? Mr Thomas will be right with you."

Megan sank into the leather settee, grabbed the copy of Fresno State Magazine on the end table and began thumbing through it. She had yet to find anything of interest when a tall, aged, and portly man came out of the hall behind the receptionist. He talked as he walked.

"Miss Holcomb, thanks for coming. I'm George Thomas, your grandfather's attorney."

She laid down the magazine and stood up just in time to take his outstretched hand. The gentle but firm clasp enveloped her fingers without jamming his hand into the fork between her thumb and index finger. It gave away his upbringing and his generation, and it went well with the sparse gray hair, the bifocals, and the three piece, dark blue, expensive, probably Brooks Brothers suit.

"I suppose you have heard it before, but I'm taken by your resemblance to your grandmother. Oh, it had been a few years since her hair and complexion matched yours, but those emerald green eyes—they never lost their youthful sparkle."

Megan smiled. "Yes, I've been told before, but never tire of hearing it. I'm sorry I couldn't be here when you met with the rest of my family. I was out of the country and came as soon as I could finish up my work."

"No apologies necessary. These things never happen at a convenient time." He let go of her hand, stood aside, took her arm and gently urged her towards the hallway behind the receptionist. "Let's go sit down. Would you like coffee, tea?"

"No, no, perhaps a glass of water."

George ushered her into a small conference room and directed her to a chair at a rectangular, cherry wood table that could easily sit four people at each side. "We'll be more comfortable in here. I'll just be a moment."

While George was out of the room, Megan surveyed the décor, which reflected a more relaxed attitude than the foyer. Photographs, mainly of family, decorated the walls. Complementary photos of orange groves that nestled under the mantle of snowy High Sierra peaks hung to the right and left of the doorway.

The receptionist came in with two bottles of Perrier. She put some ice in a glass and presented one of the bottles and the glass to Megan. "Let me know if you need anything else," she said. Before Megan could do more than say thank you, the receptionist smiled and left the room. All efficiency, that lady, Megan thought.

George entered carrying a briefcase. Not one of the old-style, leather valise types, but a latter-day version: rigid, rectangular, made of space-age metals and plastics. Probably a Samsonite, Megan thought. George punched the intercom on the phone. "Jackie, I'm going to need the 'Martin Holcomb' file. Thanks."

He sat down opposite Megan. "So," he said, "tell me what you were doing in, where was it, Prague? That would be Czechoslovakia."

Megan hesitated while she chose her words. "The Czech Republic actually. Czechoslovakia came down right after the Iron Curtain. It became two countries: the Czech Republic and Slovakia."

"Hmm, seems like I remember something about that. I was good at geography in my day. A world war, the Iron Curtain coming and going, colonialism pretty much a thing of the past, I can't keep up with it. Never have figured out what became of the Belgian Congo. But I was correct? It was Prague?"

"Oh, yes. And I didn't mean to be so precise. It's just, that's what I was doing in Prague. That is, delving into the post-World War Two situation in Czechoslovakia when Communism collapsed."

He looked at her through the top of his bifocals. It caused his chin to dip towards his throat, giving a suggestion that he was passing judgment on her.

"And what university are you at?"

"Stanford. I did my undergraduate and graduate work at Berkeley. Hopefully, my doctorate is less than a year away."

Jackie, a younger version of the receptionist, entered and deposited a folder and a gray cardboard box on the table. George thanked her and picked up the thick folder that Megan thought must be the requested 'Martin Holcomb file'.

"Unlike the ranchers who became millionaires when the inland empire south of Los Angeles filled with people, your grandparents shunned retirement in Palm Springs or Scottsdale. I have been your grandparents' attorney ever since they moved their orchard operations to the Central Valley, where agriculture is still king. As their executor, I have to dispose of the particulars of your grandfather's instructions to me." He opened the folder and took out the top piece of paper. "You must have been very important to him. Martin's instructions with regards to your inheritance, such as it is, were explicit. He always was a stickler for details, and your case is no exception. Are you sure you wouldn't want coffee or tea? A soft drink perhaps?"

I wonder, Megan thought, *would he be offering me something stiffer, something appropriate for the shot glasses on the bar, if I were a grandson rather than a granddaughter? Probably, given his age, given the generation he came from. Perhaps I unfairly stereotype him. Maybe he doesn't want any of his clients less than alert when he is going over details.*

"No. No, thank you. Water is fine."

"I feel obliged to tell you your grandmother's and grandfather's wills each stipulated you would be delivered these materials only when they were both gone."

"I appreciate knowing. I…" She felt the wet film her eyes, felt the air escape, sensed the involuntary brush of her fingers on her cheeks. "I always saw them as a single entity. In a way, I have a feeling it's better now…with them together." Before George could respond, she eked out in a whisper, "Thank you for telling me."

George turned to the bar behind him, retrieved a small package of tissues and pushed them her way.

"I always have a supply of these around. There's a frequent need in times like these."

Megan retrieved a tissue, wiped her cheeks and mouthed another soft *thank you.*

He was moved. She saw it by his involuntary lean towards the table, towards her, and by the subdued and controlled tone he used when he spoke.

"I know you were important in their lives. Why don't we get on with it?"

"Yes, why don't we?"

George cast his eyes to the paper in his hands.

"Except for relatively small amounts left to your grandparents' alma maters, all their assets, including their controlling interests in the orange, olive, and walnut ranches, have been deeded to your father and your Uncle Robert and Aunt Rachel. The grandchildren received only minor items, ones that in your grandparents' eyes had sentimental value. Like you, your brother and your cousins have already enjoyed the benefit of your grandparents' forethought and generosity. They provided for each of your undergraduate college expenses. I understand your brother and a cousin are still in college?"

"Yes, I—we—are grateful for the money my grandparents put up for our college tuition."

"Yes, good. Your grandparents gave me this briefcase and gray box. They told me their contents represent an unfinished work—a legacy—one your grandfather started but laid aside after he married your grandmother. He had the best of intentions, that is, to make something of these journals—" George reached into the box and pulled out a black book speckled with white, the kind Megan had purchased at college bookstores to record class or lab notes. "But, as he put it, 'before I knew it, living a life took all my energy.' This is the oldest of your grandfather's diaries. Some of them are leather bound, but not this one. He has bequeathed to you all the diaries, there are five, and another seven written by your great-great grandfather. Your great-great grandfather's writings are in varying degrees of legibility, what with the time that has passed and the rigors of his life, but not your grandfather's. Your grandfather took care to protect what he had written.

"He wasn't always a rancher. He held a degree in journalism, you know. And the other journals, those of your grandmother's grandfather, he lacked the training, but your grandparents said he was more than capable of recording the events and happenings of his life. Perhaps..." George paused. Megan leaned closer, hanging onto his next words. "...your inheritance involves more than what is in the box and the briefcase. Perhaps your gift for writing and research came to you from both sides of your grandparents' ancestries."

"I know. Granddad took great interest in my schoolwork, and I've seen enough of his writing in letters to the editor to know he was adept at putting words on paper."

"That he was, and he and your grandmother, they were explicit that you, only you, would decide whether the final form of this work was to be one of scholarly worth, a family memoir, or published for the public. In addition to the journals, you will receive the contents of this briefcase. I have the combination of the lock and will give it to you before you leave. Your grandparents asked that you not open the briefcase until you have read your grandfather's journals. They felt you would appreciate its contents only when you knew the story."

George handed Megan the journal. She grasped it without taking her eyes off of him. Again, her eyes filled with tears. It wasn't that she expected anything of great value; paying the four years at Berkeley was, in Megan's mind, more than she could have ever hoped.

She knew about the journals, had even sneaked a peek now and again. She had always felt that buried somewhere in those pages she would find a magic potion, a hidden talisman, or prophecy that would explain the aura that surrounded her grandparents when they were together. To have these journals in her possession touched her. She smiled through tears, then wiped them away.

"Thank you, I didn't think this would catch me this way. It's been five weeks since I heard about Granddad."

* * * *

Three quarters of an hour later, Megan piled the box and the briefcase into the back seat of her '97 Honda Civic and headed down Shaw Avenue. She merged onto Highway 99. Forty or so miles south of Fresno, she took the offramp and made her way through Visalia, then to her parents' orange ranch, eighty acres nestled at the base of Sequoia National Park's ten thousand foot peaks just outside of Exeter.

She had been in Europe for the better part of ten months. The reunion with her parents included the hugs, kisses, and excitement that always attended her return home. Her brother, Sean, was in the middle of exams at Cal Poly San Luis Obispo, and couldn't make it home.

"But he promised to be here for the weekend," her mom said.

That night, they drove over to her Uncle Robert's olive farm in Lindsay. He and his daughter were the only two living there since Robert's divorce. Robert's youngest son was flying jets off the deck of an aircraft carrier somewhere in the Indian Ocean, and his older daughter was hitting the books at UCLA. Not long after they arrived, Rachel and Dave, and more cousins and their spouses, arrived to share in the family camaraderie. They barbecued steaks in the backyard, drank air-cooled California cabernet, remembered their grandparents, and relived the great times of their youth.

The clock was pushing midnight by the time they returned to Exeter. Climbing between the sheets and falling asleep with the aroma of oranges outside her window pulled the childhood memories of Hacienda Del O'Toole, her grandparents' ranch in Southern California, into the present.

The next morning she vanquished the red wine headache with her mom's strong black French roast coffee and a toasted bagel with orange marmalade. After breakfast and after her parents left for their days' activities, she retrieved the box and the briefcase from her car and brought them into the dining room. She poured a fresh cup of coffee and picked up the top journal in the box, the oldest one, George Thomas had said.

Megan sipped from her cup and opened to the first page. Except for a single hand-penned paragraph, the page was blank.

Carefully, she read these first words. Why, she wondered, did he choose to make this single entry on the opening page? She sipped her coffee, while she contemplated, then ran her eyes over the short paragraph and read the entry once more:

February 23, 1943

By the middle of February, the Japanese had evacuated all that was left of the Guadalcanal force. Honshu and Tokyo lay beyond the horizon, some three thousand miles away, but Henderson Field was ours.

She ran the date through her head—sixty-three years and then some since her grandfather wrote the words. Thoughts of him triggered emotions that threatened to lay siege to her composure. She waited a moment, allowed herself time to conjure the familiar rush, the one that comes with impending discovery, and turned the page.

Part 1

I watch the fan and listen to the mockingbird, the one that sang in the wings of night's stage while I, like a leaf caught in an eddy, twirled stage center in alternating spells of semi-consciousness and opiate visions.

Sunday, March 7, 1943
War Casualty

I stare at the ceiling and force myself to think about how falling snow used to close school, and I would lose myself for a day or two in adventure stories. In the blizzard year, the year I turned twelve, I sat by the window and watched the snow drifts while I worked my way through *Treasure Island*, *White Fang*, and the big-game hunter's autobiography, the one that devoted a whole chapter to attacks on people by predators—lions and leopards mostly, an occasional hyena or wild dog. At the moment of the attack, all the book's victims felt fear, but no pain and no clear memory of the attacks themselves, even as claws and teeth ripped through flesh and bone. "Nature's way," the author speculated, "of minimizing death for the prey of predators."

Is that what's working in me, nature's way with prey? Is that why the attack comes to me only in vignettes—flashes of recollection between bouts of searing pain? Perhaps. Perhaps nature consigned me to the brotherhood of gnus and zebras when the mortar's fractured fragments ripped into my body. Perhaps my prey psyche took control, blocked out the snarling slayer, absolved me from the horror of the cold-steel fang that pinned me to the ground. Perhaps. Perhaps that's why only now, weeks after, I find myself in the middle of cool San Diego nights, my finger on the button that brings a nurse with brief respite in a needle.

I reach up to my shoulder and caress the bandage that covers the carnage from the bayonet's thrust. I push, feel a twinge shoot up my neck; push harder and quit before the sparkling stars in the back of my eyes explode. I lie back, wipe wet globules off my forehead, shutting my eyes to ward off the pain. For a heartbeat, visions of jungle combat upstage the stars, allowing me a glimpse of war's bounty, warriors' commission. The stars recede. The present returns. I use the pain-free interlude to contemplate my fate.

I think about marines, sailors, and soldiers who stay in the hospital at Pearl. How they are either close to death or able to undergo a quick fix and return to the front. How the rest of us, the lucky ones, alive but unable to see regular duty ever, or at least anytime soon, are ferried to the mainland as afterthoughts—ballast maybe—on airplanes and ships.

I call up images: the belly of a Navy cargo plane, a corpsman attending me and five other stretcher cases, ominous wooden crates, cardboard boxes with pictures of Phillip Morris decorating their sides, a Navy ambulance—vague visions during brief breaks from numbing pain, dipping in and out of consciousness.

I lie in sweat-soaked sheets. Thoughts ricochet off shards of white heat that slice through my brain. Then, relief. Breathing that came in gasps returns to normal. I grapple with panic, with hopelessness, with fear, push them away and force myself to acknowledge this lull, this lucid moment.

The quick grating sound of steel on flint; I turn my head and watch the leatherneck captain light up a cigarette with his Zippo. Smoke drifts out of his nose. He inhales and slides the lighter under his pillow; the smoke retreats down his throat. He holds it there. Seconds. Long enough for me to recite the ditty that pops up in my head; LSMFT—Lucky Strike Means Fine Tobacco. He smiles, as if he read the words in my mind, then laughs. Smoke chugs out of his mouth in little puffs. Another ditty, the little engine that could – I think I can, I think I can. I laugh.

We both laugh. Neither one of us knows why. At least I don't. It just beats the hollowness that is slowly turning me inside out. He takes another long drag, tilts his head back, sending a procession of smoke rings towards the ceiling.

We direct our attention to the door, watching it swing open. The captain's face registers disappointment—not Nurse

Carol. Nurse Betty, fat Betty, waddles through the door. An orderly carrying a bedpan squeezes in behind her before the self-closing door slams shut.

"Owooo!" Someone lets out a wolf call. The captain snaps up a Lucky and holds the pack out as Nurse Betty passes by. She slaps his hand without stopping. "You know I don't smoke!" She hip-sways her way down the center of the room and disappears out the far door. He pulls the pack back, tucks it under his pillow, rolls over and pulls one last deep draw, sending the smoke in a steady stream to the ceiling. The orderly stops and looks for the source of the howl.

Words waft through gauze that covers all but the eyes on the face of a stricken sailor.

"Not you, stupid—her."

I hear scattered snickers. The orderly's face flushes; he takes up Nurse Betty's trail. As he flees, another "Owooo!" followed by laughter and crude remarks. I watch him disappear and ease back on the mattress.

Nerves send searing messages. Fright flitters up and invades my lungs. Breathing is an effort. A moment of respite. I force my mind off the present, compel it to wander back to a safer time and place – my senior year at the University of Idaho in Moscow. Graduation in the spring, a degree in journalism with a minor in languages. Emphasis—German.

German—that's what brought me to Elaine.

Pain, morphine's alter ego, knocks at my mind's back door.

German—that's what should have sent me to Europe after Pearl Harbor.

A sliver shoots up from my back. I straighten my legs and arch my back. The pain retreats. I lie flat on my Navy mattress.

Elaine. German, and Elaine and studying the musical words of Goethe in his native tongue. More pain. Try moving my legs without arching my back. There. Gratitude fills me, floods me with relief.

Elaine and Goethe. A hillside south and east of the UI campus. The smell of wild flowers in May. Goethe and Kant and Remarque's *Im Westen Nichts*, and Mozart's biography written in his native tongue. Elaine and wildflowers—syringas and camas, and little white daisy-like things. The smell and touch and taste of Elaine. Below us: Moscow. Moscow and the First Presbyterian Church we'll both attend on Sunday.

"Oh shit! Where's the nurse?" I fumble for the button. Press the button. Press the button. Press the button! "God damn it! Bring me morphine for the pain!"

* * * *

I've heard that coming off a drug overdose is like waking up after drinking all night in a smoke-filled bar. Never drank all night in a smoke-filled bar. I do know that waking up from my last shot of morphine was peaceful. No headache, no bloodshot eyes, just a feeling of detached, don't-give-a-shit awareness of where I am.

The large fan that hangs down from the ceiling is out of balance. I watch each slow, shaky rotation of the blades. I watch the fan and listen to the mockingbird, the one that sang in the wings of night's stage while I, like a leaf caught in an eddy, twirled stage center in alternating spells of semi-consciousness and opiate visions. It's morning; he's stage center now, his voice full-throttled, his repertoire unoriginal and repetitious. I listen and watch the blades spin and wobble. Before long, that bird's incessant singing, his gift of mimicry, intrigues me. We don't have birds like that in Idaho. In Idaho, only sparrows sounded like sparrows, only jays sounded like jays. The mockingbird arias arouse my curiosity.

I raise my head. The barren bed that butts up to the far wall under the wooden casement window is freshly made up. Where did the sailor with the gauze mask go? I can't see out the window. I lift up on my elbows for a better look. For brief seconds, before the twinge in my back awakens my fear, I study the eucalyptus trees lining the field beyond the hospital grounds. I lie flat and wait for the twinge to surge and become that mind numbing hurt that sends me clawing for the button.

I twist on the mattress a fraction to tempt the twinge, bait the surge. I push the mockingbird out of my mind and focus on the pain. I twist again, harder this time and feel it. Not mature pain; instead—adolescent pain, tolerable pain.

My fingers brush past the adhesive tape on my right side and I touch fresh bandages. The act of discovery causes me to wince from my mutilated shoulder, and I feel new sources of hurt underneath the fresh dressing that covers my lower right back above my kidney, the one the doctors wanted to let heal before they did anything more. Cognition comes slowly, and when it does, I am washed with newfound optimism. They have removed the last of the shrapnel; I'm going to get well.

Wednesday, March 17, 1943
Recuperation

The days stretch into nights, the days and nights into a week, the week into a fortnight. Each day brings more consciousness and less pain, but cramps, chills, chattering teeth and wild imaginings. Nurse Carol tells me it's the morphine. "Doc's pulling you down," she says. "A little less each day. Painful now, but you'll thank us in the end." I buy the cramps and shakes part, but combat demons live deep in the catacombs of my mind. They stand in the stairwell, anarchists, waiting for their cue, chaffing to create chaos, anxious to disrupt the order of my peaceful state.

Between shakes and spasms and feral bouts of fear when visions boil up day and night, I'm up, mostly walking to the head, sometimes out on the steps, then back down the hall. No more living through the indignity of crapping in a bed pan and lying there while a corpsman or, God forbid, one of the nurses cleans up. Showers are still out. I continue to live with what the Captain calls whores' baths—a washcloth, soap, water in a pan and a towel. I can now take care of this myself, except for my back.

Whenever they change my dressings, Nurses Carol and Betty knead new life into both muscles and mind with magic fingers, soap, and warm, wet wash cloths. Their goal is to scrub away the dead skin and dirt, but the resulting back rubs help keep the loneliness at bay.

* * * *

Today, I venture outside and stand on the landing of the one-story barracks that has been turned into a makeshift hospital ward to handle the overflow of casualties, maimed men caught in war's inevitable outcome. Are they like me?

While their bodies heal, does war's chaos still chafe on the raw recollections like new shoes on a newly-born heel blister? Does fear wrap around their minds and repel comfort? Like me, do they constantly battle with panic brought on by sure knowledge that, no matter the healing of the flesh, wounded psyches may never mend?

Each day I look out at the white clouds and watch seagulls cavort in the wind. Each day I test a wooden step and retreat, not quite ready to risk the stairs that take me down to the sidewalk and ultimately to the street curving up from the bay, where I'm told one can see the conning towers that belong to gray ships of war.

My isolation in a building full of people consumes me at times. God damn it! My parents are a two, maybe three-day ride. And Elaine? She didn't send me one of those infamous Dear John letters. It was over before I left Moscow. Over when it had barely begun. It was as if what happened on the hillside cooled fervor, cooled commitment—hers, not mine. She still plays on my mind, a dull ache, one I force myself to when fresher, deeper hurts threaten to overpower me.

* * * *

Nurse Betty, fat Betty, has me flat on my stomach while she changes the dressing on my back. I've already succumbed to the pleasures of her cleansing massage on my shoulders. As she lays back yesterday's bandage, I sense her closeness and the naked vulnerability that comes with first-shared intimacies, which is strange, since she's exposed my wounds and cleaned them before. The adhesive rips at the stubborn hair that keeps trying to grow back; I wince. Her fingers brush my undressed skin and arouse feelings, feelings until now anesthetized by shock and pain and morphine. It's only Nurse Betty, an innocent imitation, but my excitement is real. Titillating images fill my mind.

"There you go." She pats my good shoulder. "Is there anything else you need?"

"Nope, think I'm going to get some shut eye." I reach around, wince at the latent shoulder pain, find the corner of my blanket, and pull it up enough to hide my neck, which must be bright red, given the flush I feel.

"All right then, I'll check with you later in the day."

When the far door shuts, I hear the flick of the Captain's Zippo and the smoke escaping through his pursed lips before he chuckles.

"You can come out now, she's gone."

I ignore him, lie here, confused by my maleness, not knowing if my longings are borne in "honor, not love," as Elaine said before the tears welled up in her eyes, before she left me sitting at the corner table of the Palouse Pharmacy. Or now, an even crasser possibility; the stirrings of passion. Christ! What's the difference? I turn my back on what we once hoped for before our hand-in-hand surrender of innocence on a Moscow hillside in May. What a bitter outcome!

I drive these disturbing thoughts from my mind. I can't deal with the here and now and knowing she's moved on with her life. I turn away from yesterday's whys, what-ifs, and maybes and contemplate today's realities: my loss of youthful immortality, rapidly healing wounds, visions of horror, and the bizarre antics of the Captain, who has become my safe harbor in this tossing sea of recurrent nightmares.

The Captain and I talk about home, about sports, about the weather, about women, about anything, except what circumstance brought us here. He can walk now, even though he needs crutches to compensate for the calf muscle mostly missing from his left leg.

Around us, sailors and marines come and go. A few walk out; most leave on stretchers and wheelchairs. To other hospitals? Long Beach, Seattle, who knows? Who cares, really?

One dies. A private paralyzed from the waist down. He's well and good, talking about walking again, driving a cab when he gets home to Brooklyn. Then, like that, he's dead.

The Captain and I and the rest of the ward watch the gurney come in empty and leave with the private underneath a cotton shroud. No one says anything for long moments. Then, from the back of the ward, "Shit!"

No words pass lips for a long minute or two. All the bed-ridden sailors and marines lie silently on their backs. I sense they're doing what I'm doing, contemplating the fragile circumstances that keep me alive, calculating the price of not dying: youth's credo of immortality. The fan wobbles and spins, wobbles and spins, wobbles and spins.

* * * *

"Hey, Admiral." The Captain always calls me Admiral. "Ever play cribbage?"

I look over. He is sitting up on the side of the bed. That meatless shin pokes from his pajama bottoms and splays out into his still swollen ankle. He holds a deck of cards in one hand and a cribbage board in the other. That familiar smile decorates his face.

Cards and cribbage; before I answer I let the memories fill my mind and drive the wartime horrors into a corner, where they linger, waiting their chance to counter punch.

I'm barely nine years old and anxious to be part of what exists between my father and my brother. Dad says I'm too young for hunting, except to bird-dog for him and Grant while they scour the cornfields for pheasant and quail. "Deer and elk—they'll come," my dad says, "when you've mastered the twenty-two and can shoulder a real rifle." I've consigned myself to being on the outside of the circle and looking in when Dad breaks out the cribbage board. "Let's play cards," he says. We do, an hour or two after dinner for two or three nights a week until I've learned how to play, even win once in a while, and math grades at Collister Elementary start to improve. I'm in the circle now—my dad, my brother, and me. In the years that follow, we all play cribbage, hunt up above Gramps' ranch in Long Valley, fish Clear Creek, the Deadwood, Payette, Snake and Salmon, and tinker together with ham radios in Dad's shop. On Sundays, full of Mom's after-church dinner, we sit on the porch, lazy, like the Jerseys chewing their cuds in the pasture, and watch afternoons fade into evenings. My last cribbage game? Dad and me, the night before I leave for Seattle to take up my commission, May 9, 1942. My brother, Grant? Gone to Georgia, a sergeant teaching radio electronics for the Army.

"How 'bout it, Admiral? Ever play cribbage?"

I look at the Captain and return his quizzical grin with a smile of my own. "Cribbage? Sure." I sit up, wheel my legs out of the blankets and place my feet on the floor. "Cut the deck, low card deals."

We play for cigarettes. Neither one of us has any money until the Navy catches up with our billets. Only now is the mail starting to dribble in for those of us who've been here these past three weeks. The Captain got two letters from his sister today. What about me? Does anybody know where I am?

* * * *

When morning comes, it's Nurse Carol who changes the bandages. While she finishes, I direct our idle chatter towards the object of my real concern.

"Say, Lieutenant, isn't there supposed to be a chaplain standing by for those of us who may need one?"

Nurse Carol rips off a piece of adhesive and lays it on my back.

"You know there is, Ensign. And which one will you be needing? We got us a Catholic, a Protestant, and a Rabbi. Take your pick. 'Course the Protestant and Catholic have been pretty busy. If you're not fussy, a Rabbi could be here real quick." She finishes taping.

I roll over and face her. "The Protestant will do, since I'm a church-going Presbyterian back home."

"My, my. With all the cursin' I been hearing, I'd never guess. I'll let him know. I was only part funning you. He really is busy. It may be a day or two."

Her remark about my cursing causes a momentary pause. She is right, of course. I've taken too freely to associating barracks language with God, blaming him, maybe. I return to now and Nurse Carol.

"A day or two? I bet you can get him here faster than that if you let him know a back-sliding Presbyterian needs to be pulled away from the brink."

She smiles, not the funnin' kind of smile, but the courtesy smile that puts a respectful distance between a nurse and her patients. "Well, I'll let him know."

As soon as she about-faces and works her way down to another patient, the Captain catches my attention.

"Hey, Admiral, how about I trade you your Chesterfields for my Luckys, we call it even and start over."

I reach into my stash of loose Luckys. "Seems to me I got a whole hell of a lot more Luckys than you've got Chesterfields." I toss a couple of handfuls of Lucky Strikes onto his bed covers. "Seems like you need to concede the match before we start over."

The Captain looks at the cigarettes scattered about his bed, raises his eyebrows, reaches under his pillow and tosses two empty lucky packs now filled with Chesterfields over my way. He smiles. "Done," he says. "You win."

The hours become days and days become nights and nights turn into yet other days. I collect another surplus of Luckys; the Captain really isn't a very good card player. To be exact, it's five days before Nurse Carol's chaplain shows up, but not before I drive off wild imaginings with my thrashing in the nights, not before mail call brings letters from home.

Tuesday, April 20, 1943
Letters

This morning an orderly drops three letters on the foot of my bed, the first I have received from anyone since weeks before that fateful night on Guadalcanal.

All the letters are written on that tissue-paper stuff that becomes an envelope after the letter is written, Victory Letters they call them. Two of them are from my mom or dad, I'm not sure which, and one is from my brother. I check the postmarks and lay them out in chronological order, oldest to newest, left to right. I can't help but notice the one on the right carries an address that points the mail to the Navy hospital at San Diego. My heart picks up its pace. They know, Mom and Dad, and the forwarded letters mean the U.S. Navy knows too; my personal belongings and a paycheck can't be far behind.

Grant's is the letter on the far left. I resist the writing that covers the back of the envelope and carefully tear back the seal. The letter is dated December 18, 1942, eight or nine weeks before the night I was cut down on the edge of Henderson Field.

My eyes fall on the salutation: "Hey Bud:" I stretch out on the bed. The whirling fan hides behind a sudden, inexplicable wet screen that covers my eyes.

For a moment I'm back on the farm, eleven, maybe twelve years old. The hot August sun soaks into Grant and me as we lay in green grass with our heads on Molly's side, listening to the gurgles while she chews her cud.

"Hey Bud," Grant says, "why you suppose old Molly's so peaceful out here in the pasture, lying down with us draped all over her, and pure hellion when you lock her into the manger so's you can milk her?"

I can't remember the answer, only the question and the feelings of closeness—Molly, my brother, and me—and streaking clouds off in the distance where rain is dusting off the August day—and Molly's big brown Jersey eyes blinking away a fly now and then as her jaws work mechanically sideways and up and down—and the cow smell on Molly's light brown hide—and my brother next to me, asking me dumb questions, calling me Bud. No one else ever calls me Bud.

I fight back tears and read.

Not much room to write on these papers so I'll make it quick. Got two letters from you since I last wrote, also hear on a regular basis from Mom and Dad. Getting mail is no big deal when you're stationed in Georgia.

I stop reading. Getting mail is a big deal when you're floating around in the Pacific, dodging torpedoes slicing through the water, or Jap Zeros plunging down from above. Getting mail is a big deal here in San Diego, when you're pretty much flat on your back, knocking away days by wondering why nobody writes, or, better yet, drives down to visit.

Life here continues to be good, at least as good as it can. Much better; I'm stateside and spending my time in a classroom instead of in a foxhole over in North Africa.

I got me a lady friend. Her name is Nancy, she's from Alabama. She's a typist here at the Army base. Met her at the base chapel. She's a good Baptist girl. Mom won't mind that much. Not a Presbyterian, but not like taking up with a Catholic or Mormon. Wish me luck!

Got leave between classes and went up to Alabama with another noncom who teaches Morse code and walky-talky operation. He lives on a farm not much different from ours about twelve miles from the nearest town. The river's a lot muddier than the Boise, the native hardwoods are so thick you can hardly walk through them, and a bite from a water snake will probably kill you.

Out of room—write when you can, Grant. Merry Xmas! If this reaches you by then.

I turn the letter over and scan tightly packed lines on the back.

I got me a whitetail buck. You'll never believe how. We hid up in trees and shot the bucks with rifled, twelve-gauge-shotgun slugs as they came sniffing through the woods. Don't think Dad would find that sporting. It's legal in Alabama.

I fold the letter, put it down, lie on the bed, and savor the fond memories of growing up with Grant. How strange the arbitrary hand of war, how it puts some where they need to be; the physics teacher, Grant, in a classroom—and others where it makes no sense; me, a German-speaking journalism grad, out in the Pacific war. For Grant, taking a whitetail buck on an Alabama farm is an event to remember. Me? I'm doing my best to forget the meshed images of downed mule deer and elk thrashing on Idaho hillsides among men twitching their last on a flare-lit, Guadalcanal night. I give up, lie on my Navy bed, and let in the boyhood memories: me and Grant.

The Captain has his back to me. A veil of tears makes him opaque, like I'm looking at him through the heavy base of a cut-crystal glass. He's unusually quiet, absorbed, I guess, in his own letters and memories from home.

The sun quits poking through the window, is no doubt looking down on top of the hospital roof, before I contemplate my parents' letters.

The older letter is from both of them. Dad filled up the left half, Mom the right. Like Grant's, it was written well before the incident at Henderson. It consists of the typical newsy stuff and ends with the usual, "Take care of yourself. Love, Dad," and, "Love, Mom." The other is from Dad, a week old, if the postmark is right, and speaks about my injuries.

Knowing they knew, like the tears that can't seem to quit flowing, somehow relieves the load, as if they could make this deadly business go away, like my childhood brush with the bumble bee in the cucumber field, like patching my dented ego and skull when Jim Jensen's bat ended my catching career, or like a hundred other safe catastrophes that proved my parents' omnipotence.

I finish the letter, flip it over and read it again:

Dear Martin:

You don't know how word of your injuries has upset me and your mom. Mom can hardly do her work for worry you need her there. We got word a few weeks back in a telegram that you were injured and being sent to Hawaii for treatment…

I look out across the room. Is that what they said? That I had been injured? Not that I was caught in the middle of an attack by fanatic Japs who weren't even supposed to be there? "What few's left," HQ had said, "are down at the end of the island, getting pounded to hell every time Jap destroyers try to sneak in and take 'em off."

Did anyone say these desperate, dirty Nip bastards did their best to kill me? That they damn near did, by exploding hot pieces of metal that slid into me like a kitchen knife into cheese? That one of them ran me through with a bayonet jammed into the end of his rifle? That their screaming faces visit me when I least expect it: in the middle of a cribbage game, when I'm brushing my teeth, in the still hours of the morning before sunup? Did anyone describe the different smells: decaying flesh, jungle rot, men's sweat, shit, and fear? Or the piercing screams and deafening blasts? Or the sight of a disconnected hand lying a dozen feet from the marine whose life's blood is spilling onto the tarmac and you're helpless to do anything about it? Do they know that three marines, including the sergeant who shot dead my assailant, died in a matter of seconds? All that? And I've been injured? It's too sterile, too passive, too…lacking in viscera.

For long moments the letter shakes as if I was carrying it in one hand while steering the family tractor with the other, down the wash-boarded, dirt road that fronts our house. Long seconds pass. I calm myself and read on.

...then nothing. Finally, we learned you were in San Diego, hospitalized, but expected to fully recover. We are hesitant to make the trip in the old DeSoto, what with its cracked block and all. Plus, the roads this time of year are vicious, and gas rationing would be tight. A Lt. Commander Markowicz told us you should be getting leave to come home in a matter of a few months, if not weeks. He didn't recommend visiting at this time. Really no place to stay. Snow here right now is light, but it's mighty cold. Write soon!

Mom sends her love, Dad.

Yeah, I'll write. Soon as my arm and shoulder loosens up to where I might hold onto a pen for more than thirty or forty seconds without dropping it. Can't see sharing my thoughts with one of those well-meaning volunteers who comes in to transcribe. I'll even call, collect of course. I haven't got any money, if I can ever find a pay phone. They want to come down. But, yeah, I know, gas shortage and all. I close my eyes, squeeze out salty tears, and ignore my shoulder while I pound the crumbled letter into the mattress.

Grant, Mom and Dad—they all come down on me like a tidal wave. Now it's not only tears, a sob rushes up and erupts in an explosive heave. More sobs follow, clipped off at the end while I gasp air in convulsive gulps. I fold my arm, the left one holding Dad's letter, across my eyes, as if doing so will shield my unseemly condition from my soldierly peers. Long moments pass. Recurring waves of lament rise up from the depths and crash into my solar plexus. Snot runs from my nose, where it joins with tears and slides off my chin onto my throat and neck.

After a while, sunlight knifes past the eaves and creates a windowpane mosaic of radiance and shadow on the foot of my bed. I lie on my back, bathed in peace, exonerated from internal torment by the simple delivery of mail from home, mail from Grant. I watch the hairs on my arms wave back and forth ever so slightly, driven by the force of the wind currents spawned by the revolving fan. They remind me of strands of seaweed waving in clear waters of the South Pacific.

For the first time since that awful night on Guadalcanal, I'm aware no horror waits to ambush the stillness that now occupies my mind. The tears and paroxysms have flushed the grinning Shinto masks from my memory. I can see them scurrying down the stairway into the catacombs, where they cringe in fearful obeisance to my newly found serenity. I slip, after all these weeks, into peaceful sleep.

Friday, April 23, 1943
Looking Ahead

For the last several days, I have been buoyed by my rapidly improving physical state and the increasingly long periods of absence of memories of horror.

I find myself entertaining notions about my family, friends, and all the folks in my back-home life. I see them as a whole, a memory of a life displaced from the here and now. I see them moving from yesterday's stage-center. I value them, but they are hidden behind the side curtains. I feel only a fleeting pang of disloyalty, and I'm bitter Mom and Dad haven't broken away from their routine to come to San Diego.

What about Elaine? Convinced that our feelings one for the other were once genuine, I've been confused all these months by the way she left me sitting in the corner of the Palouse Pharmacy in downtown Moscow, her glass of cherry Coke still half full. Now I understand; my timing was bad—taking up my commission so soon after. It was, in her eyes, a betrayal of sorts, one that counterfeited my promise to do the right thing, the honorable thing, should it be necessary. I see now how wrong I was and how wrong she was on both scores; my sense of duty and my love for her. I see now, because of the uncertainty, my going away, and her time of month come and gone, how she came to look at my promises and declarations as lacking in credibility. I can't get over the notion I love her still, even after all these months of hearing nothing. But, however painful, she's in my past. My instincts tell me to face the here, the now, and my tomorrows.

I'm aware of a new issue, virulent hatred. I've felt this emotion before; the badger that wantonly murdered a hundred Rhode Island Red pullets one early summer night for the pure joy of doing it, or the rattler up on the Deadwood that struck my boot before I knew it was there, but never for other human beings. Hatred of Japs replaces fear. Fear prods the hatred from the shadows then slides out of the way, like Elaine, to be handled or forgotten in a distant day at a time and place of my choosing.

Despite the periodic recurrence of vile visions when I least expect them, I sense an undercurrent of hope, of optimism. I play off the hope, even lose myself on occasion in bouts of frivolous nonsense reminiscent of those carefree years as an underclassman at UI, or even earlier, when adolescent tomfoolery led to great adventures. And when gaiety fails, when I wake up in a sweat, or steel-helmeted apparitions catch me unawares in the middle of the day, I subdue them with my hatred and suppress them with my conviction. Tomorrow hinges on living each today by my own wits.

This morning is a good day. The sun is barely out. I have already washed, shaved and brushed my teeth. I take on the stairs and stroll down the sidewalk to the street. It's while I'm standing there in my pajamas, bathrobe and slippers, flexing my still-stiff shoulder and basking in newly found freedom that I notice a Navy officer walking up the sidewalk. His brisk pace seems uncommon for a man whose belt requires an extra five or six inches to circle his waist. I do some rough calculations: five-foot nine, maybe and forty inches round. No seagoing sailor this one. He is carrying a big leather briefcase, and it swings freely at the end of his arm as he closes the distance between us. He approaches. The trimmings on his tunic tell me he's a lieutenant and a chaplain.

His arrival proves to be anticlimactic, but I'm living outside of my mind since mail from home. So, I waylay him on the curb, salute, introduce myself, and engage him in idle chatter until he pushes for resolution.

"You're the man I came to see. I'm pleased to see you on the way to healing your wounds. But I'm usually called in to deal with issues of the soul. You did ask Lieutenant Chambers for a chaplain?"

"No. No, I did ask for a chaplain. I hadn't heard from anyone, well, you know, back home since I came stateside."

"Seems she mentioned something about your being a Presbyterian. I'm an Episcopalian priest, but don't think there's much difference between our views when things need sorting out a thousand miles from home in the middle of a war."

The easy smile on his face tells me he is ready to listen.

"Yes, but what I've seen lately, it doesn't seem to be all that important what you're brought up to be, or for that matter, if you're brought up to be."

Why did I say that, push up against his calling like that? His friendly blue eyes encourage me to carry on. His silence provides me the opportunity.

"Anyway, yesterday I got letters telling me they knew I was here and why. My folks, that is. That is, contacting my family, that's what I wanted. And, well, that's been taken care of…sir."

I can tell he was spinning my words around in his mind, discerning their meaning in light of what? My previous words, maybe? Or what he already knew about me from whatever Nurse Carol told him? Or is my experience, my challenge to the spiritual status quo, not so different from all the sailors and marines away from home? He responds to my words before the silence compels me to speak.

"Well then, I expect there's no need for me." He reaches down and picks up the briefcase he had set down earlier. "I'll be moving on. You know where I am if you need me."

The chaplain walks six or eight steps, turns around, smiles, and speaks his parting piece.

"And, Ensign, God's in the chapel in the main hospital building. Not more than a hundred and fifty paces, easy paces now that you're walking. It would be a pure shame to waste your parents' Christian efforts, especially in a time like this, when you need Him most." He smiles. "Have a good day now."

He waits until I remember my protocol, something I wouldn't have been capable of not too many yesterdays past. Chastening under his mild rebuke, wanting to make amends for my verbal jab at his calling, I snap to attention and give him the closest thing to a salute my stiff shoulder will permit.

"Yes, sir. I'll get over there, sir."

He smiles again. "Good, I'm counting on it." He returns my salute, spins about and walks towards the bay.

I have no spiritual desire to visit a chapel right now. But, what the hell, in any case I can test out my legs. See if they're up to even a short walk after these past weeks of confinement. I start up the sidewalk that leads to the main hospital building.

The heavy, wood-framed glass door taxes my strength. I pull it open, step through, and move out of the door's way while I catch my breath. This doesn't look Navy, at least not the hospital Navy I've been living with these past weeks. The floor is hardwood, some kind of oak probably, and for a few seconds it moves in and out of focus. I'm not quite up to even this little stroll. But my mood remains adventuresome. Escaping with only a mild censure from the chaplain for my assault on his credo, our credo, invigorates me.

For the moment though, I lean on the wall next to the door, force myself to breathe slowly and suck in two large draughts of air.

Two women, one a matronly civilian in her early fifties and the other a twenty-something, red-haired WAVE, are engaged in conversation. They stand behind a large, deep mahogany-colored counter. I let go of the wall. As nonchalantly as my giddy state allows, I saunter over and line up with the redhead.

She and her companion ignore me. I feel fine now and allow myself to get caught up in the redhead's obvious feminine charms. Eventually, she looks up. I fall in love. Tresses, more red than burgundy, more brown than scarlet, frame a round, girlish face populated by freckles that spread out in profusion from the bridge of her nose and diffuse into scarce speckles by the time they reach the line of her jaw. Generous lips, delicately painted a light orange-red, reveal a hint of an upward arc at the corners, giving the impression she's about to smile. Tiny furrows spread out from the corners of her mouth and quickly dissipate. They give away her disposition; she smiles a lot and probably laughs too. She's tall for a woman, maybe five-seven but no match for my six-foot-one frame, and she's obliged to cant her head up when she addresses me. Doing so accentuates the scattered, brown freckles decorating her cheeks. Strange, they bring up an image of the bright red speckles on the side of a freshly caught Idaho brook trout. Modest breasts press against her Navy-issue blouse just enough to remind me, although convalescent, I am a male. Her wide-open, round, emerald eyes overwhelm ordinary eyebrows and eyelashes, despite her efforts with mascara. She exudes a robust demeanor I find very attractive, speckled trout simile and all. I'm distracted from my spiritual quest and forget about my weakened stamina.

She appraises me, starting with my head and shoulders and working her way down the bathrobe to the slippers.

"Hmm." She pauses, a well-orchestrated lull that complements the sparkle in her eyes. "I don't recall bathrobe, slippers, and blood-stained tissue as the uniform of the day."

I pick the dried-blood toilet paper off the piece of chin where the Schick safety razor smoothed off a rough spot an hour or so ago. Damn! This is embarrassing, and rank is no advantage. She's an ensign too. Why, I wonder, didn't the chaplain say something about the toilet paper?

In a move characteristic of my pre-wound self, I improvise.

"Well, I don't recall that ensigns are always informed about the uniform of the day for lieutenants." I stop, for effect and to judge whether my fish has taken the bait. Her smile is poised to disappear if its owner perceives the need to get serious. I push on. "I'm feeling the need to find the chapel, and thought maybe you could point me in the right direction…Ensign."

The smile is gone now. She's not sure if I'm a full lieutenant, a lieutenant, junior grade, or just bullshitting her. She's not taking any chances; she straightens up. I'm captivated by the subtle movement beneath her blouse. In the back of my mind, some remnant of yesterday's sullen frame of mind offers itself for my conscious comparison. Today's difference exhilarates me. I shift my eyes to hers and close with panache reminiscent of the boy before war.

"So, Ensign, if you'll be pointing the way to me I'll be about my business."

"Yes, sir." She points to her left. "Take the main hall, then the first right. Chapel's at the end of that hall…sir."

"Thank you, Ensign. That will be all." My impulse is to turn and beat an exit in the direction of the chapel or out the front door, but I'm into my role now. I wait.

She looks at me. I know what she's thinking: either way, this guy's an asshole. She gives me the benefit of the doubt.

She delivers a half-hearted salute. "Yes, sir, very good, sir."

I return the salute, wheel around, and stroll out the front door. I'm laughing, and for the first time since Guadalcanal, I know why: me in my pajamas, her not knowing what to think or do, my inventive chicanery, the sexy innuendos, those delightful freckles, beguiling emerald eyes, and flirtatious sparring.

* * * *

The Captain is sitting up in his bed, playing solitaire. The ever present cigarette droops out of his mouth.

I step up to the side of the bed and slap the covers. Cards hop in the air an inch or two. His neat rows disappear. The

Captain's stare carries with it a cold threat that promises harm for what I did. I ignore him.

"Captain, we gotta blow this place. I've been walking around. There's blue skies, green trees, and redheads out there. Let's figure out how to get some money."

The Lucky Strike clings to his lips, the ash close to his mouth. Smoke swirls around his nose. Some disappears up his nostrils. Some slides around the point of his nose and wafts past his eyes. He ignores the smoke, ignores the burning butt, and stares at me with wild, threatening eyes.

He grinds out the butt, scoops up the cards, shuffles them and deals out seven neat rows on the bed covers. He flips up the first card, a seven of diamonds. He turns the second card, the jack of spades. He lays the jack on the pile anchored by the queen of hearts and looks up at me. The words he utters catch me completely off guard.

"Get the fuck out of my life, Admiral."

I stand next to his bed, stricken to silence. The Captain stares at me. I stare back. What I see is a drawn curtain behind his eyes. It cuts off his grasp of the outside, transforms the ailing but outgoing and happy Captain and forces him to contend with warriors and wars inside his head. How do I know? I know.

Friday, April 23, 1943
Escape

Tonight, a rare event for San Diego: rain. Not a tropical torrent like the squalls that blew up out of nowhere in the waters of the South Pacific, but a steady drizzle rolling in off the ocean from the northwest. I can see the water as it slides off the eaves, rivulets made faintly luminescent by the low wattage bulbs that light each entry in the hospital ward. I can hear the drops splashing off the lid of the galvanized iron garbage can outside the wall that faces the foot of my bed—a staccato rhythm that keeps time with the varying intensity of the downfall. Inside the ward, it's quiet. It's been lights out for one hour? Two? I don't know.

The rain woke me up from a sleep made light by the contrasting events of the day. On the one hand, I'm invigorated by my outside adventures: the run in with the chaplain and the repartee with the redhead. On the other, I'm distressed at the Captain's retreat from his upbeat, cheerful self. Contrary to recent yesterdays, his state and not mine occupies my mind.

Before lights out, the Captain focused on his solitaire. The few times he was interrupted, he struck out at his tormentor with the same vitriol that brought me up short earlier in the day. I have seen his defiant look before—in the eyes of marines lying on the tarmac and in the eyes of Jim Jensen's collie after it had been hit by the mailman's Studebaker out on rural route 12.

Thinking on it, I look over at the Captain. His bed is empty. I look past the four beds beyond his that mark the end of the ward. A dim light shines over the exit door. To the left, I see the light underneath the door that leads to the head. Off to the right, luminescence slides from the night nurse's desk lamp onto the floor. I look back to the Captain's bed. A crutch is leaning against the wall. I realize now his thumping off with one crutch provided counterpoint to the rain's patter, and that's what woke me. Strange, I don't recall the Captain ever needing the head at night.

I reach a pack of Chesterfields from the small nightstand I share with the Captain and dig out the last cigarette. No one's going to know or care. Guys smoke plenty at night if the mood strikes them. I light up, take a deep draw, suck the smoke deep into my lungs, lie back and let the nicotine do its work. I contemplate yesterday's strange, conflicting events and wait for the Captain's return. Perhaps I can reach him in night's hush.

Outside, the wind drives walls of water against the windows. Images float through my mind: the one time I was on the bridge when we took up our battle stations plowing the Slot off Guadalcanal through a relentless rain storm; the sheets of water crashing into the bridge a baptism of sorts, a cleansing of the ship for the sins we were about to commit in the name of war. That chilling remembrance makes me shiver. I wonder, what transgressions need washing away this night?

One more draw and I crush the half-smoked butt in the ashtray on the nightstand. I hear the drops, big drops now, crashing against the window. The wind slides by the eucalyptus trees, creating an oscillating, baritone moan as the trunks, leaves, and branches bow and scrape. The garbage can lid clatters to the ground. Damn! That's gonna make a mess for someone to clean up. The wind abates, then renews. The garbage can lid clatters again, and again, duller this time. Maybe it's not the lid. Maybe it's the can itself.

My curiosity gets the better of me. I clamber out of bed, cross over the other side, and peer through the wet glass. Ahead of me, the eucalyptus trees bend and weave in response to the whims of the wind. To my left, faint light from the nurse's station filters through the window and lets me see the ground close to the wall. The rain and wind come harder. I look, strain to see through the opaque-with-wet window. The rain lets up; the wind follows suit. There on the ground lies the Captain's crutch. In the instant of cognition, dread numbs me. Panic follows, compelling me to reach that lone crutch outside my window, as if doing so will deny the possibility of my intuition.

I push on the casement window. It won't open! Instinct takes over. I grab the small stand next to the empty bed and smash it through the window, and, with quick, pile-driver strokes, poke out the wooden pane and remaining pieces of glass. I slide out onto the ground, ignoring the wet and the slivers of glass. The wind picks up again; the rain comes down—a torrent. One last, futile bath of absolution.

The crutch lies on the ground in front of me. I watch the individual drops of water bounce off the crutch's blond wood for a long second while I contend with its implication—its invitation—to seek the source of my premonition.

Behind the crutch, the garbage can lays on its side, its junk contents spilled onto the wet earth. Above the can: the Captain, suspended from the eaves by the sash of his Navy-issue bathrobe. He swings in macabre meter with the genuflecting eucalyptus trees.

The sight horrifies me, stupefies me. Behind the Captain's swaying body, I see the night nurse rushing down the stairs, coming to our rescue. She comes in slow motion, her pumping legs and swinging arms moving in exaggerated sluggishness, as if she were pushing herself through water instead of air.

A patient, clad in nothing but pajama bottoms, rushes down the stairs. I stumble forward, fall over the garbage can, struggle to my feet, hug the Captain's legs and lift. The frantic nurse arrives. She grovels in the trash and comes up with a soggy, muddy copy of *Stars and Stripes*, which she wraps around a shard from the broken window. She stands on her toes, reaches up, slashes in vain at the cord anchoring the Captain to the eave. Then she's in the air, thrust there by the pajama-clad patient who embraces her around the thighs and raises her.

"Let him down! I can't reach!"

I let the Captain slide through my arms a few inches then clamp hard. The nurse's hand balances on my head. I feel the patient's legs clash against mine as he struggles to hoist her higher. With no warning, the Captain is free. The dead weight of his torso slumps away from me. The three of us, caught up with the collapsing Captain, tumble onto the ground.

While I scramble to a sitting position and lift the Captain's head, the nurse works on the knotted plait with the shard. The glass cuts through the wet *Stars and Stripes*; her blood runs down her fingers and spreads from the rope down the Captain's back. The knot comes free. Frantic, I pull on the Captain's shoulders until his head lies in my lap. I can tell by his swollen face, the blood seeping from his eye sockets, the limp loll of his lifeless head—he's dead.

Wednesday, April 28, 1943
Tomorrow's Sunshine

The morning after, I was sent over to the surgeon. He dealt with a couple of loose stitches in my back, assorted scrapes, and imbedded pieces of glass in the soles of my feet. The shoulder, outside of feeling like a horse kicked me, is going to be okay, at least as okay as scar tissue and mutilated joints are ever going to allow.

In the four days since, I have taken to walking around the hospital grounds at least once a day, probably three quarters of a mile. I'm banking that doing so will strengthen my physical stamina. Oddly, the Captain's suicide has strengthened my resolve to shake away the nightmares and walk away from war with my sanity. Even so, I still wake up from horrific dreams, and Guadalcanal memories now compete at the most unlikely times with visions of the Captain.

Today was a letter day and most important, payday. I received no letters, but the paymaster finally caught up to me and I'm flush with two month's pay. My contemplation of how best to spend it is interrupted by Nurse Carol, who is leading a yeoman, second class, toting a duffel bag over his back. She motions for him to drop it at the foot of my bed. It's the one I had left behind on the Albuquerque when I went ashore for my unplanned rendezvous with remnants of the Jap army.

"The duffel bag, it was in the bottom of my footlocker," I say to Nurse Carol. "I sure hope they thought to pack it with the locker's stuff, all of it. It'd be just like them to pack the underwear and socks and leave the uniforms, letters and everything else that's important."

"Seems to me," Nurse Carol says, "you're lucky to get any of it. Aren't you kind of humiliating yourself when you slam those sailors on your ship, seeing as how six weeks or so back you were one of them?"

"That makes my case. Look at me – shot up, weak as a baby, couldn't hold a pool cue long enough to make a decent poke at the eight ball in the corner pocket. And for what? Why? To collect a story no one asked me to get anyway. I'm as dumb, dumber even, than the rest of them. My damage wasn't for cause—not like the Captain's dying—my damage was pure stupidity on my part."

Nurse Carol dismisses the sailor with a wave of her hand. He ignores even a pretense at military protocol and escapes. I don't think it registers with him that nurses or patients in hospitals are also officers. I can see why. We patients, officers or not, see nurses as angels from heaven. Officers, I'm one of 'em, sure as hell don't bunk in heaven.

"Well," Nurse Carol says. "I'm glad to see you've decided to come out of your shell. You need to stay that way, Martin. We lost one who couldn't face his mind's madness. You, above all, must know you have to put all that stuff to sleep until you overpower it with fond memories."

Calling me Martin and her careful choice of words nail with one statement all my various states of mind over the last few months. They banish the banter. I, too, become sober. I turn and pull a packet of envelopes from under my pillow.

"There's a fundamental difference between me and the Captain, Nurse, that is, Lieutenant, sir…ma'am." I hold out the envelopes. "See these letters? I found the letters under his pillow the morning after he…" I pause while I seek a palatable euphemism for hung himself, "…died. Found them right after the accident, before the interns turned the Captain's bed and took his belongings. I was searching for some of the Chesterfields he won off me."

I pull the top envelope away from the others and hold it for Nurse Carol to see. "This one is from his mom. His dad's dead. Bet you didn't know that. Died in a car accident while the Captain was finishing his senior year at West Point."

Nurse Carol looks first at the envelope, then at me, as if doing so will confirm the veracity of my words.

"That's right. He was a career soldier, one of those army boys who crossed over to the Marine Corps when he graduated. Kind of picked this stuff up these past weeks playing cribbage. Postmark's from Winchester, Virginia."

I pause, pull the letter back and place it at the bottom of the small stack of envelopes in my right hand.

"I didn't read the letter from his mom. Figured it was none of my business. Figured it probably said pretty much what my letters from home said – how they're proud of him, how they worry about him, hope he stays safe. Weather's fine, weather's bad. Shi…stuff like that."

"But this letter—" I hold out the envelope that is now at the top of the packet. "It's not personal. I read it." I hold it up so she can easily see the face of the envelope. "It's from Pearl Harbor, Naval Headquarters, Pacific Command. You might want to read it too. Explains things, I think. Anyway, the Captain's going to get a Congressional Medal of Honor for what he did on the Canal. At least that's what the letter recommends. No doubt he'll get it. The recommendation is signed by none other than General Vandergrift, the commander of Marine Corps forces at Guadalcanal."

I stop talking for a second while I let this news register. Nurse Carol hasn't moved and has followed every word. That's what makes her a good nurse: the ability to listen.

"It's all here in the general's letter. Seems back in September, when the going was really rough, the Captain held the line when the Japs counterattacked and damn near overran the airfield. Would have done it too, except for the Captain. Cost him most of his command, but the Captain held until the Navy destroyers moved in close to shore with their five-inch guns, until reinforcements could relieve him. Basically those destroyers and the Captain's men broke the back of the Jap's intended surprise attack."

I push the envelope towards Nurse Carol. "I only have to deal with my own fears and failings. The Captain was carrying the weight of all those men who died under his command that September night. This letter opened up wounds—bitter memories of the letters he wrote home to the families of men who died on his watch. That's what drove him over the edge. I know it. All that happy-go-lucky stuff—laughing, joking and blowing smoke rings—just soldiers on the ramparts, too few for the job, like that night on Guadalcanal, except this time there's no five-inch cannons to the rescue. This letter's words reinforced the demons he's been trying to keep at bay. When you've seen them, you know."

The two of us look at each other. Me? Words can't come until I chase visions of evil into the background where they can't betray their presence by trembling syllables and the envelope shaking in my hand. Nurse Carol? Who knows? Maybe she's dealing with her own demons, ones she's offloaded from boatloads of savaged sailors' souls.

Eventually, she reaches out with a tentative hand and takes the envelope.

"You might as well take these too." I hand her all the envelopes. "They'll need to go to his next of kin. Don't think he had a wife, just a mom and a sister, as far as I know."

I let out a big sigh. Nurse Carol waits on me to sort out the sequence of words that carry my next thoughts.

"Me, I'm alive, and this war and those Jap bastards aren't going to rob me of living on my terms."

She looks at me for quiet seconds before she nods her head and speaks.

"All right then. I'll see these letters are included with the rest of the Captain's belongings."

"Yes, well, one other thing. Any chance of getting me a bunk in the bachelor officers' quarters? I need a fresh look on life and kind of figure bunking in the BOQ around them that's healthy will speed things up."

Nurse Carol stuffs the letters in the pocket of her uniform while she considers my request.

"I'll tell you what, Ensign. I'll see what I can do. We could use your bed here for patients that will be coming in. But only if you do something for me. Go see Chaplain Chambers about offloading your anger. It's okay for now, hating the...Japs. It's understandable, useful even—helps fill the void, but sooner or later, hate will derail all your hopes for a future. In that case, those you hate end up destroying you."

Fact is, Nurse Carol's a real looker for a woman who left thirty behind a few years back: hair like corn silk, blue eyes, a gorgeous face and curves and bends in the right places. But she's no dumb blonde. When it comes to wisdom, she resembles my Grandma Scott, sans the gray bun and the dowager's hump. But I'm in no mood for taking other's advice. I pause, out of respect, to give the illusion at least that I'm considering her words. Nevertheless, my words carry defiance.

"That's okay. I've already ignored the chaplain's request that I find God in the chapel. Maybe I'll find Him there, maybe I won't, but I'm living outside the chapel, in the septic world, where God's turned his back of late. I'll deal with my hate here. Maybe I'll feel different someday. Down deep I hope so. But right now, it doesn't matter to me one way or the other if God comes out of the chapel to help."

I watch her eyes widen, her eyebrows arch. Color begins to flood her cheeks. Her body stiffens, as if my attack was physical, not just an affront to her authority. Her mouth opens then clamps shut. Her lips form a seal that prevents speech. She inhales, exhales, and relaxes before she lets any words escape.

"Perhaps you're right. I'll see what I can do."

She smiles, and before I can respond she turns and walks down the aisle. I watch her work her way through the ward. She stops and talks with a new patient. I see her concerned visage as the patient responds to her query. She bends down, straightens the blanket, pulls it tight, tucks it under the foot of the mattress, turns and walks out the door.

I sit down on my bed and open up the duffel bag. I search through the clothes—socks, underwear, uniforms. At the bottom I find my notebooks containing journals and my unpublished news stories. Someday, when the censors have gone away, I'll publish them and the journals.

Inside the oldest journal, I find the half-sheet of notebook paper Elaine slipped under my dormitory door three days after she left me contemplating her cherry Coke. I flip the sheet over, notice how the torn edges have started to rip into the paper, how the number two lead is starting to smudge away. It doesn't matter; I've memorized the words: "You can go to war with your head held high. No one will know. It's our little secret."

I look over to the Captain's bed. For now, I need to get these uniforms cleaned and pressed. I, too, need to walk out the door.

Thursday, May 6, 1943
Sanctuary

For once, things went smoothly. I was out of the hospital in less than two days. To my surprise, I found myself renting an apartment of sorts in a 1920's-era home in Point Loma on the north bay, a ways from the hospital. Nurse Carol couldn't find room at the inn, so to speak, so she turned to Chaplain Chambers. He's the one who found my lodging. I can pay by the week, six bucks, seeing as I'm in uniform and all. My middle-aged landlords seem more than pleased to have a young person in the house, although they still have a daughter at home, a senior at Sacred Heart High School.

Pacheco's their name. Enrique and Mariella Pacheco. I asked Chaplain Chambers how it was an Episcopalian priest found me a place to stay with good Portuguese Catholics. He came back with something about how Catholic and Episcopalian men of the cloth work together when they're in the same navy.

"Anyway," the chaplain said. "Don't be too quick to turn their offer down. You're here until the doctors release you and that will be weeks, maybe more. There's no vacancy in the single officers' quarters. Time in a home with good and willing people is a whole lot better than lying around mostly well among a bunch of sick and wounded."

I couldn't have agreed more, even if getting back to the base for checkups involved a mix of city bus rides complete with transfers and whatever charity I could pick up by hanging out my thumb.

On the second morning I discovered that my six dollars apparently bought me meals. When I wandered into the kitchen, Mariella asked me to sit down and she served up a breakfast: Cream of Wheat, which I detest, especially after it has set up in the pan and gotten lumpy. I ate it anyway, with toast and coffee. While Mariella cleaned up the breakfast dishes, she told me about the family.

I learned the Pachecos have three other children in addition to Maria, the stay-at-home high school senior. Two are daughters, married and living close by with their husbands, both of whom, before the war, fished on the high seas. Now, one's husband is in the Coast Guard somewhere in the Pacific, and the other teams with Tony, the Pacheco's only son. Together they chase tuna all the way to Peru and back. Mariella says they are sometimes gone for months at a time.

"The war don't want Tony," she said. "He messed his knee up playing high school football. He lives with his wife in his sister's house, the one whose husband is in the Coast Guard." She went on to explain that the brother-in-law, the one who fishes with Tony, is in his mid-thirties, and, for now at least, has managed to avoid the draft.

This breakfast talk has become a regular thing in the week and two days I've been here. I eat and Mariella talks while she serves me and cleans up the kitchen. Each morning I learn a little more about the nuances of the individuals that somehow seem to fit in this close-knit family.

As for Mariella, she is short—five-feet-two or three. Her dark brown eyes sit in the middle of a friendly face whose circular geometry matches that of her body. Her thick, black-streaked-with-gray, curly, almost frizzy hair tumbles like brambles in a berry patch down her shoulders and off to the side. A few tangled strands even climb up in the air from the top of her crown. She's constantly in motion, seems to always wear a smile and exhibits an overabundance of the maternal instincts and behaviors I've learned to expect from mothers. Her world doesn't extend beyond the confines of family, home and church.

The good sisters fell short with Mariella, though, so much so I find myself struggling to understand her. She has amazing ways with the English language—ones that consign double negatives and dangling participles to the realm of the amateur language butchers. This morning I mentioned that venison, both deer and elk, and other wild game were often on our dinner table back home. Mariella comes back with, "We don't eat much wild meat. Some deers and some quails once in a while. But before the war, Mr Steiner down at the meat market, well he come home with two cantaloupes from visiting family in Wyoming. He gave us some cantaloupe chops but I didn't care for them."

I didn't know cantaloupes had families, I thought, and, after deciphering her syntax, wondered why anyone would bring cantaloupes from Wyoming. I suppressed a smile.

Mariella busied herself with wiping the counter.

"Don't you mean antelopes?"

She chuckled, "I guess you're right. I never much thought about it. Figured there was melons that was cantaloupes and animals that was cantaloupes." And so it is with Mariella. I'm discovering she hangs familiar monikers on the unfamiliar, and the unfamiliar includes almost everything beyond Point Loma.

Last night I was hard pressed to hold my own in an evening chat with Maria about history, geography and even Aristotle and Socrates. I can't believe her Catholic high school education is that much different from her mother's. Yet, it must be.

At first, the evidence of Catholic commitment—crucifixes and pictures of Jesus, Mary and what I presume are saints—made me feel like a visitor to a foreign land. But I find myself immersed in a setting where the interplay between husband and wife, child and parent, is all too familiar. Before long, I see the new sights and smells as nothing more than window dressing, fringes to the common experience of Presbyterians and Catholics, dairy farmers and fishers of the sea. Overall, I find life in the Pacheco's home strangely reminiscent of what I left in southern Idaho when I went off to college.

Enrique Pacheco is a second-generation Portuguese fisherman. By the looks of him, he would do Prince Henry the Navigator proud. His face and arms are browned and furrowed by a lifetime at sea. Heavy brows hang over soft gray eyes that perpetually squint, frozen that way, I'm sure, by years of screening out the sun and salt spray. His mostly black hair and beard is flecked with gray and a tinge here and there of red, which suggests a tryst with the Vikings during some distant forefather's time. When he stands, even though he is on dry land, his knees flex and bend with the rise and fall of the deck of his fishing boat on the rolling seas, a behavior he shares with the career officers and sailors I have met in the Navy.

Enrique's offshore fishing provides fresh fare for the local markets. He's up way before dawn, rarely goes out of sight of the California or Baja coastlines, and comes back home by mid-afternoon. I know he's up because Mariella gets up with him and starts the coffee. The aroma bathes my mind with nostalgia. The coffee aroma floats into my tiny room, and I brace for my mom's quick shake of my feet through the blankets and words that order me out of bed. *Get up, there's chores to do and cows to milk.* I take note of my detached demeanor about these early memories. A scant week or two ago, nothing more than letters from home brought tears.

The other smells from the kitchen present my nose with bold scents different from the ones I grew up with. Onions, garlic and peppers hang from the ceiling over the kitchen sink. Mariella uses them with every meal, along with a variety of spices, most of which she cultivates in a small planter box on the back porch. In the few days I've been here, fish—halibut, barracuda, squid, and an assortment of others that escape my identification—all in various states of culinary preparation, have been my nose's constant companion.

Her dinnertime creations present a different fare from the red meat, potatoes, thick cream, cold pitchers of milk, and home-canned, over-cooked vegetables I grew up with. For a week or so now, I have experienced tangy pastas, spicy sausages, fish, an assortment of bright fresh vegetables jazzed up with olive oil, garlic, and I don't know what else. All washed down with glasses of strong, red wine.

"Mom makes wonderful pastries," Maria said at the dinner table one night. "Now that Lent's over, you'll see."

"Yup," said Enrique. "Your mama makes about the best desserts in Point Loma."

"Well," I said, "giving up desserts for Lent doesn't seem like much of a sacrifice to me, but then, I'm not a Catholic and don't much care for desserts. That said, I can hardly wait."

I looked around the table. Maria was watching her dad, surprised, I think, that he had voiced more than his normal three or four word sentence. Enrique was watching Mariella, who looked first at me, then at her husband, then at her daughter. She rested her fork on her plate.

"Oh, pshaw!" she said. "All your coaxing isn't going to get a dessert on this table until I get ready to make it."

She gave us all a contrived glare, moved the fork to her mouth, and hid a coy smile while she chewed. After a few seconds pregnant with quiet, we all followed suit.

For all its strangeness, dinner at the Pacheco house was beginning to feel like home.

* * * *

I can see my apartment was a post-construction afterthought. Access is via a double, glass-paned and curtained door off the living room. To gain entry, I am obliged to pass by Enrique's overstuffed chair, which, occupied or not, emits pleasant, pungent memoirs of pipe tobacco. The apartment consists of two rooms: a bedroom and a private bathroom that sports a toilet, cupboard, sink and mirror.

"You will be fine here," Maria told me the first day I arrived. "Grandma Freitas lived in these rooms for four years before she passed away. You can shower in the bathroom off the kitchen; that's what Grandma did. You might want to wait until after breakfast, when everyone who's going to shower has gone for the day."

Next to the bed: a nightstand that has room for nothing else but the table lamp that sits on top. The cheap, soft-pine dresser butting up to the nightstand sports nicks and gouges covered over by thick layers of cream-colored enamel. A hotplate sits on top of the dresser. When I hung my dress uniform in the empty closet, I discovered the bare necessities stored on the closet shelf: two hand towels, a bar of soap, a sauce pan, teapot, plate, cup, knife, fork and spoon. A crucifix hangs over my bed. A quilt of clean patches where pictures once hung creates a stark contrast to the exposed and worried walls.

My days here have served to mend my memories while I wait for the body to heal. Today I feel the urge to take advantage of the after-breakfast solitude. I need to respond to the mail that has bombarded me.

My parents' letters continue to be newsy and positive, although they've made no further mention of possibly driving down from Boise to San Diego. Dad reminds me of the cracked-block DeSoto and, "now that spring is here, it'll be calving time before long."

Grant's romance is going great. "Don't be too surprised," he said in his last letter, "if I have me a bride by the time we next see each other."

Mom tells me the down-home, newsy stuff and repeats what Dad says. Her last letter reminded me how "this war has been cruel to us all." As if she had first-hand knowledge.

I write quick, obligatory letters to Dad and Grant.

Now, with pen poised to write, I prepare to write to Mom, but my mind wanders. Visions of Elaine pop into my head. I remember the closeness, the whispered promises, the confession of private dreams, the feel of her body with mine when we discovered together the electrifying sensations, the shared guilt when we looked down on Moscow at the steeple of the First Presbyterian Church which reached up to touch us on the hillside where we lay. I can't deny these shared experiences and feelings, but neither can I duck the reality. We have no future. I feel the longing, rue my conclusion. Just another casualty of war, Elaine and me, thrown into yesterday's clutter along with everyone else in my pre-war world. Perhaps we will remain there, all akimbo with family, friends, and God until war's intensity no longer makes ardor pale by comparison.

My mind does a flip-flop. Might she yet be there? No, she's already moved on.

I put the pen to paper and write a note to Mom. I tell her I appreciate hearing from her and miss her and Dad, that I'm stronger every day, and I concur with her words that the war has hurt all of us. I add parenthetically, "some of us more than others." I talk about being home soon, and express the hope my feelings about the war's damage to me will be sorted out by then. "For now," I conclude, "distance separates us." Are my words too candid, too hurtful? I doubt she will catch my innuendo. She's so uncomplicated: not as simple as Mariella, but shares with her a straightforward, simple view of the world. No matter how she chooses to look at them, my words are honest. As honest as she is.

I pause with pen in hand, then sign off. "Your loving son, Martin."

Monday, May 17, 1943
Everyday Happenings

It's Monday, and Maria was right: her mother makes marvelous pastries. So far, the hot plate in my bedroom remains unused. I keep expecting my hosts to ask for more money; I hardly see how my rent can be paying for the food they keep putting in front of me.

I did approach Mariella after the first week. "Oh foolishness," she said. "Most of our food comes from our labor, not the store. You're not to worry none about it." So, I haven't, even though it's not true; only some of their food, fish and a few herbs, comes from their labor.

So, why should I be surprised tonight at dinner when Enrique announces, "We're driving up the coast Friday to take care of Danny's place." I have no idea who Danny is, but I gather from the drift of the conversation that follows he's got property, isn't there to take care of it and, like me, is to be a benefactor of this good family's generosity.

Mariella objects. "Why can't we go up next Saturday, or, better yet, the Saturday after?"

We eat in silence while Enrique evaluates this request.

"Can't do what needs to be done on Saturday. We'll go this Friday. Can't wait until next week."

No more is said by Enrique or Mariella. Maria asks about school, and Mariella tells Maria she can take care of herself until they get home that evening. I put the whole Danny question out of my mind when Enrique suggests we all listen to *Fibber McGee and Molly* after dinner.

It's while I'm sitting on the front porch talking and smoking with Enrique, waiting for the time to gather around the big Philco console, that a tired old International pickup pulls up in front of the house. I have seen a bevy of its relatives cruising around San Diego—all makes, even a Willys or two. Most of them are faded black and dented, almost always with a wind-burned fisherman behind the wheel.

A reasonable facsimile of Enrique, except he's maybe ten years younger, climbs out, walks around to the open tailgate, sits on it and lights up a cigarette.

Enrique wanders off the porch over to the tailgate and sits down next to him. The two of them smoke while they talk. They are too far away for me to hear, but their quiet conversation suggests it is business they are talking. The driver of the pickup flips his cigarette up on the lawn, reaches into his shirt pocket and pulls out an envelope, which he hands to Enrique.

Enrique jams his pipe into his mouth, opens the envelope and peeks inside. Then he stuffs the envelope in his back pocket and nods. The two exchange short words, and Enrique heads back to the porch, where I have lit up another cigarette in an effort to appear uninterested.

Maria breaks the quiet. "Show's on."

I ponder the night's events while Fibber's closet opens once more to predictable chaos. We all laugh with the studio audience. Before the half-hour is over, my tired blood catches up to me. As soon as the show is over I head for bed. I fend off sleep long enough to ponder the curious events of today. Who is Danny and what can't wait until Saturday? What brings a fisherman buddy to come around in the early evening with an envelope? Why did Enrique stay up past his normal bedtime to listen to the radio?

My next to last waking thought has something to do with the peace I find in wondering about the inconsequential events of ordinary people living a life.

My last thought: can I get through one more night without nightmares?

Tuesday, May 18, 1943
Pleasant Diversions

After breakfast I put on my uniform and make my way to the front door.

Mariella comes out of the kitchen still drying her hands on a dish towel. "You going to the hospital today?"

"Yes," I say. "It's Tuesday. I check in each Tuesday and Friday."

Mariella throws the towel over her shoulder. "Well, Enrique's planning on working on Danny's pump Friday. He kinda hoped you wouldn't mind coming along." She stops talking, lets the lure of her words work on my curiosity then closes the deal. "Besides, you'll enjoy the drive up the coast, and I'm packing a picnic you don't want to miss."

As if I could say no! "Sure, Mariella. I'll see what I can rearrange."

As it turns out, I don't need to take a bus. The fellow down the block sees me at the stop and gives me a lift all the way to the hospital entrance.

I work my way through security at the gate and walk up to the first intersection, take a right and then a left. A half mile up the road, I see the main hospital building. I haven't gone more than fifty yards when a beige '37 or '38 Plymouth business coupe passes me up, slows down, swerves to the right and stops.

I reach the driver's side door and glance at the open window. A familiar freckled face looks out and delivers an impish smile that goes well with her cutting yet friendly words.

"Let's see now," she says, as she scans me up and down. "Seems like today you are wearing the appropriate uniform for an ensign, Ensign."

My cheeks and ears heat up to the point I'm sure they glow. At a loss for a suitable rejoinder, I surrender. "You've got me. I give up." I hold both hands out and push them together at the wrists. "I'm your prisoner. Better take me back to the gate and hand me over to the officer of the day." I do my best to imitate the friendly side of her smile and tone.

"Well, I've never had a prisoner before. I'll figure out what to do with you after you get in." She bobs her head over to the passenger side.

"Yes, Ma'am." I can't believe my good luck. I make my way to the passenger side, open the door and hop in. She guns the engine and pops the clutch.

We drive up the road for half a block before she glances over and speaks.

"We can't go around calling each other Ensign, it gets kind of confusing. My name's Sherrill, Sherrill O'Toole."

"And mine is Martin Holcomb. Glad to meet you, Sherrill O'Toole."

She gives me a quick glance and a nod, then focuses on the road while she talks. "So, Martin Holcomb…Ensign Martin Holcomb…where you headed?"

I point straight up the road to the hospital we are fast closing on, doing my best to ignore the way she carved "Ensign" out for special emphasis. "Don't suppose you'd believe me if I said the chapel?" She refuses my verbal gauntlet; lets it lie, I don't know, between my feet on the floorboards probably, where it fell with a thud after I uttered it. Damn! Always the wise guy. I abandon my failed attempt at glib and get semi-serious. "I have an appointment with the doc. It's a twice a week thing until they say it isn't. You can't ignore doctors' orders when they outrank you. And you? You headed for work?"

She pulls up to the front of the hospital and stops. "Work it is. I'm running late."

I open the door and step out. "Well, I'll not be keeping you." I stick my head back into the car. "Thanks so much for the ride."

"Say, Ensign Martin," she says before I can pull back and shut the door. "I have a lunch break at eleven-thirty. You in for some hamburgers? Course, you'll probably have to stick around an hour or so, unless those appointment people are slower than usual."

I look at my watch. "Lunch? Sure, a hamburger sounds great. I'll even buy, and a milkshake too. Seems it's the least I can do for today's ride and—" I put on a broad smile, "—the fun I had at your expense last month." Damn! Why did I do that?

Again, she ignores my reference to our earlier soirée and returns my smile. "Eleven-thirty, right here."

I close the door and give her a wave as she drives off. Why the refusal to carry on with friendly jousting? She's the one brought up the ensign stuff. Then it hits me. Nothing she could say worked as well as me making things worse with my own words.

The doctors and nurses are unusually efficient today. I'm in and out of there in twenty minutes.

"Last week's results are in," the doctor says. "Your red blood count is still a little low, but you've finally entered into what we medical types refer to as normal—barely normal, but normal nevertheless."

Before he shoves me out the door, he gives me a green light to skip Friday's appointment altogether. Now I'm stuck with almost two hours to kill before lunch.

I decide to find out how much stamina I have built up with my daily walks around Point Loma. I walk down towards the bay where I can overlook the fleet. Somehow, watching the tops of gray ships nestled in this safe harbor gives me a sense of identity. I almost, but not quite, miss the roll of a ship's deck under my feet.

On my way back to the hospital, I think about the past few weeks and how they've culminated in this chance acquaintance, re-acquaintance really, with Sherrill O'Toole.

Despite the fact that I've been outmaneuvered by indifference, of all things, today's encounter has been energizing. I hope she's calling a truce at lunch. I can't help but notice the spring in my step as I approach the front of the hospital. Sherrill O'Toole waits in her Plymouth.

Ten minutes after I jump in the car, we order hamburgers with the works, a basket of fries and milkshakes at Bud & Donna's Cafe. While the order disappears into the kitchen with Donna, Sherrill and I pick up the conversation where we left it in the Plymouth. She pursues her interest in my Idaho origins. Behind her, I catch the flurry of activity behind the counter as Donna works on our milkshakes.

"So, how did you end up in Moscow? Way up north from Boise it seems to me. Was it the Idaho connection?"

I can't help but be taken in by the inquisitive sparkle in Sherrill's eyes. How many seconds have gone by since she stopped talking?

"They met there. My dad was studying agriculture and my mom, I'm not sure what she studied." First one and then another milkshake machine grunts then whirrs in the background. "Funny, I've never asked. Probably home economics or something. Anyway, she never finished. Married my dad instead. Lucky for me."

Donna drops the silver cans holding our milkshakes on the table and disappears. We both fiddle with the straws. Donna's back in a flash with two deep-throated glasses. I pour and spoon the milkshakes from their cans into our glass goblets.

"So, how about you? How did you manage to end up in San Diego?"

Sherrill gives a pull on the straw. Nothing happens so she takes the straw out of the glass, points it into the can, blows on it, sticks it back into the milkshake, which is almost as thick as peanut butter, and tries again. She picks up the long-handled spoon and scoops out a mouthful of mostly ice cream. "I didn't pull anything off. I walked into the recruiting office with my degree in liberal arts from USC, and the next thing I know I'm running the front office here at the hospital." She smiles, fishes out another scoop of ice cream and slips it into her mouth; all the while those tantalizing emerald eyes are on mine. Infatuation overwhelms me. My conscience calls up a quick image of Elaine. I send it back to the unconscious, the realm of my civilian yesterdays. My mind talks to itself. *You should be so lucky, it's just lunch!* Then, but it was her idea. Another fleeting image: Nurse Betty washing my back. The nape of my neck heats up. Nerve endings send out little vibrations, scouting parties, from my loins into my groin and thighs. Sherrill speaks up and saves me.

"I have a grandpa from Idaho, leastwise, that's where he spent a big part of his life."

"Really? What part of Idaho?"

"Hmm…Lewiston I think." Sherrill looks up at the ceiling. "Yes, Lewiston. He was a soldier. Got hurt in one of the Indian wars. The way grandma told it, they fell in love when she nursed him after he was wounded. So, after he went home to Indiana, he came back to Lewiston and married her. Kind of romantic, I think."

I'm intrigued by our common bond, and my nervousness demands words, any words, to stifle the silence. "Really, Indian wars and falling in love? Lewiston? Your grandpa must be ancient. I'd like to hear more about that sometime. The publisher of *The Lewiston Enterprise* was paying for my school the last two years at UI. He had pull. Said it was pure waste for a good journalist to be carrying a rifle. He helped me get into the Navy with a commission and an assignment as a PIO. 'Course, being in the ROTC in high school helped. He printed a couple of the articles I sent back home. Don't think he really thought a public information officer would actually end up in harm's way."

Sherrill stops mining the glass and watches me with those big green eyes. "And how did a…PIO is it? How did a PIO end up in harm's way?"

I look down into the milkshake miasma while I try and sort out a bland explanation, one that will satisfy her curiosity without giving the demons an opportunity, a clichéd foot in the door. The silence becomes threatening. I conjure a hurried reply and open my mouth. The words don't come. I cover my mouth with my hand. Doing so buys time to align my speaking with the inhale-exhale sequence. My hand moves from my mouth to my chest, which I pat with my fingers in a bad mime's weak portrayal of one who's swallowed too much food. A smile hides my awkwardness. The words that come out are hardly up to the clumsy dramatics that preceded them.

"It's a long story. Should have never happened. But I'm going to be okay."

Her impish smile puts me under her spell—propels me into reality's present moment. "What a coincidence," she says. "You're right, Gramps is ancient—close to ninety I think. But he's spry. You'd never know he's that old. He'll live forever. Seems to me he wrote for a Lewiston paper way back when. 'Course, he didn't have a real education. I didn't know you were an author. "

I'm grateful she has put my moment of angst behind us. I submit to her wiles, as if silence were my enemy.

"I'm thinking your grandpa has a story to tell. I'm not an author—wish I was. Just a journalism major trying to learn his trade. When I went into the Navy, the Lewiston paper asked me to keep them informed. Said they'd make it worth my while if I could shoot them some news from the front, especially if it was about Palouse boys, Idaho or Washington, it didn't much matter. About the best I could do was feed them some uninteresting OCS stuff when I was stateside."

Donna interrupts my speech with the hamburgers and fries. I pick up the hamburger and hold it perpendicular to the table. After a few seconds, liquid fat drips into the basket of fries. I can't let Sherrill get a word in. "Well," I say, "looks like Bud knows how to cook a hamburger without drying it out."

I put both hands around the hamburger and take a bite. A couple of chomps, and I jam in two or three French fries. While I chew, Sherrill intrigues me by the way she delicately picks one French fry, pokes it point first into her mouth, chews, takes a sip of milkshake, a modest bite of hamburger and then initiates the whole process all over again by selecting another French fry.

"What are Palouse boys, and what prevented you from sending stories from over there?"

I chew in silence for a few seconds. "The Palouse? You don't know about the Palouse? The low lying hills that roll out of Eastern Washington into Northern Idaho and Northeastern Oregon? Before the whites came, it was prime grazing country for horses. It's why the Nez Perce and Cayuse were so famous in those days for their horse herds. Now, it's pretty much taken over by wheat and pea farmers. Anyway, the *Enterprise* wants to know the war fortunes of any boys who grew up in that part of the country. Problem is, everything out in the war zone gets censored, so I tucked my notes away. I'll use them someday, unless someone finds them and I get arrested for espionage or something."

Sherrill O'Toole is starting to act like a female version of Edward R. Murrow or one of those other radio network truth seekers. And me, I can't seem to shut up.

"So, how'd you come to end up in the plush quarters here in San Diego?"

How deep do I want to go? Her beguiling green eyes reflect honest interest in my answer. I surrender. "I was actually researching a wartime piece when…" I pause while my mind seeks the right word. "…I got myself banged up. I guess I wanted to say something that would make a difference. Maybe let people back home know even if we got no choice, war is insane. Now I'm sitting in San Diego, too hurt to leave, too well to stay. Maybe I'll write about eating hamburgers and fries with a California WAVE."

I look across the table. Sherrill looks back. Our smiles complement each other. Damn! She's captivating! I turn my attention to my hamburger and fries. Sherrill follows my lead. Donna drops the bill on the edge of the table.

I walk Sherrill to her car before I head to the corner, where I'll hitch a ride with my thumb unless a bus comes by first. I hold the car door for her. She climbs in and rolls down the window, reaches into her purse, and pulls out a pencil and a matchbook. "You have a phone where you're staying?"

"Well, yeah, but danged if I know the number."

She writes something on the matchbook. "Here," she says. "This is the number at the hospital. Call after one and before four-thirty, tomorrow or Thursday." She sticks the matchbook through the window and looks at me with her mischievous smile. "Your lifestyle's making you kind of maudlin. You need something cheerful to write about." She pops the car into reverse, backs out and drives up the road.

I'm still standing there when I see her turn and stop at the security gate a long half-mile up the road. I look down at the matchbook. The irony of the prefix catches my attention: Prospect 2-1422.

Thursday May 20, 1943
Family Secrets

Two other fishermen arrived last night. I didn't see what happened, but Enrique stayed up and hung around the radio until they arrived. He met them at the door, and their short conversations occurred out on the front porch. Enrique went to bed as soon as the second visitor left.

This morning, I return from my after-breakfast walk just in time to see Mariella walking out of the pantry with a large Quaker Oats box. She plops it on the table. "You want to help me count this money?"

I look at the oatmeal box. "Is that what's in the box, money?"

"Yup, we're taking it with us to the county offices tomorrow. Can't go to San Diego. We have to go up to Santa Ana. Don't understand why we can't pay in San Diego. Need to count it first, though."

"Sure, Mariella. Let's get it counted." I pull up a chair.

Mariella pops the lid off; I can see envelopes. The first envelope only has a name on the outside. She hands it to me and tells me to count the money, write the amount on the envelope and give it to her. Then she scoots the oatmeal box over to me. "Do them all that way," she says. She goes into the front room and returns in a quick minute with a sheet of paper. While I count and record, she enters the contributors' names and amounts on the sheet of paper.

In all, there are nine envelopes. The next to the last one has my name on it. There are eighteen dollar bills inside. It appears I'm unwittingly contributing to this unknown cause.

I find it odd she entered the amounts in a neat column but didn't total them. Then, considering the way she butchers English, I figure her math couldn't be much better. In my mind's eye, I see Enrique or Maria doing the adding at some later time.

Mariella thanks me, returns the box with its treasure to the pantry and retreats with her list into the front part of the house. A few minutes later, I hear the Kirby vacuum roar into action. I guess I'm never going to know what this is all about.

Friday, May 21, 1943
BB Guns and Strawberries

We don't get on the road until about 6:30. Before we leave town, Enrique pulls into a bakery and buys a sack of glazed donuts. Mariella reaches into the sack between her legs and produces a large thermos jar and three coffee cups. While we head north out of San Diego, we sip on hot coffee laced with cream and sugar the way Enrique likes it, and eat donuts for breakfast.

The ride north hugs the coast. At times we are so close to the water I can see wave embryos forming behind the surf; a steady cadence of barely perceptible swells that in a matter of seconds bloom into full-term breakers that crash onto the long, sandy shoreline. At other times, the surf line is nothing more than a white shimmer that defines the break between long beaches and the Pacific Ocean. And at still others, the road skirts so close to steep escarpments that I can only guess at the crashing surf below us; all I can see is the long blanket of undulating gunmetal gray unrolling from the haze-obscured horizon.

Before long, Marines are playing at war on both sides of the road. I'm reminded that Camp Pendleton north of San Diego is the training grounds for leathernecks destined to vanquish Tojo's minions in the far Pacific. I push those disturbing thoughts out of my mind, and lean forward so Enrique and Mariella can hear my words.

"Mariella says you may need my help with a pump." We drive for the better part of a mile before Enrique acknowledges my words.

"The pump runs off a single piston and a huge flywheel. It's noisy as all get out. But it pumps a fair amount of water when it's running right. I'm thinking she needs to be greased good and run for an hour or two to make sure she's healthy.

There is nothing to irrigate, but maybe you could man a shovel to keep the water off the road."

I've never heard Enrique put that many words together at one time. "Sure," I say. "I've done a lot of irrigating. Glad to help." My mind flashes for a subliminal second to my attire: khaki trousers, khaki dress shirt and black dress shoes, pretty much standard fare for ensigns on the job, except for the open neck and missing tie, but hardly appropriate for irrigating. "What kinds of crops does Danny farm?"

We ride down the road for a while. I've about given up on getting any kind of answer, then Mariella answers my question.

"We used to get all kinds of vegetables and strawberries. But Danny don't grow nothing now. He and his family's gone away."

Enrique points the car down the road. Nothing more is said. I'm left with my unanswered questions.

By midmorning I've found out where and what Santa Ana is: a quiet little town eighty or ninety miles north of San Diego. It's the county seat for Orange County, which seems a more than appropriate name, given the zillion acres of orange groves we drove through to get to Santa Ana.

Enrique takes us to the court house, parks out front and disappears inside. He doesn't say a thing when he comes out; just climbs in, starts up the Ford and drives off. When we are back in the orange groves and headed south towards home, Mariella speaks up.

"Well, it all paid up now for another year?"

"All paid up," Enrique says.

No more is said. Before long we slow down and veer off Highway 101 and head east two or three miles, then south on a dirt road. The orange trees have been left behind. What I'm seeing now are farms – dry farms mostly. What looks like barley has already pushed a foot or so through the rich brown earth. The wood-frame houses with outbuildings, corrals populated with horses and livestock, fruit trees, tractors and assorted farm implements scattered about make me feel comfortable. After two or three miles, the lay of the land changes. Enrique slows down and turns left before the road dead-ends. We start to climb up a small canyon that was probably carved by the stream that hides in the gully coming of the nearby hills. The sun is bright. Behind us, fingers of Pacific fog cling to the ground.

A twist, a turn to the top of the hill, and we come out on yet another flat valley. It's mostly chaparral and gangly bushes with burnt sienna bark. I ask Mariella what they are, and she tells me. "It's called Manzanita. Not much down low like this. Tons of it higher up." Her answer earns her newfound respect. I had no idea she knew about anything outside the city limits of San Diego.

The field alongside the road lies fallow. Strange grasses and what will be tumble weeds in a few months disrupt the regular spacing of once carefully plowed furrows. A black-tail jackrabbit scoots across the road. In the distance, two hawks hang in the air with still wings. A wood-frame house with a green asphalt-shingle roof nestles in the corner of the field a quarter of a mile or so off the main road. Behind the house a dilapidated outbuilding struggles to stay erect. One of those trees the Californians call pepper trees and twenty or thirty distressed fruit trees struggling to put on a show of spring blossoms decorate the front landscape.

Enrique slows, turns off the road onto the long driveway and stops. Down the driveway, three saddle horses are tied to low lying branches on two of the fruit trees. I suppose Enrique sees them, but he seems unconcerned. He pops the gearshift into neutral, sets the handbrake and climbs out. He wanders off the driveway and kicks around in the bushes that cling to a small berm, one created in a past year by a side-slicing disc turning at the end of a row. He stoops down and grabs hold of what looks like a long piece of four-by-four.

I can see, as he drags it back, that a mailbox riddled with bullet holes is attached to the far end. I ponder my own youthful escapades, when one night we tipped over every mailbox on Black Cat Road. Pulling them off their posts was one thing, shooting them full of holes would have got us caught.

Enrique pulls the busted post to the road and stands it up. He kicks the ground with his hard-toed boot until he uncovers the stub of the four-by-four that goes with the one he is propping up. He lays the post and mailbox down and climbs back in the car.

"We will remount that on our way out." He shifts into first gear and releases the parking brake.

The driveway ends in front of a gate hanging on loose hinges. The gate bisects a bleached-out, white picket fence. Beyond the gate sits the front porch, a fine layer of dirt and dust covering its steps. The saddle horses watch us from what I can tell now are apricot-trees substituting as hitching posts. Enrique and I climb out of the car.

A boy walks around the back corner of the house. He is about twelve years old, the right age for someone who might be carrying a Daisy air rifle, which he is. He is dressed in typical out-west farm gear: denim trousers, plain brown-leather cowboy boots, a white t-shirt and a straw hat tilted up on the sides until the edges almost touch the crown. While he stands and watches us, a ten-year-old version of the boy with the BB gun rounds the corner and stands with his hands in his pockets.

"Hi, fellas," Enrique says.

Neither boy says anything. The younger one jams his hands deeper into his pockets.

Enrique nods towards the horses. "Those must be your horses?" Except for the shuffling of the ten-year-old's feet, neither boy moves. "I see three horses and only two boys."

The younger one shuffles his feet some more, steals a quick glance over his shoulder, and returns his gaze to the ground in front of his feet. The older one looks at Enrique and speaks up.

"Yeah, them's our ponies. The bay is mine, the pinto is my brother's." He nods to the boy standing next to him. "And the roan belongs to Wesley. He's out back."

"Wesley, he your brother, too?"

"Naw," the older boy says. "Wesley's Ma and him lives in the old house down by the tracks on the other side of the valley. Our Pa rents it to 'em." He throws his shoulders back, smiles, and emits words in a prideful tone, as if their content were revealing his own feats of heroism. "Wesley's dad's in the war—flies one of them Liberators and drops bombs on Germans."

While the boy and Enrique carry on their conversation, Wesley wanders out from behind the house.

"So, you must be Wesley."

Wesley neither confirms nor denies Enrique's statement. Enrique pushes the conversation with a question they can hardly ignore. "You boys ride over here much?"

Wesley looks at Enrique. Wesley's tone and posture, unlike the older brother's, are neither polite nor prideful. To the contrary, the smile that borders on a smirk, the erect posture, the unblinking gaze, they work to convey defiance. "No, not much," he says. "We're just out riding. No school or nothing today." His manner projects the unspoken message that none of us can help but miss: *What business is it of yours, anyway?*

Wesley is a clean-cut looking kid. He isn't wearing a hat, and his full head of blond hair goes well with his blue eyes and a fair complexion that is only slightly marred by a crop of pimples populating his forehead. He's older than the other two; I would guess fifteen or sixteen, and tall for his age, probably pushing six feet. Right now, he really pisses me off.

"I don't suppose," Enrique says in a level voice that ignores Wesley's unspoken challenge, "you would know who's shooting up mailboxes and knocking them over?"

The littlest brother speaks up. "It weren't us. All we got is Robbie's BB gun." His brother holds the gun out for our inspection.

"I can see that."

"We ain't shootin' nothing except birds and lizards."

Wesley speaks up. "Naw, we didn't shoot no mailbox, or knock it over. But so what if we did? Don't belong to no one but a yellow-skinned, slant-eyed Jap."

Enrique's face sets up hard, like an Idaho pond in a February freeze. Long seconds pass before anybody says anything. When Enrique speaks, the words come out in a meter that suggests he tastes each word before he lets it out and makes sure it has the right flavor.

"Back where we live, we have a butcher. He's a good man. Name's Steiner." Enrique stares straight at Wesley. "Lloyd, that's Steiner's first name. He was born and raised not ninety miles from here. A good man, Lloyd. Looks a lot like you."

Enrique's sober tone and spacious meter root those boys to the ground. The littlest brother stares at Enrique. The brother with the BB gun is taking his cue off of the older Wesley, and Wesley is doing his best to put on a show of disinterest. He and his protégé look past Enrique at the horses, like they might want to ride on out of here.

I don't have any idea what Enrique is up to, and I'm dumbfounded by Wesley's statement; Danny's a Jap? But down deep, I feel like Enrique deserves respect. It kind of goes with the way I was raised, kind of what a man like Enrique naturally commands.

In case these three take a notion to leave before Enrique's finished, I wander over to the apricot tree and stand next to the roan. Wesley watches me. I reach up and scratch the roan below his forelock. He nibbles at my sleeve then bares his teeth and tries for a piece of arm. I move my arm, reach up under his chin and grab both reins and hold the horse's head away while I pat him on the neck. Everyone, even Mariella from her seat in the car, watches me. The horse calms down. I direct a respectful gaze towards Enrique. We all wait on him to continue his seminar. When he's ready, he continues.

"Lloyd's daddy, he come from Germany. I'm pretty certain Lloyd's got cousins and uncles wearing Nazi uniforms and fighting over there in Europe, where your daddy's probably dropping bombs while we talk.

"So, I'm thinking maybe I oughta shoot old Lloyd's butcher shop windows out cause of what his cousins and uncles are doing over there, and while I'm at it, maybe I should follow you home and pull your mailbox down, seeing as you look an awful lot like Lloyd and his Nazi cousins."

The boys are trapped. They know now they are being lectured, and they are not sure that's all that is going to happen. As for me, I've got a cauldron of confusion bubbling around in my head. *Danny is a Jap!* My mind is kind of in line with Wesley's, except for Enrique's commanding presence, no doubt honed by skippering small fishing boats on big bodies of water. His reasoning and rhetoric, falling on deaf ears in front of him, rally my intellect and send it up against my unassailable prejudices, the ones conceived in southern Idaho and brought to term on the tarmac at Henderson Field. But I also absorbed admirable attitudes in my youth, among them respect for authority, and I defer the outcome of my internal struggle, reason versus emotion, for another day. I am caught up with Enrique and his cause, whatever that might be.

Enrique takes two quick steps towards the boys. Before they can react, his words come out strong and mean.

"You listen to me. Like Lloyd Steiner and me, and your daddies, Danny Ishisaka's a good man. He's a friend of mine. He's a friend of Lloyd Steiner. He's a friend of the Luna

Brothers and Marcus Rodriguez and the fishing fleet down at Newport and a whole bunch of others down south of there. So, you boys would do yourselves and us a big favor if you put the word out. Danny Ishisaka's place is off limits. We find out who's been messin' with it there's gonna be the devil's own hell to pay." Enrique visibly relaxes. He smiles. "I'd be thankful if you helped us keep an eye on Danny's place."

After an interminable silence, Enrique walks to the back of the car and opens the trunk. The older brother is the only one to speak.

"We didn't do nothing, mister."

Enrique ignores him. Wesley and the two brothers head for their horses. Wesley reaches for the reins, but I've got a firm grip on both of them under his roan's chin. Wesley hesitates before he opts to challenge me.

"This here's my horse." He grabs the saddle horn and reaches for a stirrup with his boot.

I pull back on the reins and lean into the roan. The horse fights the reins, tries to rear its head and then moves backwards, which throws Wesley off his attempt to mount. Wesley whirls on me with his fists clenched at his sides. Before he can do anything foolish, I attack with quick words.

"This horse ever go any but the same way home, Wesley?" Wesley's blank look tells me he's caught by surprise, impressed that I know anything about horses, dressed the way I am. "I bet not. I bet he will run straight to the stable when I move you out of the way and swat him good and hard on the ass." I've got Wesley's attention now. I've called his bluff; will he call mine? I'm not sure I can take him, given the sorry state of my condition. I press my case.

"So, here's the deal. I don't like Japs any more than you do, but you're going to pay attention to what Mr Pacheco asked of you. You agree to it right here and now, or your roan is going home on his own, and when he does, we are going to follow him to your house. We're going to tell your mom, so she can tell your dad, how you're doing your part to defeat the Japs. It's your call. But I got to tell you, where I've been, the Japs were set on killing us, not insulting us. And the men I've been with, I'm thinking your daddy is pretty much like those soldiers fighting Japs—not too impressed by them that go around irritating people for the pure hell of it."

Wesley looks at me, then over at Enrique, who stands at the trunk of the car with the picnic basket in his hands, and looks back. Wesley is whipped. "Yeah," he says, "I heard him."

"And you're going to leave this place alone, isn't that right?"

Wesley nods his head. I motion to the brothers. "You fellows better get out of here, and don't forget Mr Pacheco's advice." The two of them scramble for their horses, mount up and ride out of our reach. They stop and wait until I hand Wesley the reins of his roan.

"Thank you, Wesley."

He mounts, wheels his horse and lopes off. I turn back to the car. Mariella is still in the front seat. Her shocked look is mirrored by Enrique, who hasn't moved since I saw him open the trunk.

"Boys need to respect their elders," I say. Did Enrique get my point? This is about him, him and those boys, not about Danny Ishisaka.

Enrique and Mariella look at me for more shocked seconds before he reaches into the trunk and pulls out a red and white checkered tablecloth.

Mariella spreads her tablecloth under the pepper tree. We eat sandwiches and chase them down with the Luna brothers' home-brewed wine. It goes down like strawberry punch and kicks like a Salmon River pack mule.

Neither Mariella nor Enrique says another word about today's events. I'm itching to know the story behind this Danny Ishisaka, his strawberries and vegetables, and why a bunch of commercial fishermen are protecting the property of a probable Jap spy.

After lunch, we discover the windows on the back of the house have all been shot out. By the looks of the casings on the ground, it appears the damage was done by shotguns and .22s, although I couldn't help but notice a couple of BB's stuck in the wood siding. We check out the pump and discover there's no running it; the gas tank is full of bullet holes and shotgun blasts.

Enrique says he can't see any point in putting up a mailbox so they can knock it down, so we head for home. From the backseat of the car, I overhear a few words about getting some folks to board up the windows. But the best I can tell, most of Enrique and Mariella's talking is inconsequential family stuff. I content myself with watching the coastal scenery unfold as we drive back to Point Loma while I work on my conflicted feelings of the day's events.

* * * *

After dinner I volunteer to help with dishes, so while Maria washes and rinses and I dry, we talk. I am drying the silverware and putting it away when Maria speaks up.

"Oh, I almost forgot. A Sherrill O'Toole called and said there's a slight change for tomorrow. Said she's got a three-day pass and she's going home. Wants you to come along, so you're supposed to bring enough clothes to hold you over to Tuesday. Said to tell you her parents don't bite and you'd enjoy talking with her grandpa." She smiles and winks at me. "Got you a girlfriend, have you?"

I feel my face turn red, and mutter something inconsequential about how whether I do or don't is still up for grabs.

This change of plans idea is new to me; I didn't even know we had plans. I was late calling on Thursday and Sherrill had already left. Since I didn't have any way of getting hold of her, I left word I'd called and gave the message taker the Pacheco's phone number. Now, I'm headed to the O'Toole's, wherever the hell that might be.

But that can wait. Right now, I'm perplexed by this Danny Ishisaka thing and why Enrique and all his fishing buddies feel obliged to keep Danny's place pure. Best I can figure, Ishisaka and his kin probably got rounded up with all the other resident Japs and put behind a fence somewhere. Probably happened right after Pearl Harbor. But why Enrique's so all fired up about it is beyond me. Never met anyone who didn't figure rounding them up was a pretty sane thing to do, considering the war we're in. I resolve to push Maria for some information.

Maria rinses another dish and puts it in the drainer. I pick it up. While I'm drying it, I launch into my conversation.

"Boy, your dad sure was upset with the way Danny's place was rundown." I place the plate in the cupboard and reach for another one that Maria has stacked in the drainer. She's scrubbing on a pot and ignores me for a few seconds. She pulls the pot out of the dishwater and places it in the deep double sink that holds the rinse water.

"Dad doesn't build friends easy, but when he does, they're friends for life." She grabs another pan, places it in the dishwater, and scrubs while she talks. "The rest of the men who fish look to Dad. They know he's the best skipper on the Pacific Coast, and they know if they do right by him, he'll back them no matter what."

"Loyalty is a trait admired by all kinds of men. But how did a Jap…?" The first syllable is out of my mouth and done with. Belatedly, I sense the need to keep my objectivity. "…anese truck farmer and a Portuguese deep sea fisherman ever come to be friends?"

Maria confronts me with her eyes, her hands still immersed in the dishwater. For a few seconds an uncomfortable silence invades the room. Before the quiet becomes a standoff, she takes her hands out of the water, dries them on the apron tied around her waist and faces me. I can tell she's about to let me into the circle of familial acceptance.

"You remember Mom telling you that Tony doesn't have to worry about the draft because of a football injury?" She doesn't wait for an answer. "Well, that wasn't quite the truth. Oh, Tony was with football players all right, but they weren't playing football. They were hunting when Tony hurt his knee. Mom has a way of trimming and cutting the truth until it feels comfortable."

When Maria dropped this bit of family intrigue, I was in the process of drying a wine glass. Now I set both the glass and the dish towel on the counter and look at her. For a few seconds we exchange silent appraisals. I sense she wonders if she should say more, thinks maybe she's already said too much. She casts a glance towards the living room, as if maybe her parents might be standing in the doorway nodding their silent approval or disapproval. If the silence continues, she has control; I don't want to risk that. I reach into my journalistic training; avoid direct questions to unwilling or skittish sources. I smile, a weak attempt to hide the inquisition I have in mind.

"Really?" Then, for want of inspiration. "What happened?" That's good: a direct question, but no judgments, no accusations, just friendly interest in another's events. Maria keeps her gaze on me, then turns to the pan in the sink. While she scrubs, she talks.

"I'm not sure of everything that happened. I was only ten or eleven. I know that Tony, Terry Varnedoe and Paul Steiner, the three of them were real thick. They grew up together, all the way through grade school, junior high and high school. They all three played football. Tony and Paul didn't make the varsity until their junior years, but Terry—Terry was fast. When he came up from junior high, Saint Francis put him on the varsity team. By the time they were seniors, they were all starters. Tony was a guard and played all the time."

Maria stops for a minute and gazes at the window, as if in its reflection she could see Tony, Terry, and Paul out on the football field. I find a wine glass sitting on the back of the sink and polish it with the dishtowel. She looks down at her hands resting in the soapy suds and commences to scrub. Her story continues.

"Paul had grown into a giant by the time he was eighteen. He was center on the All Southern California first team for nineteen-thirty-eight. Got him a scholarship at Berkeley. He was smart, Paul was, and a good football player. Not that Terry was dumb. And fast, oh, Terry could run! The college coaches were after him. They didn't know if they wanted him for football, or track, or both."

I learned early in my stay with the Pachecos that Maria owned more than her share of intelligence. Now I am learning that she knows how to employ her wit to tell a compelling story.

"What about Tony?"

"Tony? Tony was good for high school because he's tough, but too little for college. Besides, Tony's Enrique Pacheco's son. Pachecos go to sea, not college.

"Anyway, Tony, Terry and Paul headed for Los Angeles in Dad's old International pickup one Saturday. Terry was invited to visit a meet at USC. Track coaches were especially hot on him, so Tony and Paul decided to go with him. They took their shotguns, said they were going by Danny Ishisaka's place to see if they could scare up some jackrabbits."

"How did they know about Danny Ishisaka?"

Maria pauses. "Danny? Every fisherman south of San Pedro knows Danny. He would show up at Newport or San Diego on a regular basis and trade whatever he'd grown for what fishermen have in their holds. He liked a lot of fish that don't sell in the markets: Spanish mackerel, shark, as well as anything else they might have.

"I think he's a Buddhist or something, but he and his family made a point of showing up whenever fishermen celebrated a wedding, a baptism or a confirmation. And he always brought something. If it wasn't strawberries, apricots, pomegranates or vegetables, it was some crazy seafood dish Yoshi, his wife, made. Every fisherman on the coast thinks Danny is family."

Maria is wiping up the sinks. I'm standing there, re-wiping the counter next to the drainer, basically doing nothing but absorbing the answers to all the questions I had harbored for the last week or so. I decide to quit the charade and sit down at the kitchen table. Maria joins me.

"Anyway," she says, "they dropped by Danny's early Saturday morning. Danny told them to stay off the fields— they were just planted, but if they drove up the road, into the hills a little ways they would come to a spot where the road crosses the gully on a wooden bridge. I can almost hear Danny telling them to 'Hunt up that draw. There's lots of cottontails this time of year, and cottontails taste good. No one going to eat the scrawny old jackrabbits feasting on my crops.' Probably told them to drop back by and pick up some goodies on their way out.

"That's what they did—drove up that canyon about eight o'clock in the morning to hunt cottontails."

Maria stops talking. I wait. I think it's her sense of theatrical timing. She's a natural storyteller. But that's not it: she's lost in her thoughts.

I wait. Her eyes wet up. I wait.

"They told Danny they'd be back by ten-thirty. Said they needed to get on the road if they were going to make it to the meet by one-thirty. When they don't show up, Danny figures they might have had car trouble or something. So, he jumps in his flatbed and drives up. He finds Tony limping down the road. He's babbling about Paul and Terry.

"I don't know how it happened exactly. The three of them jumped a coyote. Heard something about Terry kneeling to shoot and standing up in front of Paul as Paul fired." She pauses, looks at me; her quivering chin prevents her from talking. I am aware this is more than a story, it's a venting. I reach out and place my hand on hers. Visions from her mind's eye pop up in my head, along with similar scenes on a dark night on the edge of Henderson Field. I feel for the first time in weeks that hollow panic pressing from the starboard side of my subconscious, threatening the safe harbor where I had moored it weeks ago.

Maria turns her head away and looks at the floor. She pulls her hand out from under mine, reaches out and touches my forearm, searching, I think, for consolation.

"When we get there, Mom, Dad, the Steiners and me, there's Paul lying on the couch, wrapped in a blanket, his head on Yoshi's lap. She's so small compared to Paul. Yet, she's coaxing the anguish out of him, letting him cling to her waist like she was his own mom. Yoshi is rubbing his shoulders and back and singing a quiet lullaby none of us had ever heard and couldn't understand. But it calmed Paul down, stopped the wild thrashing and banging that had bloodied his forehead. It was a strange sight. Paul's six-foot-four-inch frame wrapped in a blanket, his blond hair buried in Yoshi's lap, and little Yoshi stroking his head and shoulders while she sang that soft song."

The room takes on an uncanny solitude. I hear the mantle clock in the front room. Each tick accentuates the silence. For some reason it reassures me, reminds me of early mornings when winter's quiet is broken by the muffled and metered ring of Dad's axe splitting stove wood out behind the shed. I let the seconds tick off while I compose my thoughts. "What about Terry's mom and dad? What about Tony?" Her fingers press on my arm then slide away to the edge of the table.

"They had gone on to Santa Ana. That's where they took Terry. As soon as they took Terry away, Danny somehow got Paul out of his clothes and wrapped in that blanket.

"Tony got off easy. His knee was wrecked by the pileup when he drove the pickup off the road going for help. Tony's small like Danny, so Danny put Tony in a pair of his coveralls. Then he went back up with his John Deere and pulled Dad's pickup out of the gully. By the time we got there, the clothes were gone and the pickup was in the front yard with no sign of anything—well, it did have a bashed in left front fender—but no blood.

"Judy, Danny's daughter, had arrived from town with clothes for Paul. She told us her dad threw the bloody clothes away and washed the pickup. That's like Danny, always thinking about other people."

I feel the floor shake and hear footsteps coming from the front of the house. I suppose Maria can also. "That's about it," Maria says. "If Danny wasn't a friend for life before, he was now." I can tell this interview is coming to a close, so I come back with a quick summary for her, hoping she will correct any errors.

"So, when Danny and his family got sent to the Nisei camps, your dad, Steiner and all these fishermen kept up his payments on the property tax, is that right?"

"Something like that," Maria says. "Dad says Danny's going to have his farm when this war is over."

Mariella steps into the doorway. She's attired in her nightgown, which is covered by a terrycloth bathrobe. "My, aren't you two the gabby ones tonight."

"Yes," I say. "Doing dishes can actually be fun when you have good conversation." Mariella seems oblivious to Maria's flushed complexion and still wet eyes.

"Well, if you're gonna keep on talkin,' you might hold it down. Dad's done reading and headed for bed." These words from Mariella turn off story time. Maria says something about needing to put her hair in curlers before she goes to bed, and I mumble about a big day tomorrow, say my goodnights, and head for my room.

After I pack up enough underwear and socks to keep me going for three days, I pull out my journal and write the story while it's fresh in my mind. It belongs with all those high-seas notes I've recorded for some future time, when perhaps I can sort and separate war's events, depersonalize them, digest them, relate them in a way that makes a post-war audience cherish peace.

I know this: Maria's story puts violence in perspective—death comes not just from the chaos of man-made designs, but also from carefree, innocent pursuits.

Before I turn out the light, I give my story about Danny Ishisaka and Enrique Pacheco one more careful reading.

Now, I lie in bed and think about the day's events. I think theirs is a unique brotherhood, one requiring tough men to stand up in the face of virulent public pressure. Had I not witnessed Enrique in action, I wouldn't have believed Maria's tale.

After today, I have even more respect for Enrique Pacheco. The nagging notion that Danny Ishisaka deserves the same pulls at my conscience.

* * * *

I'm on a hillside, the one above Moscow where Elaine and I lie in the grass. She's next to me, her head resting on my shoulder. I kiss the top of her head, whisper familiar endearments to her. She snuggles closer. I stroke her hair, kiss it. I slide out from under her resting head, roll over and lie next to her, my head not quite even with her shoulder. My left hand props up my head; my right arm rests across her breasts and reaches to her cheek, which I caress. I move to kiss her.

That's when I notice the strawberries. I look about. I'm
no longer on the hillside. Well, maybe I am, but the ground we
lie on is cultivated strawberries. I hesitate, hold off the kiss. In
the distance, a grove of apricot trees surround a lone pepper
tree. Above the trees, two hawks hang in the air over the edge
of the valley. They swoop my way. I'm mesmerized by their
graceful flight. I watch them glide. They are over us now. To
see them I have to tip my head back until it rests on the top of
my shoulders. I look down at Elaine. Her eyes are locked on
mine, inviting me—waiting for me. I caress her cheek and look
back at the sky. The hawks slice through the air. I blink, look
again. I see the red circles on the wings, the boxy, yet
contoured fuselages; hear the scream of the engines as two Jap
Zeros dip into a dive straight towards Elaine and me in the
field of strawberries. I turn back to Elaine, lean over her, close
my eyes, kiss her tenderly on the lips. Kiss her forehead, then
her eyes, the tip of her nose, her cheek. My hand wanders
down and fumbles with the buttons of her blouse while my
cheek rests on hers. In the fringes, the Zeros are shooting at us
but I don't care. I kiss her again on the cheek and open my
eyes, scan down to her jawline. I see the freckles, the ones that
remind me of an Idaho brook trout. I look into her eyes:
emerald green. The Zeros are of no concern right now. How
did Sherrill O'Toole get into my dreams?

I wake up and look over at the alarm clock ticking on the
nightstand: 3:50. Jeez, I don't have to get up yet. But the dream
perplexes me. It doesn't frighten me like my recent dreams,
just heightens my emotional state and arouses my…curiosity.

I climb out of bed, pull on my pants, and fish a
Chesterfield out of my shirt pocket. Quietly, I work my way
out of the bedroom, through the living room to the front
porch. There I light up, watch wafting smoke curl off the
porch into early morning's dark, damp air. I hear noise in the
house, turn and see the light creeping down the stairs, petering
out before it hits the floor.

I flip my burning cigarette butt and watch it arc out onto the lawn. Might as well eat breakfast with Enrique; he has fish to catch and Sherrill will be along in a couple of hours.

Saturday, May 22, 1943
Allures of Home

Sherrill pulls up about ten after six. I stuff my duffel bag on the floor behind the passenger seat and climb in, feeling a little awkward decked out in Navy casual: dungarees, shirt, and boots. This is the first time I've seen her in anything but her uniform, and she looks like every sailor's girl back home. Her light green skirt covers her knees and goes well with her plain white blouse. Around her throat, a green scarf complements the skirt. Her red—leaning-towards-auburn—curls, held back this time by barrettes, frame the face that disrupted my dreamy dalliance a few hours past. There's something else I can't quite place. We're out of Point Loma and headed north before I figure it out. She has exchanged the hint of red-orange on her lips with what the advertisements call Victory Red. Every sailor knows about Victory Red. I comment on her choice.

"It's my patriotic duty," she says. "It's not enough the war-time production gurus allow the manufacture of lipstick. 'Good for the morale of men and women,' they say. Besides, Victory Red carries a promise: victory for the Country and victory for the wearers as well as their beaus."

She glances over at me. I'm beginning to understand what I like about Sherrill O'Toole, her flair with words that goes so well with her vibrant appearance. But I don't let my admiration prevent me from seizing the opportunity.

"Well, let's pray neither the Country, nor wearers, nor beaus are disappointed." She looks at me for a few seconds, throws back her head and laughs.

"The Country? Let's pray for the Country. Wearers, too. Beaus? Don't know that praying is going to help." The Plymouth picks up speed and veers around a slow moving truck while I make a mental tally of the score: wearer—one, beau—zero.

For the next seventy miles or so, we retrace yesterday's route, the one I had taken with Enrique and Mariella. At some point between the cutoff to Danny Ishisaka's place and Santa Ana, we turn east. Before long we are driving up a wide canyon. The roadside out my window is a steep wall for the most part. On Sherrill's side, the riverbed runs flat for three-quarters of a mile or better. I think there's water in it out in the middle where the oaks and cottonwoods hang out, but can't tell for sure. Sherrill assures me there is water. "It's the Santa Ana," she says. "It's probably thirty or forty feet wide right now. You'll be able to see it when we get about halfway through the canyon. In the summer, you can jump across it. It was lapping at the edge of the highway one winter six or seven years ago."

"So, how far is it to Riverside?" She has already told me her folks live on an orange ranch outside of Riverside.

"Another twenty-five, thirty miles." She looks at me. "Why? Getting nervous to meet my family?"

"I don't know. Depends on how they feel about their daughter bringing home sailors for long weekends."

We drive on in silence. For once I think Sherrill is at a loss for a flippant rejoinder. Could it be she's never brought home a beau or a beau-maybe? Could it be my verbal jousting has carried me across the carefree boundary into no-man's land? It would be a hell of a note, I think, to get dumped out in the middle of this canyon and have to thumb hike back to San Diego.

Before long, she comes out of her reverie. "Funny, I have no idea what they are going to say. I'm not even sure they know I'm coming home, never mind dragging along a Navy officer from, of all places, Idaho. Idaho! How does a guy from Idaho end up floating around the Pacific Ocean in this war? You're supposed to be in the cavalry or something." She thinks my laughter is in response to her quip. I know that's only part of the truth; the rest lies in the way hilarity hides relief.

Before we get to our destination, we pull out of the canyon and drive through Corona, which could be any one of a dozen small towns in southern Idaho: Rupert, Meridian, Burley, Gooding. A few miles out of Corona we work our way through a series of county roads, most of them paved. Driving past small farms, big orange groves, a few walnut orchards, we come to a dirt berm that defines the bank of a canal. A couple of miles on the top of the berm, then down onto yet another paved road until it forks. The right fork consists of two ruts in the dirt that slant down a side hill into a small valley until they give out on the shore of a proportionately smaller lake. Sherrill stops the car. "That's Mockingbird Canyon, and that big pond, as you might guess, is called Mockingbird Lake. There's fish in it. We used to ride our horses down there and look for the boulders with Indian pictographs on them."

We look at this peaceful scene for a long minute. My mind flashes to that morning in the hospital in San Diego when the canyon's namesake warbled and woke me from my anesthesia. Is it a coincidence that Sherrill's intuition compels her to stop here and reminisce? Perhaps the mockingbird's incessant repertoire was a harbinger of a good thing to come. Perhaps Sherrill O'Toole is the catalyst; perhaps she is the good thing.

Sherrill nods her head towards the fork that leads away from Mockingbird Canyon. "Up there, that's home." She cranks the wheel and guns the engine.

Home—I haven't thought about home in quite some time. Getting there—home, follows a painful path through war's wasteful carnage, forces me to face my conflicted feelings about duty, honor and Elaine—compels me to accept the transience of my safe and happy childhood. My destiny is in today, in tomorrow.

The Pachecos: that's home-like, but I can put my finger on crucial missing elements.

Home? I don't know. Does home lie at the end of this ribbon of road that plunges into a forest of orange trees? Maybe, maybe so.

Saturday, May 22, 1943
Memories

When we turn off the narrow pavement I am confronted with a sign that arches over the entrance to the graveled road. The words burned into the wood catch my funny bone: Hacienda Del O'Toole.

I laugh. "Only in the good old US of A would one find a sign that spans roads and cultures all at the same time."

"Well, that's my dad's work. He's got quite a flair for off-the-wall expression. He picked up his Spanish and his sense of humor in the groves instead of the classroom. You'll like him."

Yes, I already like him.

We make a sharp right. The walls of orange trees on both sides of the car give way to a parking area that fronts an expanse of green lawn. A white 1920s vintage, two-story wood-frame house sits behind a rose garden that borders the far side of the lawn. A second-story balcony hangs over the portico that graces the entrance. To the left of the house, a black Packard sits outside of a detached garage. The garage is big and both double-wide doors are open. Parked inside are an International Farmall tractor and a one-ton, stake-side truck, a Dodge, I think.

In the time it takes for me to take all this in, Sherrill parks and jumps out of the car. "Come on," she says. "Let's see who is home."

I pile out and catch up to her about the time we reach the rose garden. A tall woman in a dress and apron opens the screen door and stands on the porch steps with her hands on her hips. It's clear by the emerald eyes, the auburn hair fighting off the streaks of gray, and the blended freckles on her face, that she is Sherrill's mother.

"Sherrill O'Toole, you ever hear of the telephone? We have one, you know."

Sherrill meets her mom at the bottom of the porch and kisses her lightly on the cheek. "I know, Mom. It was kind of a last minute thing. Mom, meet Martin Holcomb from Idaho. He's a writer. I thought maybe Gramps might enjoy talking with a writer from Idaho."

A sharp bang somewhere behind the house, a .22 by the sound of it, interrupts Mrs O'Toole's welcome. "That would be your grandpa. He's out at the apricot trees trying to kill off the ground squirrels." She puts out her hand. "Pleased to meet you, Martin."

Before I can say anything, she takes up the grandpa story where she left it. "Says he doesn't begrudge the birds a few apricots, but the ground squirrels strip the trees while the apricots are still green, which leaves nothing for either the birds or us humans. Course, he can't see worth a darn—safest place for one of the squirrels is in front of Grandpa's barrel."

She stops talking, but continues to hold on to my hand and looks at me with her warm, sun-browned, laugh-crinkled face until I acknowledge her greeting.

"Come into the house," she says. "I just put a pot of coffee on. Dad should be back anytime for a mid-morning cup."

We sit in the kitchen, talk, eat toast spread with cream cheese and homemade orange marmalade, and drink hot coffee. Now and then the .22 disrupts the comfortable conversation.

Getting to know Sherrill's mom is easy. I'm halfway into my second cup when the crunch of gravel directs our attention to a Dodge pickup with a shaggy yellow dog in the back. The dog and it's well-built but smallish, middle-aged master head for the backdoor. Before long, Sherrill's dad is in the house and joining us for coffee and conversation. His red, almost orange hair and mustache are tinged with gray. Unlike his wife and daughter, his eyes are clear blue. Like theirs, his have a friendly cast about them. They look out from under heavy brows and a creased countenance caused by a lifetime out of doors. His physique reflects an active life. Even in middle-age, his muscled and proportioned shoulders taper to a flat belly. His suspenders are more than decorations; without them his Levi's would slip past his nonexistent waist and hips to the floor. His easy manner, like Sherrill's mom's, makes conversation relaxed and enjoyable. In them—her mom, her dad—I think I've discovered the source of Sherrill's fun-loving slant on life.

Eventually, Sherrill's mom works around to Sherrill's earlier declaration about Grandpa, Idaho, and a writer.

"So, you're a writer? What kind of writing do you do?"

"Strictly speaking, not a writer—a journalist. At least, that's what my degree says."

Sherrill's dad gets into the conversation. He leans back, his left arm looping off the top of the chair, his right holding his coffee cup: a friendly, disarming pose. "What does a journalist do in a war-time navy? Journalist, huh? What college?" His questions, rapid-fire and direct, like a prosecuting attorney's, are nevertheless couched in a friendly tone and bracketed by a hint of smile.

I return his smile with one of my own and answer the questions in the inverse order they were asked. "University of Idaho. I traded in my degree and ROTC time for a Navy commission. I was stationed on the fleet's flagship. In addition to my communications-room battle station, I created and released communiqués about fleet activities for the press." I leave out the part about censoring sailors' mail before it went home.

"And was your ship attacked?" But before I can respond, in a low-key, friendly way, "Was that how you got hurt?" He sips his coffee, apparently deciding by my silence he's assumed too much. "That is, were you hurt? Is that what got you to the hospital in San Diego?" He is boring in, hot on the trail. I've been there before: fielding questions from a father who wants to know his daughter has nothing to fear, but never when the daughter is a Navy officer and a graduate of USC. Nevertheless, I struggle to construct words that pass muster.

"Uh, no, sir. That is, no ship was attacked. Well, actually we were attacked, but that's not when I was hurt." I pause. How do I tell the story without conjuring up painful images, which would only make things worse? "I was on shore to interview some Marines for the *Stars and Stripes*, that's the armed forces newspaper." Evidently that quells his curiosity.

"Well," he says, "we're glad to have you as Sherrill's guest."

Sherrill stands up, grabs my left hand and pulls. "Come on. Let's go see if Gramps has managed to keep the squirrels out of the trees." I cast a helpless look at her parents and allow myself to be towed out the back door, where the yellow dog intercepts our path and exacts a toll of scratches and rubs before he lets us proceed.

"Shadrach!" Sherrill says. "You stay—don't want you chasing squirrels when Gramps is out there with his gun."

Shadrach follows us as we move off behind the garage, where I discover a small stable complete with corral. A half-grown Hereford heifer is pulling hay out of a manger next to the near corral fence. Her roommate, a bay gelding that looks a lot like a thoroughbred except he's maybe a little smaller than average, stands in the middle of the corral and watches us, his ears pitched forward at that familiar angle that tells me we have his full attention.

"That's a good looking horse. What kind is he?"

Sherrill turns and points towards the house. "Shadrach!" Shadrach stops and watches her. "Go home!" He turns, tucks his shaggy yellow tail between his legs, droops his head into a mournful hang, trots towards the house then turns back and looks at us. "Go home!" Shadrach resumes his disconsolate trek. Sherrill takes my hand.

"That's Gramps' horse. He's not a Thoroughbred. Standardbred I think they call him. They're bred for harness racing."

We walk behind the corral and through a gate that provides entry to a two or three acre pasture, quarters for another horse, a pinto by its size and powerful chest, a quarter horse and two sheep. We walk in silence. I don't know what's on Sherrill's mind. I'm reflecting on her command to go home and trying to get comfortable with the whole idea of holding hands with her, innocent as it seems. Elaine still wanders in my mind. I shake off my daydream and break the silence.

"Shadrach? Where on earth did you come up with a name like that?"

Sherrill swings our arms in playful arcs, to and fro. "Some more of my dad's shenanigans. See this big pinto?" She points her hands to the horse grazing in the pasture. "That's Meshach, even though she's a mare. The bay in the corral is Abednego. The sheep are not ours, so who knows what their names are? But the cat, she's Dolly, Dolly Madison. Over the years we have had Admiral Farragut, Salome, Isabella and Ferdinand, Poncho Villa, Genghis, and I don't know how many others. No Spots, Dukes, Fidos or Socks at our place. We are attended by the famous and infamous. Don't be surprised if Dolly's next litter doesn't have a Tojo, Mussolini, and Hitler in it."

"So, what's the story with Grandpa and squirrels? Do they really eat the green apricots off the trees?"

"They really do."

We reach the gate and go through. A well-worn path leads off to the east and plunges into a gully. I can't see in the gully, but beyond it are eight or ten fruit trees. On the near side of the orchard I see Sherrill's grandpa sitting in a fold-up deckchair. I turn and close the latch. We continue to walk.

"Oh, there's plenty left. But Gramps says it's not fair—eating apricots before bird or man can enjoy them. Mom says there's more to the ground squirrel and Grandpa hate relationship than apricots. Mostly, it keeps him busy and feeling useful."

As we approach, Grandpa raises his slide action Winchester—it's like the one Grant owns. He squeezes off a shot. I look in the general direction where the barrel is pointing. A squirrel sits on a low branch. Another shot. No sign the squirrel's hit or, for that matter, even aware he's being shot at. He sits up on the branch and grabs a green apricot. A third shot. This time we are close enough to see a few leaves up in the branches shower to the ground. The squirrel jumps down with the apricot in his mouth and heads for the far end of the gully. A fourth shot kicks up some desert dust about six feet in front of the scampering squirrel.

"Grandpa needs to lower his sights," I say.

"Probably so. That's Dad's twenty-two. He's probably set the sights up for a long shot at a coyote or something. Wouldn't much matter. Mom's right – Gramps can barely see the squirrels at that distance, never mind see well enough to actually hit one.

By now we are on top of Sherrill's granddad. He sees us out of the corner of his eye, turns in the chair, and ignores the cane his leg bumps onto the ground. The way his smile smoothes out the creases and gullies that spread out from the corner of his mouth, takes years off his countenance.

"Who's your friend, Sherrie?" Sherrie—I like that.

Sherrill bends down and kisses him on the forehead. "Hello to you too, Gramps. This is Martin. He's from Idaho like you, and like you he got himself banged up in the war. I thought you might have things in common."

I reach out my hand. While he responds in turn, I take in his features. Old? Yes. His face is weather-beaten, with tiny red veins splayed under the skin, like feeder creeks on a topographical map of any forest in the West. Drugstore glasses perch low on his nose so he looks over them to see me. Blotches of brown on his face and the top of his head match those on the back of his wrinkled hands. Skin hangs loose under his chin like a turkey's waddle. Sparse gray hair on a barely receding forehead complements a full, gray mustache. All of these reveal his aged state. Yet his interested and lively demeanor conveys a notion that he lives with a young man's optimism. Is it his undisguised interest in meeting me, the exuberance in his smile, the sparkling eyes? Or is it the clean trousers and wrinkle-free shirt, the flushed face and arms, as if they had just endured a robust scrubbing in a hot shower, or the neatly trimmed sideburns, and freshly shaved face? Maybe it's the way he reaches out to me from his seated position with a slightly palsied hand, eager to grasp mine and, when he does, the way he tests my mettle with a firm grip. I instantly like him.

"Glad to meet you, Martin. What part of Idaho?"

"I am pleased to make your acquaintance, Mr O'Toole. I was raised in the Boise Valley on a dairy farm, but spent the four years before joining the Navy up at Moscow."

Before I can go on, Sherrill jumps into the conversation. "Gramps isn't an O'Toole, Martin." She looks at her grandfather. "He's Mom's dad. Ramsey is his name."

"Hmm, I shouldn't have assumed. So, I'm pleased to meet you, Mr Ramsey."

"You can call me Isaac. Nobody in years has called me Mr Ramsey."

"Isaac it is." I cast an eye out to the apricots. "So, are you going to get any apricots? I've really never heard of ground squirrels eating tree fruit."

Isaac raises the rifle and touches off a shot. I watch a goosy squirrel hug the ground then scamper back to the gully.

"Me, either. Must have learned about eating fruit because they are surrounded by oranges. Anyway, they sure do like green apricots."

"You know," I say. "Seems like your sights are too high."

"Maybe so." He squints down at the rear sight, takes his thumb and pulls the sight's elevator back down. "Sean must have set it up."

I look at Sherrill. "Sean—that's your dad?" She nods but doesn't have a chance to say anything. Isaac keeps right on talking.

"You want to try it?" He holds the Winchester out to me, the barrel pointed down and away from Sherrill and me. "Go ahead. Maybe your young eyes can put one of these rascals out of commission. Maybe doing so will send a message of caution to the ground squirrel town on the other side of the gully."

I take the rifle, check the safety, and slide another bullet into the chamber. My own .22 was a heavier Savage bolt action, but I'd pushed plenty of rounds through Grant's identical version of this pump-action Winchester. Despite the visions of guns' damage that haunted me not so many weeks past, the little .22 feels good in my hands. I look off in the orchard. Fortunately, Isaac's shots have driven his prey into hiding. I don't want to face the angst of shooting one. Although, I'm comforted that the idea could at least float around in my consciousness without unleashing bouts of panic. Perhaps I'm healing. Perhaps.

I raise the rifle and the instincts born from a lifetime of shooting course through my body. My dad's counsel whispers in my ear: learn to put the sights on the target and squeeze the trigger as soon as the butt rests squarely on your shoulder. The little rifle barks. A twig jumps off the limb to the left of the leaf I laid the sights on. I pump another bullet into the chamber without lowering the rifle. Another bark. The leaf flutters to the ground.

"It shoots a little to the left," I say, handing the rifle back to Isaac. "If you want, we can make a target out of a paper plate or something and fix that."

Isaac takes back the rifle. "No need, it's been shooting that way for years. You'd mess Sean up something terrible if you moved those sights." He chuckles. "Although, that could be funny—" His mind wanders to a private place for a few long seconds. Then he finishes off his thought, "—watching Sean scratch his head at why his eye's gone bad." He chuckles, smiles, looks at me, then Sherrill. I return his smile. His sense of foolishness matches what I grew up with. "You shoot like you're familiar with the process," he says.

I've got Grandpa on my side. "I grew up with guns. Most of them were twenty-twos."

And so it goes for the next little bit: Sherrill's grandpa and I bond over the love of chasing ring-neck pheasants in fields of Idaho corn and stalking mule deer across steep canyons covered with sagebrush and scattered pines. While we share these stories and wild lies about feats of marksmanship we have witnessed, Sherrill waits and watches, her hand resting on Isaac's shoulder, her fingers absently playing with his collar. Me? For the first time since that awful night, I'm relishing the step back into pleasant yesterdays, feeling optimistic when words about fallen deer or pheasants don't trigger the arrival of demons or images of the Captain swaying in the night.

Sherrill's Gramps obviously struggles with more than feebleness brought on by his advanced years. His right leg slants outward below his knee, an unnatural appearance even for an old man—hence, the cane. It's a slow walk back to the house.

Saturday, May 22, 1943
Extended Stay

In the late afternoon we all sit down for a home-cooked meal. Despite its California setting, the smells from the kitchen don't bear much resemblance to the Pacheco dinner times; instead they call up recollections of family meals at home. But the camaraderie around the dinner table feels both like home and Point Loma. We no sooner get past the blessing on the food, one familiar to my Protestant upbringing, than Sherrill's grandfather embellishes the story about the screwed-up sights. In between passing the fried chicken and the peas, he adds some stuff about how I, not he, thought it would be a great joke to fix the sights and then sit back and watch Sherrill's dad think maybe his eyes are going bad.

Sherrill's dad picks up the line. He slips into the story so smoothly, I'm sure he and Grandpa have played similar scenes at the expense of other initiates, friends of Sherrill's maybe, who had the audacity to pass under that ridiculous Hacienda Del O'Toole arch.

"Might be," Sean says, "I'd become another Annie Oakley with sights that worked. Course…" He pauses with a fork full of peas and glances around the table. "I can already shoot the eye out of a crow whilst it's still in the air."

Their repartee works two venues. One builds on good-natured ribbing to extend an unspoken invitation to enter into the fringes of family intimacy; the other flings down the gauntlet, dares me to pick it up, condemns me if I don't. In my youth I'd been similarly tested—by neighbors, uncles and older cousins. Among them were ranchers and homesteaders, cowboys and sheepherders, miners and lumberjacks, men who learned their mockery and leg pulling techniques from tough dads and granddads who opened up the West. What Sean and his father-in-law are throwing at me amounts to greenhorn stuff. And now, for a moment, I'm home; freed from the travails of the last few months, caught up with friends and foolishness and carefree conversation.

I pick up a chicken leg, raise it and, like Sean's fork full of peas, let it hang midway between my plate and my mouth. My drumstick points across the table at the tines of Sean's fork, two culinary epees at en garde. "You know, I had an uncle like that. Some argued he was the best shot in Idaho. Then one day my dad zeroes in Uncle Van's rifle. After that, Uncle Van was so deadly he didn't even bother buying bullets. When Idaho jackrabbits, which stand about a head taller than these little bitty things Sherrill called deer on our way up from San Diego, when those jackrabbits heard Uncle Van was out in the fields, they just rolled over and surrendered when he pointed his gun and hollered, 'BANG!'" I keep my chicken epee at point until Sean looks at his father-in-law and breaks the silence.

"Well, run up the white flag, Dad, we can't top that." Sean laughs and pops the peas into his open mouth. Gramps laughs. I laugh and bite off a mouthful of my erstwhile epee. Tomfoolery feels good after these past months of misery.

Sherrill's mom laughs. "He's from Idaho all right. You've been bested by the best, Dad." Sherrill hides her mirth with mashed potatoes. I think I have passed muster at the O'Tooles'.

* * * *

After we help Sherrill's mom clean up the dinner dishes, Sherrill says we're going into town for a movie. "Take the Packard," her dad says. "That big old car seems safer on these back roads at night."

Sherrill grabs the keys off the hook by the back kitchen door. "Thanks, Dad. We'll be back before midnight."

Sherrill's mom enters the conversation. "We haven't had one since I don't know when, but if there's a blackout, pull over and stop. Don't try and drive without lights."

Sherrill waves her hand in response to her mom's request, opens the back door and heads for the Packard. I look at Mrs O'Toole, who smiles and pats me on the arm. "She'll be safe with you. I don't like her driving around on these back roads at night by herself."

I follow Sherrill through the door, wondering why I can't shake off the feeling there's more in Mrs O'Toole's words than worry about blackouts.

The drive to Riverside is uneventful. On the way, we pass a fenced-in orange tree. Sherrill points it out and tells me it's the parent naval orange tree, the Adam and Eve of all the naval orange trees in California.

We park and buy two tickets at the De Anza Theater, which sits a few blocks past a giant white statue Sherrill says is a likeness of a Spanish explorer named Juan Bautista De Anza, the theater's namesake.

The show is a double feature. The first one is some crazy Red Skelton thing about baseball and the main feature stars Teresa Wright and Joseph Cotten in an Alfred Hitchcock thriller called *Shadow of Doubt*. We sit in the back row. Sherrill pulls my arm around her, and she leans back against the seat while she eats buttered popcorn and giggles at Red's nonsense. Later on, when Hitchcock's tension builds on the screen, she snuggles up close. Her pleasant smell, recently shampooed hair tainted by the residue from cigarette smoke, mine and hers, mixes with the aroma of the popcorn and calls up familiar recollections of other nights in other theaters with other girls, even Elaine.

On our way home we stop at Tuxie's drive-in and get hamburgers and milkshakes. It strikes me odd. We're both over twenty-one, but burgers and shakes seems a comfortable thing to do in lieu of bellying up to some bar. I never was much of a drinker, and evidently neither is Sherrill. Although we are outnumbered by teenagers, Sherrill bumps into a couple of high school friends. She introduces me as a colleague from the Navy in San Diego, which I appreciate; doing so avoids the strained atmosphere while people figure out how to deal with the war's reality brought on by wounds.

We retrace our steps to Hacienda Del O'Toole; down Magnolia Avenue, the main thoroughfare going our way, for three or four miles, then left on a dark road flanked by orange trees. We come to a stop sign. I can't quite read the street sign, but remember it was Victory Avenue when we stopped here in the daylight.

"Close," Sherrill says. "Actually, it's Victoria Avenue, as in Queen Victoria. The Victoria Country Club flanks it a mile or so from the center of town. That's where the ranchers meet the professionals, doctors, lawyers and the agents who insure everybody's homes and ranches, for golf and gala events. That's where I learned how to play tennis.

"Did I tell you I was on the varsity squad at USC? Well, at least for a couple of years. But being the last one on the traveling team in my junior year didn't seem worth the effort when decent grades took so much time."

I start to reply, but her sudden deceleration stops me. She continues to coast, touches the brake a little and downshifts. She pulls over, stops, and turns the engine off.

"What's wrong?" I ask.

She doesn't answer for a few seconds, just keeps her eye on the rearview mirror. I turn and look behind me in time to see the red glare turn off. A sheriff's deputy climbs out of his car. "Oh, nothing, probably," Sherrill says. "I think it's Alfred. I was hoping we could avoid him."

Before I can ask who Alfred is, he's leaning into the window Sherrill has rolled down.

"Well, I thought that was you," Alfred says. "Saw you driving in earlier in the evening. Almost missed you in your dad's Packard."

"How are you, Alfred? Things so slow on a Saturday night you can just stop folks to chat? Or did you catch me driving too close to the side of the road or something?"

I wasn't sure if it was fear, dislike, or a little of both, but Sherrill's banter bore none of her hidden humor. Her normally playful lips flirted with a snarl, and the acidity in her tone eroded any notion of friendliness in her words.

"Not so slow," says Alfred. He leans back, assuming an almost boastful pose. "Fact is, I stopped Freddy Soliz over on Victoria."

"Has Freddy changed? We didn't call him Steady Freddy for nothing."

Alfred's self-satisfied smirk flashes to a frown, then restores itself. "Well, he's a Mexican. Mexican, nigger—don't make much difference—I figured I'd find something if I pulled him over. Did, too! Had an open bottle of Pabst in the back seat."

Sherrill looks up the road, ignores Alfred for a second or two, then turns her head towards him and smiles. "What would this country be if we didn't have you to protect us from Mexican banditos? I feel safer now. You going to cite me, or can I be on my way?"

Alfred's smile turns into a straight line. "Just wanted to say hi, for old time's sake. Thought maybe we could have a drink up at the Oasis, for old time's sake." He steps back, leans into the car door, looks past her to me. "Who's your friend? You drag him home from the war?"

Sherrill's tone is no longer etched with acid, it's floating in it. "Who my friend is, Alfred, is none of your business." She turns on the ignition. The Packard jumps to life. "Isn't there some kind of rule about drinking on the job?" She puts the car in gear. "It's been nice talking with you, Alfred…for old time's sake." She pops the clutch. Alfred steps back from the door as the Packard moves down the road.

"What was that all about?"

Sherrill ignores my question while she moves up through the gears until we're moving down the narrow road in high. She flicks the high beams on. They create a luminescent conduit through the citrus trees crowding both sides of the road. A gleaming set of eyes slows her down. A cat crouches and waits while we pass by. We ride in silence for a half-mile or so before she speaks up.

"It's an old issue. Alfred's full of himself, as if he actually earned the silver spoon in his mouth. His dad and granddad run the biggest law office in town – Wilson, Thomas & Wilson. Estate planning, wills, partnerships—all that business stuff. I dated Alfred a few of times. A couple of movies, double dates both times, but he hit the sauce pretty heavy, even in high school. While I'm no prude, I didn't have time to deal with his obnoxious behavior."

Sherrill quits talking while she negotiates the Y that leads to Mockingbird Lake on one leg and the road home on the other. We drive into the dark. She slows down for another set of luminescent eyes.

"What in the hell was that?" I ask.

"You never seen a possum? Guess not, coming from up north. Well, you have now." She turns up the gravel driveway, and picks up the story. "Alfred was a big man on campus. Party boy, went both ways on the football team, track star. He asked me to the homecoming dance. I turned him down. Told him I'd already been asked and accepted. When he found out I went with my cousin, Michael, he was really irritated."

Sherrill pulls into the garage and turns the engine and lights off.

"Anyway, I'm home for the Christmas break in my junior year at USC, and Alfred comes driving out to the ranch one Saturday afternoon when Mom and Pop were shopping in San

Bernardino. Just Gramps and me sitting at the kitchen table. Alfred is plastered. I could tell by the way he placed one purposeful foot in front of the other as he made his way to the back porch. I told Gramps to tell him I was still in bed, and I disappeared upstairs. Gramps stopped him at the porch. Alfred said he'd come on in and wait. When he opened the screen door, Gramps grabs the twenty-gauge from where Dad kept it in the porch closet, points it through the door at Alfred's belly, and tells him he isn't invited in." She pauses. I think she's searching for words to fit the scene she is resurrecting in her mind. "When Alfred says he's coming in anyway, Gramps puts a round through the door next to the floor."

"Jeez! Your Grandpa plays hardball!"

Sherrill chuckles. "Yeah, he's kind of known for that. Anyway, some splinters and a couple of pieces of shot peppered Alfred's legs." She chuckles again. "Sobered him up pretty quick. He decided not to come in after all. Mumbled something about having Gramps arrested for attempted murder." Now she laughs, a crescendo of hilarity. Sherrill can hardly talk she's giggling so much. "I'm hiding at the top of the stairwell. Gramps tells him, 'Go ahead, Alfred. Sheriff knows me well enough that if I'd attempted murder you'd be dead.'"

"I need to take notes," I say. "This is the stuff of a Steinbeck novel. So, that's what this is all about? He's still carrying the torch for you and trying to live down being run off like a common drunk? What's the story about Freddy Soliz?"

Sherrill has both hands on the steering wheel and is looking out the front window at the back wall of the garage.

"Freddy's a Mexican. What with all the trouble with the gangs, the pachucos and the service men in L.A., lots of people around here think that's the only reason you need to make their lives miserable. Alfred's one of them. But it's more than that. Freddy made the mistake of humiliating Alfred. Alfred doesn't handle humiliation well, since he's better than everyone else, especially wetbacks and niggers. And Freddy's a wetback—his words not mine."

It's not like I've never heard those words before, even used them a few times myself. But it seems so out of character for Sherrill, even with her caveat at the end.

"So, where does the humiliation come in?"

"Goes clear back to high school. Alfred's the big track star. I don't think Freddy made it past his junior year, but that year he was a sophomore. He never had time for sports and wasn't much of a student. But he ran in the interclass meet—that's during school time, a spring assembly of sorts. Anyway, Freddy runs and beats all comers, including the big senior star, Alfred, in both the one-hundred and the two-twenty. Alfred Wilson has his reasons to be on Freddy's case." She emits one last chuckle.

"Gramps, he finished off his version of the Gunfight at the O.K. Corral by standing on the front porch with that old, rusty revolver of his as Alfred drove off." Sherrill looks at me. "Dad, he gives me the Packard, hoping Alfred will ignore it thinking Dad's behind the wheel. Otherwise, Alfred always stops and harasses me when he's on patrol. Scares Mom. To tell you the truth, he kind of scares me, too. He's known to get violent. Put one of the field workers in the hospital a year or so ago when somebody called for help at a bar. Hit that poor guy so hard with his club he fractured his skull."

The silence that follows allows us a moment of quiet reflection. We look at each other. The only sound is the occasional creak of the Packard's block as it begins to cool in the night's air. Sherrill's beguiling countenance intrigues me, and the ever present hint of a smile, that upward turn of her mouth's corners; the effect is alluring. Even in the dark, I see her captivating emerald eyes. They sparkle, refracted by the veneer of glistening wet between them and the faint moonlight that creeps into the front seat of the Packard through the open garage door.

The combination of eyes and seductive demeanor create an open invitation to come close, but she's the one who slides over and leans into me. I'm so taken aback, I almost blow the opportunity and hesitate before I reach my left arm around her and draw her closer. My eyes close. Her presence comes to me: cool, soft lips, fingers that wander by my cheek and nest in the hair at the back of my head, the essence of her gender sneaking past the latent suggestions of buttered popcorn, cigarettes and the drive-in fare. She holds the kiss long enough to convey caring while holding passion in check. Her words don't break the mood, they set the boundaries. "Thanks for a wonderful evening, Ensign Martin Holcomb."

This tender moment melds with the carnal instincts spreading through me. They call up recollections of the past, combine with the day's events to dissolve my resolve to live in today and tomorrow, and create longings to replicate passionate yet caring moments from my yesterdays. Right now, with whom is of no consequence. I suck in air, catch my breath, place my fingers under her chin, lean forward, and kiss the tip of her nose. "We better go inside before I do something to ruin the night."

We haven't crossed the kitchen into the hall that leads to the formal dining room before her Mom comes tip-toeing down the stairs in her nightgown inquiring about the movie and cups of chocolate before bedtime. I think Momma thinks Sherrill is still in high school. I decline. I want the taste and smell of Sherrill's lips to linger, like the lilting words in a lullaby, until I fall asleep. Perhaps they'll let me defer the debate in my mind about causes I suffered wounds to defend, that the Alfreds of the world might carry on their charades of justice. Perhaps I'll come to terms with feelings, ones I once held only for Elaine.

Part 2

Seventh infantry's fighting up in the Aleutians. That's the same Seventh Infantry took on the Nez Perce at the Big Hole in '77 and nearly came away like Custer's Cavalry.

Sunday, May 23, 1943
Gramps

The futile, muted attempts to begin a meal without making noise wake me. Before long, bacon sizzles. I smell coffee. My eyes open and peer past the yellow curtains framing the front bedroom window. I watch cottontails nibble grass on the front lawn. Upstairs, a door opens, bare feet pad across the floor. The stairs creak. The front door opens. I track the progress of the feet by their soft shuffle until I see her: Sherrill, clad in her bathrobe, at the steps of the porch. She claps her hands and shoos the cottontails away. She watches, her hands in her robe pockets. Last night's front-seat interlude creeps into my consciousness. I've felt this before. Infatuation? I wonder.

Protest breaks my spell: a squeak of hinges, like a badly played C note on an out-of-tune fiddle. It is the screen door that leads onto the back porch from outside. Grandpa's thumping cane accentuates each careful step into the house. Voices, his and Barbara's, waft through the walls, the words muffled beyond recognition, but their tone speaks volumes about comfort and caring.

Sherrill disappears back into the house.

The mood around the breakfast table carries the same frivolous banter as yesterday's dinner. Bacon, eggs, and hash-browned potatoes washed down with coffee are consumed before Sean gets around to the day's agenda. He takes the first sip of his second cup of coffee and looks at Sherrill.

"Your mom and I are going to try to make the eleven o'clock service. Do you and Martin want to come, or do you have other plans?"

Sherrill casts a glance my way. "Do you want to go to church? It lasts about an hour and twenty minutes. Takes about fifteen minutes to get there."

I don't feel comfortable with the idea. I pick my words with care.

"One thing I didn't pack was any dress clothes. If I'd been thinking ahead, I could have brought my Navy whites."

Sherrill's mom offers a way out. "Well," she says, "we Methodists don't put too much stock on appearances, but even Dad puts on a coat and tie when he goes to church. I bet he wouldn't mind staying home." She stops long enough to let her words settle in. "So, Martin—why don't you stay and keep Dad company?"

I look first at Sherrill's mom, then her dad, then Grandpa, then Sherrill. I find no help; they're all waiting on my opinion of the stay-with-Grandpa idea.

"If he wants to go, I'm sure I can find something to do," I say. I sense this is not the answer they were hoping for. Repenting, I offer up one more possibility. "Or if casual's okay, I'd love to go."

This time it's Grandpa who comes to my rescue.

"Barb's got the best plan. I'll stay here. Maybe Martin and I can take a spin in the buggy."

That's the first time I've heard anyone refer to Sherrill's mom by any name other than Mom. Barb. Barb fits. Feels good, like his earlier use of Sherrie.

So it's settled. Barbara, Sean, and Sherrill pile into the Packard and head for the Arlington Methodist church. As they drive off, my mind plays with what Sherrill's mom meant by, "and no racing with the buggy."

Gramps disappears somewhere out back. I discover him surrounded by strips of leather, and assorted awls, knives, and punches, out in the tack room that's hooked to the stable. My presence blocks the light coming through the doorway. He looks up at me and reaches over to the switch screwed onto one of the two-by-four studs. The single light hanging from a cord over the workbench turns on. I step through the door and watch for a moment. Isaac measures out a piece of strap,

Dan Strawn

using a long piece of rein attached to a halter as a template. He picks his pocket knife up off the bench and slices the leather.

"Gonna take Abednego out," he says. "Got to have reins without cracks in the leather. Told Sean we needed to oil up the harness after the last outing. Got rained on and it already had cracks."

He picks up the new piece of rein and sizes up the harness.

"Let's see," I say. "Abednego would be the bay, right?"

Isaac punches a couple of holes in the leather and threads it through the halter. He stops his work, looks at me, and smiles. I've seen that happy grin before on his granddaughter's face, the one she puts on when she's enjoying the present moment.

"I see you met the livestock. Paid attention, too. Abednego is the bay. A fine piece of horse flesh."

Isaac buckles in the final strap and holds up the halter portion so I can see the attached blinders.

"This here's a harness for a one-horse shay. Call it a sulky where I come from. That is, if the racing cart only carries one person. But we got us a cart built like a sulky. Modified it myself so it carries two at a time. Ever ridden in a cart pulled by a finely trained pacer?"

Before I can answer, Isaac turns, grabs a hank of cotton lead rope, grabs up his cane, and limps for the door. "Let's go get him," he says, "and I'll show you what pacers are all about."

Isaac may be old, he may be crippled, but he doesn't lack for energy, and he knows his way around horses. While Abednego nibbles on the carrot Isaac fished out of his pants pocket, Isaac snaps the lead rope on the big bay's halter. We walk back to the stable. Isaac explains more about pacers.

"Pacers are racers, but instead of having the jockey on top, he rides behind in a sulky. The difference between trotters and pacers lies in the way the horse runs. Trotters lift diagonal

108

front and rear feet when they trot, while pacers lift the front and rear feet on the same side when they pace. I tell you, it's a thing of beauty to watch well matched high steppers, trotters or pacers, moving out."

Isaac and I pull the modified two-wheeled cart from one of the paddocks and hook up his horse. I feel a little tentative about whether an old man is up to handling an animal of the size and obvious spirit of this horse. But before I can say much, Isaac is on the seat and motioning with his cane for me to climb up beside him.

There's barely room for the two of us on this cart born of a sulky. A click and slap of the reins and we move out of the corral and head towards the driveway that leads to the road. All the while, Abednego is throwing his head and pulling at the traces and his gait is a fretful walk. Blue veins stand out on Isaac's trembling and wrinkled old hands.

Watching the thousand pounds or so of horse flesh revving at the fringes of an all-out bolt makes me more than a little edgy. Visions of fighting to hold spirited horses pop up in my head. I recall the big gray that carried me wherever he wanted to go after my seven-year-old hands dropped the reins. I see the buckskin mare that never failed to dump me in the water trough at the end of our daily bareback rides in that summer between the fifth and sixth grades. And it was in the summer between my junior and senior years at UI that Dad brought home the thoroughbred gelding only a jockey could handle. The image causes me to chuckle: the farmer standing on the porch, wide-eyed, his pipe's stem held in front of his face, mouth agape, and the big Preakness-wanna-be with me holding onto the saddle horn like a greenhorn. I cleared the picket fence, dug out huge divots from the farmer's front lawn, and disappeared through the apple orchard behind his house.

We move down the road at a controlled walk. No doubt about it, this old man knows his horses.

Before long we've passed the turnoff to Mockingbird Lake. The road moves on top of a berm that follows the canal. The berm is straight, only disrupted by minor wrinkles for what has to be a mile or better. Isaac pulls the goggles that have been riding high on his forehead over his eyes.

"Hold on! I'm going to open him up."

The no-racing counsel stirs around in my mind. I grab the side of the seat. "You think we ought to do this so close to the canal?"

Isaac makes a little clicking noise and sends a wave down the reins. His horse responds and I'm thrown back as the cart lurches forward.

"Gid up!" Isaac says as he sends another signal with the reins. Abednego kicks into high gear. "How's that?"

I'm holding onto the edge of the seat with both hands. My thighs jam my feet into the rests. I entertain a forlorn hope that maybe there's glue on the soles of my shoes. "I said," my voice edging up a few fear-induced octaves. "Don't you think we're awfully close to the canal to be running a horse like this?"

Isaac ignores me. We ride the top of the berm at a wild clip. The pneumatic tires, not unlike bicycle tires, sing a high-pitched tune against the hard dirt, and the scenery slides by in a way that is different from riding in a car or train. It's an intimate thing, as if the trees, bushes, canal and road were part of us and are being peeled off as we race forward. Our steed's mane and tail reach back towards us. I'm mesmerized by his precision and speed. The fore and back legs of one side reach forward and search for the ground while those of the other side pull us down the road. It's not as fast as a gallop, and it doesn't rock like a gallop, but the mile-eating pace is smooth and exhilarating.

My head tucks into my right shoulder, a futile attempt to avoid the dirt and small rocks shot my way by flying hooves. I resign myself to the moment, let the wind slip by, and commit my fate to the hands of this wild jockey and his grounded Pegasus.

We pace for what has to be close to a mile before Isaac applies a gentle pull on the reins. Before long, tail and mane have ceased their flying, which is just as well since the road cants at a steep angle down to the bottom of the berm. It winds in gentle curves, following the natural bend of the canal around the south edge of the little valley shared by a dairy on one end and a walnut orchard on the other.

For the moment, Isaac is preoccupied with bringing his horse down to a sedate gait. After a furlong or so, he finally responds to my question.

"Horses aren't cars. They're not going to plunge themselves into harm's way, even if you try pointing them there." We cover another eighth of a mile. "Course, any horse can get spooked by a dog, a butterfly, most anything, but that's why we got those blinders on him. That said, horses doing what I least expected have caused some grief in my life."

Pleasant pastures pass by. No words punctuate the clop of hooves on hard dirt and the low frequency zing of tires rolling down the road. When Abednego has blown out from his run and settled into his walk, Isaac picks up the conversation.

"Sherrie says you been through some rough war stuff. You dealing okay with it all—your injury—your buddy dying in the hospital like that?"

I'm caught off-guard. I'm not sure I can verbalize a response, even if I wanted to. I had no idea that Sherrill had been so open with my story or even knew about the Captain for that matter.

When I say nothing, Isaac pushes on. "Been through a bit of that myself. Know what it's like dealing with the mind issues after the bones and flesh are long since healed. Even today, better'n sixty years later, I still have me a bad dream now and then. Course, my wounds didn't come at the hands of my enemy, not directly anyway. But I lost me some good friends. War's not finicky about who it puts down and who it spares."

A horse neighs out in the pasture that takes in part of the walnut grove. Abednego lifts up his head and blows through his nostrils. Isaac takes up the slack on the reins and gives them a little jerk.

"Whoa, now!"

A pickup towing a stock trailer approaches the intersection from our right. Isaac reins in a good fifty feet from where the two roads intersect. While we wait, my mind fills with fear, the kind born of the war and Japs and what they did to me and the Captain. My hands tremble on the edge of the sulky's seat.

Shit! I'm losing control!

The pickup slows down and turns our way. It creeps up to us; its owner tips his fingers to the edge of his straw hat as he slides by. Through the slats of the trailer, I see familiar flashes of a brown cow. Home comes to mind. Not since the hospital, before the Captain, have I had to fight back mindless despair.

"Gid up!" Isaac puts us back on the road. At the intersection, he wheels around. Horse and cart take up the road home, trailing the dust of the pickup with its trailer. "The battlefield," Isaac says, "has a way of making men see the world in a different light. More times than not, they come to face truths about themselves. Some good, some not so good. Things they'd never know without getting cozy with the prospect of imminent, violent death. Me, I found out bottling stuff up put a miserable slant on the future. Messed me up something awful until Sherrie's Grandma showed me how a little hope and humor makes life joyful."

More road slides by.

"Didn't mean to pry."

We ride in silence. I force my mind off the war and the Japs and try to decide how I feel about Sherrie sharing my past with her Grandpa, and who knows who else. Her parents, probably. And now I'm calling her Sherrie, too, like Grandpa. He must be getting under my skin. But I like Sherrie, it sounds good, and thinking on it lets the tremors and shakes recede.

Isaac slaps the reins. Abednego starts up, then settles back into his walk. The way Isaac stares ahead, the reins hanging loose in his hands, it's like he's caught up in some private memory.

I watch Abednego's ass end as each rump tenses with the effort of pulling us up on top of the berm. Doing so allows my mind to wander off the angst and onto ways I might turn the conversation back on Isaac and away from me.

"You were right. Riding behind a pacer is a thing of beauty. How'd you come by owning one?"

"Owned his mama. Shipped her out from a breeder in Indiana. Abednego's daddy belongs to the Wrigley family over on Catalina. I learned about pacers on my folks' ranch in Indiana. Course, my dad only kept pacers around for fun. He raised draft horses, Percherons mostly."

We're coming down off the Mockingbird turnoff before I come up with a good tack for my next inquiry.

"So, what brought you out West?"

We ride on in silence. I can see the turnoff now, with its Hacienda Del O'Toole arch.

"Came out when I was eighteen with the First Cavalry. Cavalry rode horses then, not like this war, where we traded steeds for steel tanks. Started out from Walla Walla on that grand chase of the Nez Perce in 'seventy-seven, but got myself banged up before we even left Idaho.

1877! I do some quick math. He has to be as close to ninety as he is to eighty!

"Course, getting banged up turned out to be a good thing. That's how I met Sherrie's grandma."

We pass under the arch. Abednego is pulling at the reins, no doubt sensing the bag of oats that waits for him at the end of this chore. Like him, I, too, am pulling at the reins, anxious about what lies ahead: Cavalry, Nez Perce, Percherons, pacers, and Abednego; they tell me there's a bridge between horses and Indian wars and love affairs with Sherrie's grandma. I'm beginning to understand why this old man, Gramps, owns the heart of the O'Toole family. I'm anxious to ferret out the stories.

And Sherrie? Has she moved into my heart? The prospect scares me. Dare I? If so, will I bungle this like I did with Elaine? And how can I deal with this and Asian ogres grinning between the explosions in my mind?

Isaac loosens up the reins enough so we're pacing about half speed when we spill out of the gravel road and veer past the Packard to the stable area behind the house.

Sherrie's mom, clad in men's blue-denim trousers and a blouse, stands at a table in the backyard. She's plucking the feathers off a chicken that obviously came out of the scalding pot sitting on the table. A second chicken, minus its head, waits its turn next to the pot. She stops her pulling and waves as her father and I drive through the open corral gate.

More home-fried chicken! A wave of familiarity washes over me, like that inspired by the dairy cows riding in the trailer back on the road. But first, there's a horse to rub down, feed and harness, and a cart to put away.

When I walk back into the house, the headlines on the Sunday newspaper bring me back to the present: "Seventh Infantry Takes Attu!"

Gramps misses lunch. Says he's tired and going to take a nap. Sherrill's mom says that's pretty normal after a ride or most anything else nowadays. She puts some chicken, mashed potatoes and gravy in the oven for him.

After the dishes are done, Sherrill catches up to me on the front porch. Sean is tinkering with some kind of spray rig that's hooked up to the Farmall in a row of orange trees on the other side of the driveway. I can hear Barbara still moving around the kitchen. Sherrill sits down in the chair next to me and immediately strikes up the conversation. Like her mom, she changed into farm girl clothes after church: men's Levis, a red and white checkered three-quarter-sleeve blouse, and tan leather, over-the-ankle riding boots. Now, as at the dinner table, her attire makes her appear more relaxed than normal, and more intriguing.

"You have to admit, Mom's is a whole lot better than Navy grub."

"No doubt about it, but I haven't been eating Navy grub. I've been enjoying Mariella Pacheco's cooking." I let that notion sit while I lock onto those fetching emerald eyes. "But your mom's cooking reminds me of my mom's. Same kind of food, fixed pretty much the same way."

Sherrill prefaces her next remarks with that engaging smile. "I'm glad you could make it. Glad it makes you feel at home. Glad you felt like taking a risk on a gullible WAVE from behind the front desk."

We both look at each other. Bunches of emotions compete for my attention: Mom and her cooking, the milk house smell of Dad, an inexplicable hint of bleach and milk and scoured concrete that's almost sour to the nostrils and won't go away no matter how hard he scrubs; Elaine; a hard to resist urge to kiss again the tip of the impish nose that now confronts me. I settle for a serious expression of gratitude.

"You know, I'm glad—glad I came. Your family's incredible. Your mom. Your dad. Your grandpa. Sitting here smelling orange trees is therapeutic. It puts aside all the…stuff I've had to deal with lately."

Sherrill reaches over and puts her hand on mine, which is resting on the arm of the wicker chair.

"So, Mom, Dad, and Gramps are incredible. Well, that's a good start."

I'm in the midst of deciphering the innuendos suggested by the dual effects of her hand on mine and the 'good start' when she changes the subject.

"So, tell me about your ride with Gramps," she says.

"Gramps? Oh, yeah, Gramps. Well, there's more to Gramps than being a spry old guy. For one, he knows a lot about horses, and he's pretty damn clever at raising issues, good and bad, around horses without revealing anything you can…how should I say…?"

"Hang your hat on?"

"Exactly. Hang your hat on. I mean, first he loves horses, thinks they're the calmest critters in God's creative plan, as well as the prettiest and most intelligent. In the next instant, he's talking about grief they've caused 'cause they're so damned unpredictable. Then he's praising them for shaping his life. And before I can digest that, he's asking how I'm doing with my wounds and the Captain. I didn't know you knew about the Captain. How'd you know about the Captain?"

"Martin, everybody at the base knows you found the Captain." She takes hold of my hand, the one she has been resting hers on, and squeezes it. "I didn't mean to—"

"No, that's all right. I mean, I guess I should be upset, everybody knowing and prying into what I'm doing. But your gramps, he says it so casual and knowledgeable. He caught me by surprise, but it was okay. Kind of like, 'Gee, I heard you had a boil on your ass. I've had one of those. Hurt like hell. But it's okay now. How's yours?'"

Sherrill looks at me, at a loss for words. I cover my embarrassment with a laugh and quick words. "Where'd that ridiculous metaphor come from? Boil on my ass?"

Sherrill doesn't laugh, but she does smile. The next thing I know she's standing behind me with her hands on my shoulders. She bends down and slides her hands around me until her arms encase my upper chest and lower throat, and her face presses next to mine. We hold that joint pose as if we were sitting for a portrait. I feel her soft lips on my cheek. For the moment I'm speechless, lost in the tenderness. Another kiss, gentle lips brushing my cheek followed by words in my ear. "Ensign Holcomb, don't you know, he's been there?"

"There?"

"Yes, there. That place where only those hurt in war hang out. He's felt the wounds, faced the foe, looked death in the eye, all that stereotypical and clichéd stuff used by the rest of us because only warriors comprehend what they've been through, and there are no words for it. He's lived it and found the good in it. Your metaphor is not ridiculous." She pauses and emits a hint of a chuckle. "Although, it is funny, coming out of your mouth like that. To Gramps, now, today, all that stuff is a boil, a hurtful pain in the ass, a reminder of what long since has gone away. Someday, it will go away for you too." She snuggles her cheek next to mine. "Don't you know?"

I'm caught in a cauldron of different emotions. I've recovered from the embarrassment, but the boil on the ass idea has still got my funny bone. Does finding humor mean I'm getting better or worse? I feel safe wrapped in her arms like this. Yet, I've let my guard down and set myself up for events I'm not sure I'm ready to handle. I push everything back but the humor and use it to wedge us onto firmer ground.

"Well, whatever. Boils or whatever, I would love to hear more of his story about horses and Indian wars and your grandma—and how they all intertwine."

Sherrill rests her cheek on mine while she deals with my shift in the tenor of the conversation, then stands up and returns her hands to my shoulders.

"I can tell you some, but Gramps will tell you the whole thing if you hang around long enough."

I look up at her. She tosses her head. Loose locks of hair uncover her eyes so she can look into mine, which she does; a friendly, caring dare to ask away.

I stand up next to her. We both look out at the green grass, the roses, and the straight rows of orange trees beyond. I search my mind for what I want to know first. "Your grandpa said getting hurt was a good thing because that's how he met your grandma. How did that play out?"

In the next ten minutes or so, I learn how Isaac came rolling into Lewiston in the back of an ambulance pulled by army mules. How, as soon as he could move around on crutches, the Knight family took him in to make room at the surgeon's tent for more wounded flowing in from the Army's chase of the Nez Perce. Sherrie tells me Dorothy Knight caught Isaac's eye, which is what caused him to work his way west after he returned to Indiana, "just to court and marry Grandma Dorothy," Sherrie says.

The story is interrupted when Shadrach wanders from the side of the house. Sherrie calls him over to her. He wags his way up the porch steps, sits at her feet, and points his head up to her, a pose every loved dog assumes when they know their head is about to be scratched. While Sherrie scratches and talks to him for a distracted moment, I can't help but wonder about Dorothy Knight and how she salvaged Isaac. Would Sherrie become my Dorothy? Is that what she's telling me? Or is there an ironic twist that I might someday write into a latter day Greek tragedy or, worse, a comedy? After all, I asked the question, she only answered it. My mind bounces from what I've learned about Isaac to my earlier ride on the berm.

"So, how did Isaac get hurt? He said he wasn't wounded in battle."

"Broke his leg. It's a complicated story. You'll have to get him to tell you. He's much better than me at storytelling. Besides, his old mind still remembers things I never knew." She grabs my hand and pulls. "Come on, let's go find Gramps."

We find him sitting at the kitchen table, downing the last mouthful of mashed potatoes and perusing the Sunday paper.

He gives us a quick glance when we enter the kitchen from the front of the house. Sherrie steps up behind him and places a hand on his shoulder. Her words, like those of all this family when they address Isaac, transcend respect; they carry in their tenor a tone approaching reverence.

"Gramps, how was your rest? Do you want some more milk to wash that down?"

Isaac picks up his glass and swirls it as if he were Enrique Pacheco tasting his wine. He downs the last bit of milk, sets the glass down, and wipes his mouth with the bottom of the napkin tucked under his chin. "Have you seen the headlines? Seventh infantry's fighting up in the Aleutians. That's the same Seventh Infantry took on the Nez Perce at the Big Hole in 'Seventy-seven and nearly came away like Custer's Cavalry."

Sherrie moves around and sits opposite her Grandpa. "What a coincidence, since we were wondering—Martin was wondering—if you could tell him some about the horses, the Indians, and how they brought you to Grandma Dorothy."

Isaac looks at me. His eyes throw off the same sparkle I see when Sherrie looks at me, but their hazel hue pales in comparison to the emerald of his granddaughter's. "Picket pins, that's what dug those holes that broke my mount's leg. Picket pins they were! Ever hear of picket pins? Least that's what we called them up in the panhandle. You have them down south in your part of Idaho? They're little fellows about three-fourths the size of the ground squirrels eating my apricots, and a whole lot smaller than the prairie dogs I saw out on the plains in the Dakotas and Montana."

"We have them," I say. "That's how my dad taught me the rudiments of hunting and shooting—picking off picket pins with a twenty-two."

He silently appraises me, like he is considering whether to hire me or something. I'm a little embarrassed. He breaks the silence with quick, friendly words. "Sit down." He points to the chair next to Sherrie. "Your circumstances, being so fresh and all, kind of brings my own fate to mind. I got it all written down, but it's scattered in six or eight journals. I kept journals, you know. Don't know why, except I learned it from my momma. Anyway, sit down. I'll tell you about me, and Dot, and Nez Perces and horses." He's done it again: Sherrie, Barb, and now Dot.

Ever the journalist, I beg a few seconds to dash back to my room for pen and paper. I retrieve my own journal and the pen from my duffel bag and return to the kitchen.

As soon as I return, Isaac begins to talk.

"When I think on it all these years after, it's like my life's story spun off events that had to do with horses. I mean, horses in a roundabout way's what got me into the army in the first place. And my ability with horses, my ability to ride, is what set me up for getting all busted up out in the Bitterroots at the mercy of the fellow who found me. He was a Nez Perce, one of them we were chasing. But he was only one of the Nez Perces that got me in trouble. I'd spent the better part of two days trying to shake three others before I run up on this fellow."

For a long pause, a minute maybe, Isaac stretches his wrinkled fingers out on the table and looks at them before he goes on.

"Anyway, I'm getting ahead of myself. Let's cover the horses first. We'll get to the Indians and Dot later. I think I already told you I was brought up on a ranch in Indiana that bred draft horses. When I was coming into my own, fourteen or fifteen, horses made me an orphan."

Sherrie reaches over and touches Isaacs's hand. Isaac pauses, lets the gesture settle in before he continues. The silent affection between him and his granddaughter melds into the story, makes it personal, even more poignant than before.

"It wasn't the draft animals—the Percherons—it was the Morgans my dad kept to take us into town. Had 'em hooked up to the surrey, a matched pair of dark bay Morgans. They were something to see. Anyway, he and my mom took them on Sunday to go to church. My parents, they never did show up. My brother and I were already there. We found them underneath the surrey on the ride back to the ranch."

"What happened?" I ask.

Isaac's quick answer tells me it's no longer an issue riding on the cusp of his mind. "Don't rightly know what happened. Something, a dog maybe, or a rabbit running under their feet, something spooked those Morgans. Shouldn't a been any problem, except the harness come loose on one of them. We, my brother and I, we found the surrey dumped off into a thicket. One horse was half-loose and standing there, the other still in the traces bucking and pulling, trying to get away from that surrey that was spun clear upside down and wedged into a downed alder."

Isaac pauses, looks again at his fingers splayed out on the table. I notice the shake in his hands that bothered me so much when he was handling the pacer. Is that old age, or do the memories bother more than he earlier indicated? Is that why all his attention went to new reins before we went out on our buggy ride?

"Anyway, they were gone, my dad thrown into the thicket. Looking back, I think he was pulled right out of the seat by his tight grip on the reins. Mom was underneath the surrey. They were both gone. I stayed on at the ranch and helped my brother and his wife for a few years, but things weren't the same. Not bad, just not the same.

"So, one morning I hitched a ride into town and signed up with the United States Army. A few months later, I'm attached to the First Cavalry in Walla Walla, Washington. It isn't long before I'm mounted and off to Idaho. Seems the Nez Perce, who I'd never heard of, were fleeing, and General Howard, our commander in chief, was hell bent to stop them before they caused more trouble."

Isaac stops here. This time his eyes close while he draws little circles on the table top with the middle finger of his left hand. The circle drawing stops. His eyes remain closed. Sherrie is fixed on her grandpa. Has he fallen asleep? His eyes pop open, and he begins speaking as if nothing happened.

"So, horses. I grew up with horses. Runaway horses killed my mom and dad. Now I'm in the cavalry chasing Indians who own the finest horse herds in the West. That one-armed general of ours, old Howard, he decides he wants a message sent up to Weippe and then to Lewiston. Somehow, I get picked to be a courier. Why? I don't know why. The sergeant says it's because of, you guessed it, I'm good with horses and I know how to read.

"Anyway, I take off with a 'treaty' Nez Perce, one of the good guys, and head for Weippe. The next day, when we was maybe fifteen miles from where the soldiers were supposed to be, we got ourselves ambushed by three non-treaties on the prowl. My scout's horse was shot out from under him. The scout, he lived, although at the time I figured he was a goner."

"What happened to you?"

"Me? Me, I headed east, hell bent for I don't know where. Anywhere except where those red devils might corner me out on the prairie. To the east, off in the distance, I could see trees and mountains. Those three Nez Perces pursued me until I finally lost them in the mountains in the middle of a rain storm.

"That mare, she carried me all day and all the next day. Looking back, what saved my bacon was thinking to beg a bag of oats off the mule skinner before I took off on that ride to Weippe. Those oats gave her the extra oomph that got me up the steep slopes of the Bitterroots and away from them Indians."

Isaac stops here and asks Sherrie for a glass of water. After a long drink, he smacks his lips, as if he had just quaffed a half glass of cold beer. He sets the glass on the table and wipes his mouth with the back of his hand. Sherrie and I wait in silence. In his own time, at the moment of his choosing, he continues.

"Me and that mare, we ride over the summit of I don't know how many ridges and down their far sides. About the time I figure we've given them the slip, I've got one of 'em confronting me not fifty feet away, sitting on his horse, looking at me, an arrow notched into his bow. I figured out later, it probably wasn't one of them that was chasing me.

"Anyway, I whirled that mare around and put the spurs to her. That's when she stepped into a picket pin hole. She and I suffered broken legs. The Indian, he stood over me with my own pistol in his hands. I figured I'm done for, but he put the horse out of her misery, splinted up my leg, and hauled me on a travois back down the mountains. Left me there in the path of an army patrol and skedaddled. Dangdest thing I ever had happen to me.

"The surgeon said that while my leg's always gonna be bent—it had started to mend by the time the docs got a hold of me—that Indian splinting it up probably saved it from poking through my skin, saving me from getting the gangrene and dying.

"So guess what? That little mare, the one who carried me out of danger only to break her leg? When that patrol finds me, I'm strapped onto her hide. That Nez Perce carried me out of danger using my own horse's skin as a travois blanket. That mare, she's had a special spot in my heart all my life.

"So…I'm eventually loaded in an Army ambulance pulled by mules, and they hauled me to Grangeville."

Sherrie interrupts, "Weren't you taken to Lewiston, Gramps?"

Isaac quickly retorts, "No, it was Grangeville. I didn't get to Lewiston until I was on my way to being discharged. Your grandma's daddy had a farm right outside of Grangeville. That ambulance took me there, picked up a couple of really sick soldiers in Grangeville and went on to Lewiston. They didn't want me around those sick guys in the wagon, so they left me in Grangeville. That's when your grandma's daddy took me out to his place to recuperate. For the next three weeks, I'm stuck at that farmhouse outside of Grangeville. That's where I met Dot."

Isaac stops talking. Trembling hands make little ridges with the tablecloth. His eyes are shut. I'm fearful the interview is about over. After maybe a minute, he opens his eyes and looks at Sherrie. He takes up his story as if he'd never stopped.

"Her mama's good food put the meat back on my bones while Dot stole my heart."

Again, Isaac's eyes close, his fingers push more ridges on the tablecloth, but only for a few seconds.

"Before long, three, maybe four weeks, the army loads me up on another ambulance and I'm bound for Lewiston, Fort Vancouver, and the long train ride home."

"How did you get back to the Northwest?"

Sherrie and I wait out another long pause. I've decided Isaac's pauses are caused less by fatigue than the time it takes for him to reach back in his mind and haul out the pieces of his story.

"Took three years. Oh, Dot and I passed a few letters back and forth, but I was pretty much on the move. Life on the farm wasn't the same, not since my folks died. When that leg got well enough that I could limp around pretty good, I got me a job in a dry goods store and moved into town." Isaac chuckles. "But that didn't last no time at all. I had Dot on my mind. Besides, the West had kind of crawled under my skin.

"Even though my leg was all screwed up, I was young and strong and determined. I got me a job on the railway – the Atchison, Topeka, and Santa Fe, and worked my way West. It wasn't the Northwest, but it was West. Shoveling coal is what I did. Spent two years at the mouth of the furnace pouring coal into the fire so's them engines could wind their ways across the prairies. In a pinch, we'd use wood until the coal caught up to us, or we to it.

"One way or another, I kept in touch with Dot. At Albuquerque, I sent her a wire. Said I had three hundred dollars saved and a job lined up with the Northern Pacific that would take me all the way to Spokane. Would she marry me? It'd been three and a half years since I saw her, but I knew she wasn't married yet 'cause she was still writing now and then. Long story short, she said yes. I worked my way back to Chicago. Took my leave of the Santa Fe and signed on with the Northern Pacific. Less than three weeks later, we're standing in front of the Presbyterian preacher in Lewiston.

"That first year was rough. I got me a job teaching school to the Nez Perce at the old army fort in Lapwai. We made do with that meager job and what we could grow on a little patch of ground behind the house. The house was part of my pay. Anybody who had any learning at all back then was qualified to be a teacher. Course most of them were women. But, the reverend who married us knew the need in Lapwai, knew I was literate, and knew I needed work. Besides, I never did feel any angst towards the Nez Perce. Figured that fellow who hauled me out of the Bitterroots kind of reputed all those wild Indian stories I grew up with. In a strange kind of way, I figured I owed that Nez Perce something for not leaving me up there to die, or doing the job himself. Wouldn't have blamed him, the way his people and the Army were going at each other."

Isaac seems unaffected by these memories and pushes forward as if he were rushing to a point he wanted to get to.

"But things weren't all good. I contracted consumption. The docs consulted about my coughing and hacking and spitting up blood and concluded I had to get out of this wet country or I was a goner. Think they thought I was done for either way. So, Dot and I moved to the desert, hoping the dry air might save me."

I prompt him with more questions. "How did you survive? That is, what did you do for money?"

"Can't believe that Dot. Never been more'n half day's ride from Grangeville, yet she hitched herself to a dying man, and she doesn't follow, she takes me in tow and drags me out to California. Some woman! Didn't have much. I'd met a rancher from California when I was working the Santa Fe. Helped him a couple of times. Took care of some breeding stock he was transporting out West. He took a liking to me and said to look him up if I ever got to Los Angeles. When the consumption came on me, I wrote and asked about where I might find a place on the desert. He wrote back and made me an offer perfect for my situation, keeping an eye on cattle he's got roaming out on the high desert east of the mountains, not more than eighty-five or ninety miles from where we're sitting right now.

"Next thing you know, Dot and I are staked out on the Mojave in a one-room shack. My job – keep the coyotes and mountain lions away from a couple hundred scruffy heifers roaming the canyons that flow out of the San Bernardino Mountains onto the desert floor. Our pay was the shack, a reasonably good cow pony, an old army-issue Sharps carbine, a Colt forty-five, water we had to boil before we drank—it came out of the Mojave River—and food. It wasn't much, but the air was pure and dry. If I was going to beat this thing, it was my only chance.

"So Dot and I, we became cowpunchers on the desert. And my benefactor, he saved my life. Said he didn't expect much, just being there might cut down on the losses. But Dot and I, we took the work seriously. Never did get me a lion, although, I did get me a black bear, and come across lion tracks and bear tracks the likes of which I knew was grizzly. But after five or six months, the coyotes that were left made themselves scarce. Kind of figured all the ruckus our presence made moved most of the lions and that grizzly back up into the hills.

"You obviously recovered from tuberculosis. So it must have worked," I say.

Isaac smiles, takes a long drink of the water Sherrie brought him earlier. He empties the glass.

"You're getting ahead of me, moving too fast. It was a windy, blustery midday in March. I was working a canyon coming out of Deep Creek. I come across what looked like horse tracks that weren't mine. This horse was unshod and a little fellow. I figured it out later. I think he was one of them burros gone wild when some prospector up and died or went back to civilization. Anyway, I got off my horse to look at the tracks when the horse shied at a piece of something flying through the air about head high—probably a piece of sage or Joshua tree. I lost my grip on the reins, seeing as how I was bent down looking at these hoof prints, and the horse reared back and trotted off.

"I couldn't get close to him. He moved down into a gully crossing the desert floor and up the other side. When he stopped to nibble on a little bit of something struggling through the sand, I took off running to catch up to him. About the time I got to the bottom of the draw, that horse trotted over the horizon. And so it went. I chased him down and up three or four of these little canyons, gullies really, and wasn't any closer to catching up than when I started. I was winded. My side ached. I started to cough.

"In a couple of seconds, I was coughing so hard I couldn't stand straight. I was hunching over, then standing up, then hunching over, anything to get air, all the time coughing. In between the racking coughing, I could see blood on the desert dirt. Red droplets at first. Then splashes of red, like spilled paint off the end of a brush. Then I was doubled over with coughing spasms. Blood poured out of my mouth. I was on my hands and knees, coughing and hacking, the sand wet and red with my life's blood. I began to spew out great hunks of what looked like black tar. I could feel the insides of my chest coming apart. More black gunk and more blood. I lay in the sand. I knew I was dying."

Isaac pauses—for effect maybe, or to collect his thoughts.

"I must have lain there for an hour or more. I think I actually slept. Anyway the wind had let up and a warm March sun beat on my back. When I opened my eyes the blood had seeped into the sand. What little didn't was dried. That black stuff, that stuff that come up out of my lungs, it was laying there next to my face. I thought it must be blood clots, but when I touched it I saw it was solid, like a clot of mud, which is what it was – big globs of coal dust I'd sucked into my lungs while shoveling fuel into the maws of those engine ovens.

"Dot, she found me. Got worried when I didn't show up for midday lunch. Next day, that horse, he was standing at the corral waiting for his morning's hay. From that day forward, I started getting better. We stayed on that spot of arid Eden for all that year and part of the next. When Dot came in a family way, we moved out. Our benefactor found work for me on one of his farms over by what is now Redlands, about eighteen miles from here. That's where Barb's older brother was born.

"So, there you have it. I've probably left some stuff out, but the important stuff you heard. Horses? If it weren't for horses, I'd never come out West, never met Dot. Horses took my parents, but they saved my life, once up on the Bitterroots and once on the Mojave Desert. If that horse hadn't run away from me, that coal dust in my lungs might have laid there 'til it killed me."

I'm overwhelmed by the story and Isaac's skill at telling it. More questions bounce around in my head. For the moment, I'm taken out of the here and now, and lost in Isaac's yesterday. I prod him.

"And what about the Nez Perce? I'm surprised you went to teaching their kids after all they did to you."

"It wasn't the Nez Perce did me harm. It was people not getting along did me harm. That's what put me in harm's way. It was a Nez Perce saved my bacon. Got no axe to grind with the Nez Perce, although I'm a bit put out at how some's turned to low-based white habits, alcohol and all. But, that's enough for now, I'm gonna' finish reading that story about the Seventh Infantry in the Aleutians in Sunday's paper. Did you know the Nez Perce gave the Seventh Infantry a pretty good mauling at the Big Hole in eighteen-seventy-seven?"

The interview is over. Isaac's forgiveness overwhelms me. Will I, like him, ever quit hating?

I would love to get my hands on those journals, but don't dare ask. Who knows, maybe later. For now, I've got a ton of notes which need to be read and refined.

Monday, May 24, 1943
Danger In Eden

We rode in silence, each of us consumed by our private thoughts.

Sherrie drove east, past the orange groves, past Camp Haan, where soldiers waited in makeshift billets and practiced antiaircraft warfare, and past rows of B-17's lined up on the tarmac at March Field. In an hour or so, we were climbing through the range of low mountains headed southwest, maybe fifty miles from the Santa Ana River canyon we had driven through the past Saturday. Not a hundred words had passed between us since we left her parents' home for San Diego.

Sherrie? What were her thoughts? Were they twisting around Alfred's unscheduled appearance and the news he brought? Or had she pushed them out of her mind and focused instead on the winding road?

Me? My mind was a jumble of conflicting realities and suspected causes, bitter ironies and biased musings. I couldn't help but contrast random violent events in this Shangri La called California with the purposeful havoc of war. The causes of my wounds and the Captain's suicide were obvious: planning by a determined foe. But what is the sense behind a harmless hunt for cottontails and the tragedy that came down at Danny Ishisaka's place?

And just before we left, Alfred brought news to the O'Tooles in his '39 Ford patrol car: Rosa Lopez found molested and murdered alongside the canal. What's the rationale for that?

"Everybody," Alfred said, "knows she'd been seeing Freddie Soliz, and now he's dropped off the face of the earth." Then Alfred inquired as to whether we had seen Freddie or Rosa over the last two days.

Of course, we hadn't, and that's what got my mind going as Sherrie and I drove through the mountains in silence. Why hadn't we? Isaac and I rode that canal on Sunday. Alfred said the dairyman found her next to the road late Sunday afternoon when he drove up on the berm to check the flow gates for the flume that led to his place. Why didn't we see her? We didn't go to the flume, but it was only a hundred feet or so from where the road left the berm and slanted to the valley floor. I remembered seeing the water rush out of the flue on our return trip. I didn't see a body. Could I have been so taken with Isaac's wild ride I didn't see a dead person lying next to the road straight ahead of me? That's hard to imagine, but I must have.

We stopped at a Flying A gas station in a pleasant little town called Escondido. Sherrie disappeared into the ladies' room. By the time she came out, I had completed a similar trip and purchased a Dr. Pepper and an orange drink from the cooler out front. I handed her the Dr. Pepper and we climbed into the car. By the time we'd pulled back onto the highway, I felt up to broaching the subject with Sherrie.

"You know, your Gramps and I went right by there on Sunday morning. Why didn't we see her body?"

Sherrie shifted the Plymouth into third and took a pull on her Dr. Pepper. We had left town and started down the long, western slope to San Diego before she answered.

"I didn't figure Freddie for that kind of nonsense," she said. "Course, Mexicans and whites don't mingle much, but Freddie and I talked a few times out at the ranch when he was with his dad and mom working in the grove. My dad made his dad the foreman when it was orange picking time. Dad says Mexicans are like everybody else. Some are good and some are rotten, and the Soliz family is good. And Rosa, I did know her. She finished high school and had a job as an usherette at the Golden State Theater. My cousin worked there. He told me she gave her whole paycheck to her mom and dad. Doesn't sound like the kind of girl who would waste her time on a loser, or even be allowed to."

Before long, we came out of the mountains. In the distance I could see the towers and fences marking off Miramar Naval Air Station.

"Freddie's a good looking peon," Sherrie said, "whose future is tied to what he can earn with calloused hands and a bent back. Like all his compadres, he likes to play when he isn't in the fields. He probably urges fun on with a six pack, a bottle of tequila, or a little marijuana, that crazy weed the Mexicans bring in from across the border, whenever he gets the chance. Drive down any field or grove side road on a Saturday at midnight and you can scoop up a sack full of Freddies sleeping off the weekend's fun, but none of them are rapists and murderers. Neither is Freddie."

We drove on in silence.

My mind flipped back to last Friday night and Alfred's braggadocio bust of Freddie for possession of an open container. Sherrie was right, that's not even minor trouble. It's a giant leap from hiding a Pabst to rape and murder. I said as much to Sherrie. We drove on, keeping our thoughts to ourselves until she stopped out front of the Pacheco's place. We parted with an in-the-car hug and a quick kiss.

"Call me," she said. "We'll feel more sociable in a day or two."

Now, I'm lying in bed, trying my damnedest to focus on Sherrie and her family, and failing. I've never been this close to a senseless, non-combat murder, and can't get Rosa's body on the berm out of my mind. I don't need this; dangerous dreams still envelope me at night. I put my mind on Sherrie, on the Pachecos, Danny Ishisaka—anyone or anything besides Rosa. I know the night's going to be rough.

Maybe tomorrow. Maybe tomorrow I'll feel more sociable.

Thursday, May 27, 1943
Secrets

I figured on finding time to see Sherrie when I checked in with the doctors. Maybe we could do the hamburger shack thing again and talk about this last weekend. But my Tuesday visit to the docs was postponed. They wanted to see me on Thursday, instead. So, rather than a bus trip to the base, I wandered into the kitchen where Mariella was cleaning up the breakfast dishes. She poured us both a cup of java, and we sat at the table and talked.

The front doorbell interrupted our morning chat. Mariella responded while I sipped on coffee. She exuded nonchalance, or tried to, when she came back into the kitchen.

"There's a sailor out there wants to talk with a Lieutenant Holcomb. He won't take a seat. You better go see what he wants."

He got the name right. But lieutenant? I thought it might be a joke, one Sherrie contrived to get back at me for that nonsense when we first met. But jokes weren't on our mind when we last talked, and the sailor, complete with his Shore Patrol armband and billy club, was for real; so was the Navy Jeep parked out front.

Khaki pants and a short-sleeved undershirt don't reveal rank. When I produced my identification, he saluted, handed me an envelope and said his orders were to wait until I had read the envelope's contents and then take them back from me.

I motioned for him to sit on the couch, which, unlike Mariella's request, he obeyed. I sat on the old rocker Mariella usually occupied. Mariella, who stuck with me like syrup on one of her Aunt Jemima flapjacks, plopped herself in Enrique's chair. I guess she figured what goes on in her living room is her business, whether the United States Navy thinks so or not.

The envelope contained two sealed letters, both addressed to me as Lieutenant, Junior Grade Holcomb. As it turned out, I managed quite by accident to open them in the order they had been written. The first congratulated me on my promotion. I was a lieutenant, retroactive to April 1, 1943. It went on to advise me I had tentatively been cleared for non-combat duty and it ordered me to remain in contact with the base provost at San Diego until I received additional orders.

The second envelope held my additional orders. For once, it appeared the Navy was abandoning its hurry up and wait strategy. I was now attached to Naval Intelligence. Further orders would be cut when my medical status was clarified. Ah, I thought, here's the wait part.

In the interim, I was to answer the questions in the enclosed personal profile. I took a quick look at it. The form's title was appropriate, it really was personal! For example: who I'd dated and what we'd done? Who, besides me or her, could care? I was, the orders said, to surrender the personal profile only at the request of my commanding officer, one Commander Tucker here at the San Diego Base Naval Intelligence Command, or to cleared-in-advance Navy medical officers or FBI agents. I'd seen enough B movies to ID an FBI agent, but wondered what a cleared-in-advance medical officer looked like. But that wasn't all. I was advised to be sure all my various uniforms, from pea jacket to working khakis and dress whites, were in order. My injury, I was told, had qualified me for a purple heart. It and the other campaign ribbons I'd earned would be presented to me at an appropriate ceremony in the near future.

Who gives a shit about campaign ribbons? I thought. My mind flitted to the Captain and his medal of honor. I couldn't believe it eased his mother's grief because he had a medal.

The letter reinforced the sailor's words about returning it to him. I was also to make sure he sealed it in a new envelope, which I soon found out he had with him. Both he and I were to sign across the seal before I dismissed him. Finally, I was to relay nothing about the content of these orders to anyone, except at the request of my commanding officer, Navy medical officers, etcetera, etcetera, etcetera.

So, here I am on Thursday, waiting for Sherrie to come out of the hospital so we can go to lunch. Not since the courier came to the Pacheco's have I given much thought to my past troubles, Isaac's story, or that sad business about Rosa. But Sherrie, Sherrie and going home, share equal billing with secret orders for Naval Intelligence and all that leaving San Diego portends.

In any case, hamburgers taste as good on Thursday as Tuesday, my appointment isn't until 2:30, and the sky is clear—no overcast, no clouds. I feel good. I've already been to the Base Exchange and purchased lieutenant's bars and sleeve and shoulder stripes. I thought about picking up my campaign ribbons, but the letter said they were going to present them to me. The bar on the collar is part of a regulation khaki uniform; I pin it on.

Sherrie comes down the walkway in her WAVE uniform. Damn she's beautiful! Arm in arm, we walk to her car.

I entertain a flippant notion: what about our conversation, does it need to be cleared in advance?

We're halfway through our hamburgers and milkshakes before Sherrie notices the lieutenant's bars.

"Are you impersonating a superior officer again?" She takes a sip of the milkshake and waits. Like Maria Pacheco, she has a wonderful sense of theatrical timing. It's a trait that must run in California girls, maybe the proximity to Hollywood.

I smile. "I thought you'd never notice. Nope, these are legal as of over a month ago. I'm a lieutenant, junior grade of course. Only five more promotions and I'm an admiral."

That word, admiral, sends me back, serves as a call to cause for the hollowness, the loss, the dread. God damn it! My mind duels with that fearsome duet: my past plight, the

Captain's death. I prop up my smile with willpower. Sherrie reaches out and touches my wrist, the one whose hand holds my milkshake.

"I'm happy for you."

"Me, too."

"No, you're not. It makes you sad, your promotion. Why?"

Damn it! I'd hoped the future's promise would put these sudden bouts behind me. More visions: vignettes of marines vaporizing before my eyes, screaming banzai warriors, a rain-soaked *Stars and Stripes* wrapped around a glass shard, the nurse's blood spreading over the wet type as she saws at the Captain's tether.

"What is it that resurrects the war and your wounds? That's it, isn't it? I can't ever understand, but it might help to talk. I'll listen."

I'd found out bottling stuff up put a miserable slant on the future. That's what Sherrie's Grandpa had said. Should I risk it, sharing my secret horrors with someone else—with Sherrie? While the risks ricochet through my mind, I stare down at the table, then look back up at Sherrie. Her freckled cheeks go well with the intriguing, not-red, not-brown tresses. What sways me is not her obvious physical beauty, but the compassion in her emerald eyes. I surrender and let out my private hell.

"Sometimes words, like 'admiral'—the Captain always called me Admiral—sometimes dreams, sometimes views from the porch, they hit me. Words, smells, sights – they bring up that night on Guadalcanal and…other shit. Sometimes—" I force a pathetic smile "—I think about hitting the bottle just to kill the ache, the nightmares. Don't like to talk about it. Never have. Talked about it."

We let those words hang between us. She's holding my wrist, the one she touched earlier. Our silence drowns out the surrounding noises. I've exposed myself to her whims. I'd promised myself I'd never again make myself vulnerable to someone else. But dealing with war's terror like it was lost love? Her gramps is right: going it alone with war can be as fatal after the battle as during.

"Why don't you?" she asked.

"Why don't I what?"

"Hit the bottle. If you think it will kill the ache, why don't you give it a try?"

I stir the milkshake. My words are directed at first to the frosty miasma in the glass. "I'm not so lost I can't recall the misery hard stuff does when you let it get a hold of you in weak moments." I look up at her. My lips take on the hint of a smile. "Besides, except for good beer and a glass of wine, I can't stand the taste of the stuff."

"You're tougher than you think. Otherwise, you would have taken that route. You would have followed a whole armada of wounded sailors and leathernecks. I see them every day burying memories in cheap versions of Jim Beam."

Silence.

"Know why the Captain called you Admiral, Lieutenant? To the Captain, it was a term of endearment. He cared about you. I might start calling you Admiral for the same reason, Lieutenant." Care coats her words, like butter dripping on a roasted ear of July's sweet corn. I can almost see the gears grinding behind her forehead. I know what she's doing: she's weighing the risk, choosing the words to match her thoughts, just as I did not so many seconds past.

She squeezes my wrist. "I don't know where this war will take us. That is, together or apart, it's too soon. But I do know being here…now…like this…with you, will be one of the good memories. Congrats, Admiral, on your promotion to lieutenant."

"I guess—" A hybrid sob-laugh rolls out of my mouth "—I'll have to call you Admiral, too."

Now we both laugh. In her mirth, she shakes my wrist and milkshake slops out of the glass onto the table. We laugh some more.

Relief boils up. I've gambled and not lost. Winning? Who knows? Who knows what winning looks like right now? But Sherrie's words, like those she uttered after that kiss a few nights back, they set limits and hint at possibilities. More importantly, they reinforce my resolve. I'm beginning to see that her attraction is more than undeniable good looks. It's that, and something to do with quiet confidence, an innate sense of self, and a view that sees promise in every situation. A hidden notion sneaks into my mind: maybe losing Elaine wasn't as devastating as I've made it out to be.

* * * *

The San Diego skyline slides by my bus window. I'm lost in contemplation of the day's irony: sharing with Sherrie what the Navy psychologist sought in vain at my afternoon appointment, the one I didn't know I had until the surgeon sent me there after a quick exam and a donation of blood and urine for the lab. Despite the psychologist's training, he failed to learn much, except that I feared and hated Japs. I wondered if he was my cleared-in-advance medical personnel. If so, he could hardly fail me for fearing and hating Japs; everybody feared and hated Japs. I put his impressions in with the campaign ribbons and the purple heart: I couldn't give a shit.

What I cared about today was the candid sharing with Sherrie the inner torments that visited me at times. Other than that maternal twist of logic about hitting the bottle, she hadn't consumed me with mother-hen concern, hadn't rushed to be my savior. Yet, she stuck her own neck out because she cared and admitted to a spark, one that might yet catch fire. My inclination is to rush ahead, push ignition, and fan the flame. But Sherrie is right; it's too early for that. One thing is for sure, the fire that burned all these months for Elaine is out; a wisp of regret lies in the ashes.

I push these thoughts out of my mind and focus on the next visit with Sherrie at Hacienda Del O'Toole. By then, I want to have gone over my notes on Isaac's story. There are questions I need to ask. And Rosa, a murder that close to Sherrie's home, unnerves me. I don't want Sherrie wandering around the orange groves and bare hills, at least not until they corral Freddie Soliz or whoever did this.

Up ahead is my stop. I pull the cord and wait until the bus slows down before I stand up and squeeze between the seat in front of me and the lady seated next to the aisle. The bus comes to a stop, the doors flop open, and I step onto the sidewalk.

This has been a good day.

Friday, May 28, 1943
Hope

I no sooner get back to the Pacheco's from my day spent at the base than another courier shows up. This time he hands me a sealed envelope and disappears. I hide behind the shut door of my room before I open the envelope. The orders inside advise me that at 0800 hours, 31 May, 1943, I'm to report to Commander Brandon Tucker, Naval Intelligence, Pacific Command, San Diego Naval Base. May 31, that's Monday morning.

The only phone is in the hall, so Mariella, who's whipping up some pasta in the kitchen, has an easy time of eavesdropping on my end of the conversation.

The operator puts me through, and I wait out the five rings before the Base operator responds and plugs me into the hospital office. Luck's not with me, but the WAVE on the other end of the line says she'll look for Sherrie at the evening mess and "give her a message if you like."

"That'll be great. Ask her to call Lieutenant Holcomb if she gets a chance."

Sherrie calls after dinner while Maria and I are teaming up on dishwashing. With Maria in the kitchen and Enrique and Mariella sunk in their living room chairs, privacy in the hall is again impossible. After the initial pleasantries, I launch into the news.

"My orders are heating up. I'm to report to Naval Intelligence here on the base Monday morning. I wondered if you could swing any time off."

Sherrie's response is quick. "I'm not sure what I can do; I've pretty much used up the normal supply of three-day passes. Let me make some calls and see if I can work out a trade. If nothing else, I've got Sunday off. We can make a trip to the beach or something. You really think you'll be leaving that fast?"

"I don't know."

I turn to the wall and talk into the phone with my chin on my chest, a meager attempt at privacy.

"I really want to work a pass to go home. The letters are newsy enough, and I've managed a couple of phone calls, but you can't say much, even with a pocket full of quarters to feed the till. And, I want to see you again. You know the Navy. I could be gone Monday afternoon or cooling my heels, waiting for more orders until the end of the war."

"I want to see you too."

'I don't know', she had said earlier today, 'where this war will take us.' Maybe it's just as well this phone, for all its convenience, is not up to meeting my sudden need to hold her in my arms. Maybe the proximity of my curious Portuguese foster family will hold back the compulsive words that I feel the urge to unloose. I manage soft words that pass over the phone's transmitter and disappear into the bib of the full length apron I had put on to wash dishes.

"I hope you can work it out," I say. In the back of my mind I'm thinking, Work it out; I hope we can work it out.

"I'll get back to you. If not tonight, in the morning. Call me at work if you don't hear by noon."

I hang up the phone and return to the kitchen. Maria demonstrates diplomacy beyond her years. She keeps scrubbing and rinsing while I dry and put away. We engage in idle talk. All the while I'm contemplating the unknowns: tomorrow, the long weekend, maybe alone, Monday's meeting, Naval Intelligence, which seems to me a contradiction of terms, Rosa's murder, Sherrie and me, and going home.

The phone rings. It's Sherrie. The conversation turns out to be pretty one-sided.

"I've traded with my C.O. I didn't even have to ask. She heard me talking about it out on the veranda outside of the mess hall and volunteered. She's a pain most of the time, but says she'll give me a three-day pass and cover for me. How about another run to my folks'? Maybe stop at the beach on the way, maybe do some horseback riding, maybe talk with Gramps...and bring your whites. I might want to show you off at a fancy lunch or church. I'll pick you up at oh-six-hundred hours. That's six A.M. on your civilian clock." I hear her chuckle, and then, "Goodnight." Before I can answer, she clicks off.

I hang up the phone and stand in the hall while I mull over her words. Beach? Is she thinking swimming? It doesn't seem that warm yet. At least, not South Pacific warm. Horseback riding? That sounds okay, and for the sake of appearances and respect for her parents, I'd better step up to church if I'm asked this time.

* * * *

Sherrie rolls up with Navy punctuality. Enrique's mantle clock is striking six when she pulls up in front of the house. The ride up the coast is foggy, and we elect to skip the beach business, except to pull off at a wide spot north of Oceanside to smoke and watch the waves crash on the beach.

Sherrie called ahead this time and the O'Tooles and Isaac have waited breakfast on us, even though it's closer to nine than eight. After breakfast, I find out Abednego is broke to ride.

"But he doesn't neck rein," Sherrie says. "You take the pinto. I've handled Abednego before." She throws an English riding saddle on him, a stuffy contrast to the Western saddle with the heavy fenders and saddle horn that go on my mount. The pinto's tack comes fitted with a saddlebag. Sherrie tucks in a canteen with water, a handful of unpeeled carrots, and a couple of peanut butter and jelly sandwiches.

Back in a saddle, the first time in three years, feels good, feels natural, except the pinto's rough gait sends painful but tolerable reminders of shrapnel that lived in the small of my back not so many weeks back.

Sherrie takes us through the orange trees, where the smudge pots stand guard over the long rows. Their short, squat bodies remind me of poverty-stricken, midget pot-bellied stoves sans the ornamental feet and handles.

"Do those things really work?" I ask. I can't imagine they'd generate enough heat to do much on a cold winter's night."

"You get the whole countryside fired up with smudge pots and they work well enough to save fruit on a cold night or the trees on a really cold night. If it gets severe cold for very long, nothing works. When they're fired up, you know it before you wake up. The smell of burned kerosene is in the air. Get out of bed and blow your nose and your handkerchief will be wet and black."

We ride out the backside of the property, past the ground squirrel hangout and into the rolling hills. Before long, the groves are behind us. Except for a B-17 coming in low to land at nearby March Field, we could have been riding in 1843 instead of 1943. Now and again, cottontails explode from the bushes at our feet. Their cousins, big black-tailed jackrabbits, never let us get closer than forty or fifty yards. I've seen this a zillion times: a big jack bounding out in front of me until he gets to a rise, a dip, a clump of brush, any place safe to stop in a wild rabbit's mind. As we ride, I bring the subject up with Sherrie.

"You know those jackrabbits run in circles," I say. "Coyotes know it. They'll team up, one chasing and one hanging around where the chase starts until that old jack comes rounding back. Then, wham! Soup's on! Jackrabbit stew!"

Sherrie's unimpressed. "I didn't know that. I can't imagine wanting to eat one of these wormy old jackrabbits. Gramps said he'd as soon eat his boot. Now cottontails, that's something else. I'm told they can be good eating. In the spring, while the cottontails still have meat on them, Dad lets some of the field hands come in and shoot them."

We ride on, sometimes talking about inconsequential scenery, sometimes comparing it to my home, sometimes contrasting the University of Idaho's country campus to USC's big city setting; always moving closer to knowing and caring for each other.

Sherrie, like the jackrabbits, has been taking us in a circle. I tumble to the notion when we come over a rise and look down on the east end of Mockingbird Lake.

"Let's ride down there," Sherrie says, "and eat our fancy lunch."

I like the setting: a quiet spot in the grass, a pretty lake, sharing with a pretty girl. In lieu of cabernet we enjoy a canteen of water. Could there be fancier? Yes, but more romantic? More quixotic? I doubt it. We sit on the ground while the horses stretch their necks and pull at the half-green, half-brown grass. In between passing the canteen back and forth and washing down our peanut butter and jelly sandwiches, we make idle chatter. We talk about the lake, the rock art that's supposed to be down here somewhere, the kids who sneak in on occasion and try for the monster bass that's rumored to be patrolling the lake, my ass end and how its stove up from the saddle, and how I'm going to be stiff in the morning.

"I'll be stiff, too," Sherrie says. "It's been six months or so since I've been horseback riding." She takes one last sip of water and hands me the canteen.

We stand up to leave. Sherrie steps close, puts her arms around my neck, stands on her toes and brushes her lips on mine. She takes my hand and we walk to the horses. When we reach them, I steal a real kiss. We cling to each other. Sherrie rests her forehead on the top of my chest for long, trembling seconds before she sighs, plants a quick kiss on my cheek, and turns her attention to the pinto's saddlebag.

She fishes a couple of carrots and waits while each horse bites the carrot down to the tips of her fingers. I hold onto the pinto's reins with one hand and rest the other on the small of Sherrie's back. Does she sense the tremor in my fingers on the swale where waist gives way to hips? A gentle pressure and Sherrie leans into me while Abednego nibbles the last little bit of carrot off the flat of her open palm.

We ride the dirt road in silence. I can tell Sherrie is lost in thought. What is she thinking about? I have a strong sense it has to do with what's filling my mind: the clash of passion with care these past few hours, these past few minutes, and how close passion came to winning the day five minutes ago. It wasn't a one-sided affair, not just me who trembled while resisting ardor. I'm guessing it was mutual and magnified by caring—for each other and what we have going here. How to deal with this? What if I lose her?

We ride in silence. Should I say something? Perhaps I should wait for her to say something? Perhaps there's nothing to be said? Have I made a bigger deal out of it than she has? Based on the intense moments of the last few days, I don't think so. Not worst case scenarios, but not knowing for sure puts me at a loss for words.

So, I bide my time by losing myself in the steady clop of hooves, the jerky gait of the pinto, and the clear blue sky looking down on a vista of orange trees that reaches to the horizon, all the time willing my pounding heart and wild imagination to calm down.

The straight rows of trees are arranged in squares and rectangles, no doubt defined by the grant deeds of the respective ranchers. They remind me of the Roman phalanxes I read about in the humanities course at UI. With a little more imagination, I might be in Italy and the orange groves could be contesting armies spread out on the broad Etruscan plain. An odd thought distracts me from my current dilemma; there are similarities in the way humans organize their pursuits, whether growing fruit or waging war. Sherrie interrupts my philosophical reverie.

"Do you remember Frederic Henry and Catherine Barkley?"

I run those names a couple of laps through my memory and draw a blank. "Can't say as I do."

"Did you ever read Hemingway's *A Farewell To Arms*?"

What in the hell has Hemingway got to do with us? "Nope, let me guess. Frederic and Catherine fell in love in Ernest's story."

Sherrie's mount lowers his head and snorts through his nostrils. She pulls his head up and shifts in the saddle. The clop of our mounts' hooves provides a steady meter that works to connect the pause with the words that follow when Sherrie at last responds. Her wooden body, her measured words which are carefully contrived, I think, to contain the emotion betrayed in the hint of hesitation released with the words, they heighten my sense of trepidation and expectation.

"You and I have something in common with them. They were both caught up in war – World War One. Like us, they met during war and were attracted to each other."

Attracted to each other. Those words cause me to look away from the road ahead toward Sherrie. She is watching me, testing my response to her off-hand confession of feelings. We exchange expressions which convey humor; not quite smiles, but hints of smiles like safe acknowledgements. The allure is mutual.

Now, it's me who measures out the words, a scouting party to validate my perception.

"There has got to be more to it than that. I have read other Hemingway stuff. His characters don't meet, become, as you say, attracted to each other, and live happily forever after."

Again, no words; just the steady thud of hooves moving us up the dirt road that takes us away from Mockingbird Lake. Sherrie's words, when they come, move away from intimacy to an almost clinical analysis that connects Frederic and Catherine's plight to us.

"Frederic and Catherine, they are both steeped in the notion that there is no universal moral code, which means there is no room for abstract notions like justice, equality, fairness and the like. Frederic has to learn painful lessons about character, lessons Catherine had already come to know. She downright denies the existence of God and goes out of her way to deny religion and defy its moral precepts. Seems to me that's one of the big points Hemingway makes. Frederic, if he believes in God at all, thinks God is irrelevant. Therefore, personal behavior is of no concern from Frederic's ethical point of view. Even though he's in this war, Frederic has no stake in its outcome."

Is she comparing me to Frederic? I hope not. But why wouldn't she, given the things I've said about God's role, or lack of a role, in my troubles? I don't want her to see me that way, and down deep, I'm hoping I'm not.

"It seems to me, except for meeting in wartime and caring for each other, we aren't like Frederic and Catherine at all. You have a moral code bound by a belief in God. That's pretty clear to me. And me? Well, I certainly was raised that way. What's happened, I will admit, has caused me to wonder where He was when I needed Him most."

I'm shaking inside. We've come this far, she and I. Is this the moment when my words will define a different fork for her than the one I take? "But I'm not driven to abandon the values I've grown up with, not yet anyway." I ride in silence. Guilt floats up; I repress the memories of my recent impulse and that afternoon on a hill south and east of Moscow. The horses' hooves move us forward.

"You are right, of course," Sherrie says. "We are different from Hemingway's characters. We hold onto guideposts driven by a universal God-given code. Nevertheless, there are similarities between us and Frederic and Catherine. We care about each other and we're moved by…" Sherrie stops talking, reaches down and pats her mount on the withers "…desires to, well, fulfill that caring."

I have no counter. No words pass between us for a minute, maybe two. Sherrill reins her horse in. I sense she's doing so to gain my attention. I stop and back my mount until Sherrie and I are even with each other.

"I want you to know," Sherrill says. "I do care." She stops talking and looks into my eyes, partly, I think, to relay her sincerity, partly to read my reaction. "And I have the same wants you do. But I'm not Catherine and you're not Frederic." Her jaw line becomes rigid. No tears, but little pools form in the corners of her stunning emerald eyes. "I don't want us to lose what we might have by letting this war's uncertainties lead us to their fate, on the chance there's something real and lasting between us."

She kicks Abednego in the sides and urges him down the road.

The pinto moves to follow, but I rein her in. I'm stunned, overwhelmed and perplexed. I won't know for sure what their fate was until I read the novel. Nor am I sure what ours will become. But her meaning is clear: she cares for me! I urge the pinto forward. She cares for me enough to build boundaries until the long-haul potential is known. The other message is more subtle: life with Sherrie hinges on sharing those core values she touched on. However uncertain that might make me, I'm buoyed by her candid confession of affection and the potential for affection to become intense, meaningful, and lasting. Her mastery of resolve intrigues me. Above all, I'm consumed by the intensity of my feelings for her.

Sherrie waits for me at the fork that leads to her home. "We can go home later. First, I want to show you something." She rides up the spur that follows the canal. Up ahead is the flue; on the side of the road is where they found Rosa's body. A two-by-twelve plank crosses the canal before the control gate, which sits a foot or two ahead of the spillway that takes the canal down twenty feet or so. We rein our horses and stop.

"You see that board? We used to cross over it and hike up back of the dairy. When we got older, sophomores in high school, we'd lay in the grass by the canal, listen to the water spill down the hill, and learn about romance. I got my first real kiss lying in the grass next to the canal. Now, it's all ruined."

Sherrie looks at the far side of the dirt road. "Someone, an assassin, a thief in the night, murdered Rosa and stole this Eden and all its innocent memories."

We look at the grass next to the road where Rosa must have lain. A long moment passes. I dismount, hand the reins to Sherrie, and walk over to the side of the road. I pick up a weathered Baby Ruth wrapper and an empty tin, one that held sardines from Norway. Over at the edge of the grass where it starts to drop to the main road, I reach for a green Rainer Ale bottle and an empty bottle of Pabst. Three feet of black-and-red banded snake slithers away and brings me up short. "Whoa! What kind of snake is that?"

"It's a king snake. We don't kill them around here. They love to eat other snakes, including rattlers."

The snake disappears into the grass. I place the trash in the saddle bags and mount. Both Sherrie and I are somber and quiet as we turn up the road and head for her home.

I decide to run for the pure, carefree joy of doing so and lean forward, dig my heels into the pinto, and urge her into a gallop. The wind playing in my face, the joy of an all out gallop, the rows of orange trees flying by, they resurrect a carefree moment of my youth, one devoid of uncertainties and fears brought on by men and their violence.

Dan Strawn

Sherrie catches up to me as I'm beginning to loosen the cinch on my mount's saddle. I watch her enter the corral, dismount, and walk back to close the gate. Abednego follows the reins that trail from her hand. Watching Sherrie conjures up a thrill, its origins housed in that first crush when I fell for Kay Kendall in the seventh grade. A thrill since matured by passion in its prime, tempered by the gall of having loved and lost, and made real by my wartime lesson. Neither passion nor love will last longer than my last breath. For a moment, I'm overwhelmed by the need to hold her in my arms and lose myself in hers until the uncertainties are smothered.

She turns and leads the big bay towards the stable. I'm rooted to the ground, mesmerized by the fluid movement of her hips, the flippant head toss that throws tangled locks away from her face, the press of breast against blouse when her mount pulls taut the reins and noses the ground in pursuit of a renegade wisp of hay.

Odors: a hint of orange from the groves, hay and straw, the earthy aroma of horses and their sweaty leather saddles. Sherrie: fumbling with the cinch on her mount's saddle. Isaac: in the outer edge of my vision, hobbling across the pasture towards the corral. The combination draws me like soft iron to a magnet. It promises robust living, hope of sustained caring, surety of a safe harbor in sea-tossed tomorrows.

At this instant, I know. I will bide my time, but I love Sherrill O'Toole.

Saturday, May 29, 1943
More Gramps

Isaac's nimbleness never ceases to amaze me. He climbs through the corral railings, walks up and places a caring hand on Abednego's neck. I notice how his ring and middle fingers shoot off from their second joints at oblique angles. I'd seen that in my Grandma Scott's old hands. "Arthritis," she had said. "Too many winters of bone chilling cold." She left us at eighty-two. How old is Isaac? If he joined the Army at eighteen, he has to be eighty-four or eighty-five. I figured that out the other day. For Isaac, it seems all these years in warm California winters came too late. Do his withered fingers shake from old age while he strokes the sorrel's coat? Yes, but more than that, I think their vibration comes from the exchange of deep down devotion between this old man and his horse.

"Well, how'd my pacer do with a saddle on his back?"

Sherrie answers while she heads for the tack room carrying the English saddle. "He did fine, Gramps. He's such a smooth ride, no matter whether you're trailing behind in a sulky or riding on top."

Isaac nods and looks at me as I work the pinto's coat with a curry brush.

"And you? Your ride was okay?"

I put the curry brush down, stand up, and face him. "The ride was great, but I'm afraid tomorrow's going to be painful." I lean back on the hand I've slipped into my back pocket.

A smile disrupts the splayed red veins on Isaac's weathered cheeks. "Yep, you don't do it regular, that first horseback ride can be painful."

I nod. Neither one of us comes up with the right words to keep the conversation going. Isaac's fingers roam up to Abednego's mane and forelock and linger there. Sherrie comes out of the tack room, sneaks up behind Isaac and kisses him on the cheek. I like seeing that; liked it before in the apricot orchard. It tells me what she feels for her grandpa transcends respect. There's love between them. Love between all of the family at Hacienda Del O'Toole. Respect too, and I see now it all springs from this old man, whose every action, like his caring caress of this middle-aged pacer, spreads affection.

"So, Gramps, you going to fill Martin in on the untold parts of your story from last week?"

"Well," he says. "Sean and his truck aren't even home yet. Let's do it now before dinner."

The three of us sit around the picnic table in the backyard. Sherrie and I sip Schlitz out of long-necked bottles. Isaac contents himself with a bottle of cola and turns on his storytelling charm. Sherrie leans her head on my shoulder and alternates her gaze between her grandpa and my open journal, which I retrieved from the guest bedroom as soon as Isaac agreed to talk.

Isaac takes a sip of his drink, sets the bottle down, and runs quivering fingers across the edge of the table.

"It was Lapwai, that's where I taught school down on the reservation. The Presbyterian reverend in Lewiston knew of the need for someone literate enough to teach those Nez Perce kids. He also knew I needed work now that I was married and home-bound. My bum leg held up pretty good shoveling coal into the maw of those steam engine boxes, but it made me unattractive for the honest labor I was likely to find on a ranch or a farm. The reverend set the whole thing up.

"Dot and I, we moved into this little house not too far from the fort where the school was set up. It wasn't much, a lean-to really. The slant on the roof made the back side of the one room about a hand's width shorter than me, although I could stand straight up in the front half.

"We had us a wood stove, a bed hewn out of white pine, a mattress stuffed with corn husks, a table someone must have brought from back East, and three chairs. I made us a couple of shelves to store food and clothes."

Isaac takes a long pull on his drink and wipes his mouth with the back of his hand.

"Out the side door I dug us a well and fixed up a bucket on the end of a long pole. I anchored that pole on the side of the well housing so Dot could dip the bucket into the well and bring it up by using the pole as a lever. I was pretty proud of that – took a lot of the back work out of getting water.

"The outhouse wasn't much good, so I dug us a new one first thing after the well was finished. While I'm doing all this digging and fixing, Dot's working the ground up. It was spring, so we needed to get some crops in the ground or we would be mighty hungry in the months to come. My pay was twenty-four dollars a month for ten months, the lean-to, and whatever food we could grow out back.

"At first, there weren't many students. I don't think those Nez Perce kids were any different than white kids when it came to drumming up reasons to avoid school. But it was more than that. There was the natural distrust of anybody white.

"Most of the Nez Perce on the reservation back then were Christians, treaty Nez Perce who considered Joseph, White Bird and the others trouble makers. All the non-treaties, the ones who survived, were scattered—some in Kansas and Oklahoma, some escaped to Canada, the rest hiding out with the Umatillas over in Oregon. Nevertheless, the reservation Nez Perce had suffered under the rule of the whites and they distrusted us. And not without cause. Their land had been stolen, the only safe place for them was on the reservation, and despite their differences with the non-treaties, they considered it a family squabble and resented the loss of friends and relatives back in 'seventy-seven.

"On top of all that, the local whites in Lewiston, Grangeville, Pierce, and the like figured one Indian was the same as another and treated them all pretty much the way the worst of them deserved. Being white meant I was always on trial, had to prove I wasn't a…" Isaac glances at Sherrie "…son-of-a-bitch before those kids and their parents would have much to do with me."

He takes another swig out of the soda bottle.

"So, students came slowly at first, but when September rolled around I had me a full classroom. That is, until the steelhead and salmon lured them away, and there wasn't much use in having class when their families headed to the camas fields for the roots. Course that was okay with me. I liked salmon and steelhead, too, and when they cleared out, I'd either go fishing myself, or borrow me a rifle and kill a deer, a goat, or an elk to go with Dot's vegetables. When the kids were there, I taught them what I knew about reading and writing and ciphering. Most of them learned hardly at all, some better than others. We didn't have any books, so we did everything with slate boards and chalk."

Isaac stops talking. He rotates the pop bottle with the trembling fingers of both hands while he contemplates. I have no idea what is rolling around in his mind. Some lost narrative he's obliged to go back and pick up maybe? Or is he basking in the warmth of reliving fond memories? Whatever, his silent reverie comes to an end.

"So, that's how it went for better than two years. Then the consumption, or at least what we thought was consumption, hit me, and we came to California. You remember me telling you that story? I told it to you, right?"

"Yes, Gramps," Sherrie says. "You told it to us when Martin was here last week."

Isaac looks at Sherrie, then back at the pop bottle, which he has resumed revolving between the fingers of his hands. "Yes, good. I was sure I had."

Before he loses the urge to talk, I stoke the conversation with questions.

"What happened to that Nez Perce, the one who saved you? What's that all about?"

Isaac looks at me and then at Sherrie. "This boy you brought home doesn't miss much, does he?"

"Not much, Gramps. Besides being a sailor, he studied journalism in college you know."

"Yes, I know. He told me about it last week when he was here." He shifts his gaze from Sherrie to me. "Did I tell you I wrote for the newspaper? *The Lewiston Enterprise*. They still have the *Enterprise* in Lewiston?"

We had this conversation last week, but I couldn't see the point of telling him that. "Yes, it's still around. In fact, *The Enterprise* paid for my last two years of college, and I wrote a Navy article or two for them after I left the university."

Isaac's eyes widen, and a smile spreads across his face. "Well, it seems we share more than our admiration for this little filly sitting across from me." He looks at Sherrie and winks. "In those couple of years I spent in Lapwai, I wrote maybe ten or fifteen articles for them. Local Lapwai and Kamiah stuff: school and other interesting reservation news, steelhead and salmon runs, rancher and lumberman happenings, stuff like that. They paid me, too. Not much, but then I wasn't earning much teaching, either. Every little bit helped." He rests the juncture of his thumb and index finger at the bottom of his chin, and strokes the sides of his clean-shaven face, the area where the well trimmed mutton chops were in the old family photograph in the living room. "I'll be darned. Guess I better show you a bit more respect."

"Oh, Gramps, you already respect him. Mom told me this morning you'd taken a real liking to what you called 'that sailor from the dairy farm in Idaho.'"

Isaac talks in the third person, as if I weren't sitting right next to Sherrie taking down every word he said. I know what he is doing, saw him do it last week at the breakfast table. He loves pulling a man's leg, mine or Sean's, doesn't seem to make much difference. "Yeah," he says, "truth is—I do like him. But he still can be a bit of a nuisance when he gets hold of something and won't let go."

He turns back to me. "What was it you wanted to know? Oh, right…"

We wait. We've grown accustomed to the periods of silence that have come to characterize these storytelling sessions with Isaac. This time he leaves the pop bottle on the table and taps barely audible rhythms on the edge of the picnic table.

Are these delays caused while his mind searches for some word, for all his wanting to use it, he can't remember? Sometimes, I decide, but this time is different. This time he's working harder at concentrating. I think he waits on feelings, not words.

"It was that second summer at Lapwai. Dot and I were out back working on the garden when Jesse Denning came riding up in his one-horse shay. Sitting next to him was this old man."

I look at Sherrie. She arches her eyebrows and shrugs her shoulders.

"Don't let his Anglo name fool you. Jesse Denning was Nez Perce, one hundred percent, an elder of the reservation church over at Spaulding. He came by often enough, bringing news and sometimes some fresh fish or meat. A good man, Jesse. That day he brought Otter, the old man on the seat next to him. I learned from Jesse this Otter was an old storyteller and holy man from Joseph's Wallowa band. Joseph, you heard of Joseph?"

I nod my head. "Everyone from Idaho knows Joseph. He's the most famous Indian in the Northwest. I grew up hearing the stories from the old timers about how the army called him the Red Napoleon, which is no wonder, the way he outwitted them before he finally surrendered way up next to the Canadian border."

"Right. Anyway, Jesse, he might be a good Christian, but he was Nez Perce, and even though this Otter was one of the non-Christians I could tell Jesse held him in reverent esteem. Probably 'cause of his age. Nez Perces respect their elders.

"Otter's clothes were as worn as he was. His hair was blanketed with gray and done up in the traditional non-treaty way – braids and a high pompadour in the front. His shirt was store-bought, and his pants too, but his moccasins were hand crafted. They'd seen plenty of wear, and pieces of the once fancy beadwork were beginning to unravel. And his skin? Well, I got to tell you, I'd never seen an Indian with skin as dark and worked over as his. Looking back on it, knowing he'd spent a lifetime walking and riding in steep canyons, knowing he'd warmed himself in wet, cold winters by facing a thousand fires inside the longhouse, knowing what he had endured crossing those Montana plains, it wasn't just being Indian made his skin that dark. It was being Indian and, I don't know, seventy or eighty years of seasoning and burnishing that came from repeated dousing in cold winter air and smoke and wet. The creases on his face came from wind and smoke and cold, but also from mourning brought on by death's constant presence, and seeing the suffering always hanging around the corner."

A short silence descends, as if Otter's presence in Isaac's words has consecrated the picnic table in preparation for words to come.

"Jesse helped the old man out of the buggy. Once he hit ground, he seemed pretty spry. Dot and our guests sat in the chairs I had brought outside. I tipped over an old wooden crate and used it. We'd no sooner made ourselves comfortable then Otter began to talk. It took a while, what with him speaking in his native tongue and Jesse interpreting.

"Otter said he'd come to see the limping soldier who taught the children. I have to tell you that brought me up short. The teaching part was pretty plain for anyone to see; so was the limping. But soldier? How'd he know about me being a soldier?

"Otter talked and those Nez Perce words rolled out of his mouth. Jesse could barely keep up. We sat in awe, Jesse, Dot and I, like three travelers waiting out the grandeur of a summer storm in a high mountain pass. Once Jesse started translating, he spoke the words in English exactly as they came out of Otter's mouth, except there's some words in Nez Perce that don't fit in English, and I could see they slowed Jesse up when Otter used them. For all I know, some notions he couldn't put in English never got said."

"'My brother was a great warrior,' Otter said. 'His wife died bringing a son into the world. My brother died hunting buffalo with the Flatheads. I took my brother's son into my lodge and put him at my wife's breast. The boy, grown to a man, came to pray where your horse fell down on top of you. I, Otter, taught him well. He knew anyone could kill an enemy with a broken leg. He knew there was no honor in killing an enemy held captive by his horse. Even though you were a soldier, he helped you. He took your gun from you. One morning at the Big Hole, he killed a soldier with your gun. The soldier wanted to shoot the women and children. He shot a Bannock warrior with your gun. The Bannock wanted to kill a Nimiipu mother and her baby. Other Bannocks killed the warrior who took your gun.'

"While Otter talked, he looked at me. I couldn't help but notice how old and worn those eyes were: the cloudy pupils, cataracts maybe; the dull black irises; the flecks of yellow breaking up the white, which wasn't white at all, but off-white moving towards dun. I got to tell you, his story so far unnerved me a bit, but Jesse should've prepared me for Otter's next words when Jesse repeated them in English.

"'I saw you in my dreams that summer of the war. I looked through the window of a white man's house,' Otter said, 'and saw the limping soldier showing Nimiipu boys and girls how to write words with white rocks on thin gray rock. You were the soldier, the one whose horse rolled on him north of the Lolo Trail.'

"I don't know about Dot and Jesse, but what kept me quiet was dealing with the notion of a latter-day seer who saw things in dreams that hadn't even happened yet. After all, even Hamlet's visions were merely fabrications of a gifted playwright, and the dreams of both the Old and New Testament Josephs were ordained by a Christian God. Nothing in my past prepared me for an illiterate red man's personalized powers of prophecy.

"After a bit, I told Jesse to wait. I went into the cabin and returned with my Remington revolver. Now, it was my turn to talk. The gun was loaded, so I kept the barrel pointed to the ground as I sat on my wooden crate and told the revolver's story.

"'This is my gun,' I said. Old Otter looked at the gun. His face gave away nothing, was as uninvolved as a wrinkled, burnt-sienna limb of the manzanita that grows in the hills around here. I told him a soldier friend brought the gun to me in the winter after the horse broke my leg. I related the story of the gun and how it was taken from the dead body of a young warrior the Bannock scouts shot on the plains between the Missouri River and the Yellowstone, and how the soldier who gave it to me knew it was my Army weapon before it belonged to the dead Nez Perce.

"Otter looked at the gun for a long time. Eventually, he reached out and stroked the barrel of that Remington revolver. He never did ask how the soldier knew the gun was mine, never questioned whether the dead Indian it was taken from was his adopted son. After a while, Otter took back the conversation. His story continued in a long string of Nez Perce words.

"'My son prayed in the valley where he found you trapped by your horse. He prayed to his Wyaken, his spirit helper. His

Wyaken heard his prayer and showed him his real father astride his favorite spotted horse, wearing the wolf-skin coat his wife had sewn for him. A coyote-skin cape shielded his head and shoulders. I saw my brother on the cold winter's morning he rode away from the longhouse to hunt buffalo with the Flatheads. He was astride his favorite spotted horse, wearing his wolf skin coat, wearing a coyote skin cape to keep him warm in the winter snow. The warrior who saved you, the son I raised for my brother, was a baby then. His father never came back to the Wallowa; Old Buffalo hooked him with his horns on the prairie east of the Lolo. The warrior who saved you, his purpose in that valley was holy, that's why he saw his father. That's why he saved you and put you where the soldiers could find you.'

"I learned me a basketful of lessons that summer's day I met old Otter. Like a man's deeds, killing a man or saving another, can both be noble if the circumstance is right. Like war and God and how He doesn't pick sides in man-made wars, but comes to any warrior of any color who bothers to ask. And Bibles and visions? There's no point in God talking to a man through the Bible if the man can't read; so it's not mens' Gods that are different, but God coming to men in different ways so they can understand. I learned me a lot that day, but it took a while to sort it all out."

Isaac stops talking. He looks past Sherrie and me, past the corral and pasture, past maybe even the apricot orchard and the desert and hills beyond. His fingers don't play with the cola bottle; they rest on the edge of the table. For the first time in the brief weeks I've known him, his fingers don't tremble.

"I remember lying on that hillside hurt, moving in and out of consciousness, while my savior, a Nez Pierce boy, he couldn't have been more than twenty, opened his arms to the setting sun and prayed. The words were strange, made no sense to me, but even in my sorry state, I had no doubt he was offering up prayer. The thing is," Isaac pauses, takes in a draught of air and lets it out with a sigh. He brings his eyes off the distant horizon, back to the table, back to Sherrie and me. "Until the end of old Otter's story, I thought that warrior, the one astride the spotted horse, the one wearing the coyote skin cape and raising his bow in a silent salute, I thought he was nothing more than pain-induced hallucination."

Sherrie's fingers, the ones resting on my forearm, wrap around and squeeze. I stop writing. Isaac takes his old blue handkerchief out of his trouser pocket and wipes his brow. Behind Isaac, I see a mother quail and her brood scurry across the backyard and disappear into the rows of orange trees. Each swish of the fronds in the palm tree that anchors the far corner of lawn is a response to the beck and call of the blowing afternoon breeze. My mind is a thousand miles and six decades away. I'm with Isaac, there on the banks of the Clearwater, facing his yesterdays, dealing with the contradictions.

A distant drone becomes an interloper. It breaks the silence that follows Isaac's words at this hallowed altar, this picnic table in the backyard at Hacienda Del O'Toole. The sound comes from the west, beyond the orange trees, perhaps beyond the rolling surf, the setting sun.

Isaac takes the blue handkerchief from his forehead and looks to the far horizon. The drone is strong now, and I turn my head, face west. Sherrie's chin rests on my shoulder; her arms wrap around my chest. The specter of a warrior mounted on his spotted horse gives way to the Flying Fortress in the sky over the distant hills, her flaps down, her wheels locked, preparing to land at nearby March Field. Her four engines throb, a low-in-the-throat, feline rumble poised to roar when the hunt is on. She passes overhead. Machine guns poke out of the clear bubbles on her belly, nose and tail; tight-lipped doors seal from sight the cavernous maw that holds her bombs. Betty Grable lolls on the aluminum fuselage just forward of the wings, underneath six-inch royal-blue letters that spell out St.

Louie Liz. The Fortress flies low over our heads, flies beyond the orange and apricot trees, beyond the ground squirrel town.

The wayward afternoon breeze lifts the edge of my half-filled journal notes. I look at the straight lines on a blank page. What will I write of my tomorrows? My yesterdays? I close the journal and lean back in Sherrie's embrace. Her cool cheek lies on mine. The Flying Fortress, her flaps down, her wheels locked, drops below the horizon. Old Isaac bows his head and wipes the nape of his neck with his blue handkerchief.

Part 3

I Should Be So Lucky

Tuesday, June 1, 1943
Trip Home

Monday's interview was not what I'd come to expect in the Navy. I was ushered into Commander Tucker's office as scheduled, 0800 hours. By 0825 hours I had my orders and travel vouchers.

Afterwards, I called Sherrie and made a date for lunch. We drove down to Bud and Donna's and ordered up hamburgers and fries and split a chocolate milkshake. I told her the news.

We parked next to the bus stop, smoked a last cigarette together, and talked until the city bus crept up behind. A kiss, an embrace, another kiss, a final hug, and I was out the door into the bus. I watched through the back window as Sherrill O'Toole made a U-turn and drove the Plymouth back to the Navy hospital. Maybe it was the influence of going with Sherrill and her family to the Arlington First Methodist Church on Sunday. Maybe it was the acknowledgment of a spiritual necessity in Isaac's touching tale. Maybe it was both, but I found myself praying, albeit self-serving, for the first time since leaving the South Pacific. "God, I love her. Please, in my coming absence, let her heart stay fond for me."

* * * *

I climbed on board a Continental Trailway bus. We crawled through the coast range on that familiar route that goes through Escondido and into downtown Riverside, which I had somehow avoided in my visits to Sherrie's folks' place. After we dropped off two Army Air Force enlisted men, we drove to San Bernardino and picked up an old lady who could easily pass for Little Red Riding Hood's grandma. For some reason she ignored the eight or ten empty seats and sat next to me.

We climbed out of the valley through what the old lady explained was Cajon Pass, which would take us through the San Bernardino Mountains to the desert. Probably the same desert Isaac talked about in his story of TB and tending livestock.

We've been driving away from Cajon Pass for the last hour or so. As far as I can tell, the next fifty miles of eastern California will look like the last fifty: a brown vista that reaches to the horizon, a forest of scraggly Joshua trees, which strike me as poor compromises between honest desert cacti and legitimate trees. The macadam ribbon we ride on points in a straight line toward the Nevada border.

I'm anxious for family, and I've been given a fourteen day leave before I report for duty in, of all places for a Navy man, Papago Springs, Arizona. Besides, my timing turns out to be great. I learned when I called that Grant arrived yesterday afternoon. I'm not surprised to learn he'd up and married Nancy, and she's there with him. Time with Grant appeals to me even more than time with Mom and Dad, and I'm anxious to meet the Dixie beauty that claimed his heart. The whole prospect takes me, if only for a time, to home's safe haven, away from war.

Since I'm dressed like a civilian, the old woman on the bus won't give me any peace until I explain why I'm not in the service doing, as she puts it, "your part to keep those tyrants off our shores?"

"I've got me a son, three sons-in-law, and a grandson in the army, and another son flying planes for the Navy." She pulls a fried chicken leg out of the sack on her lap and takes a bite. "Seems we all need to sacrifice. That's what the good Lord expects—that's what duty demands." She chews while she lets those words soak in, probably hoping she'll shame me into stopping the bus and enlisting at the nearest recruiting station.

I wonder, what is her version of sacrifice? Is it putting up her sons for cannon fodder? Will she be as bent for bound duty when one or all of them come home in various versions of dismemberment or in flag-draped boxes?

Vignettes play through my mind: eruptions—sand and body parts shower the airstrip. Marines kneel in slow motion and spout blood. A wild Asian face looms behind his rifle, behind the hilt of his cold steel bayonet. The Captain swings at the end of his bathrobe sash.

I lean my head up to the glass and watch the Joshua trees fly by the window. The old lady finishes her lunch and loses herself in her bring-along reading. After a while my mind goes back to last weekend, back to Sherrill, and, inexplicably, back to Isaac, his story, his sacrifice, his healing almost seven decades past. While I ride this half-full bus headed for home, Isaac and his recollections calm me and restore hope in my tomorrows.

Isaac took me into his bedroom after last Saturday's dinner. He wanted to show me the Remington revolver, the one that he featured so prominently in his afternoon story.

"Barb won't let me take it out of the bedroom," he said, "seeing as how I keep it loaded and all."

The top of Isaac's dresser was an altar of sorts. The Remington revolver sat in the middle, framed by a five-by-seven picture of Sherrie's grandma at the end next to Isaac's bed, and a big worn Bible on the other.

He picked the gun up, and with a seasoned warrior's reverence for weapons of war, held it with one hand on the grip and the other hand placed palm up under the barrel, which was pointed at an oblique angle to the floor. "My daddy always said there was only one use for a pistol and that was defending yourself. Shucks, can't see any way to defend myself with an empty gun, so, if I'm gonna have it, I'm gonna load it. Course,

I haven't fired it in forty years or so. Don't even know if it would fire." He pointed the barrel perpendicular to the floor and cocked the hammer.

Now, with that critical old lady reading what my casual inspection finds to be a Book of Mormon, and the growl of the gears grinding down a few octaves as the Trailway grapples with a drawn out grade, my apprehension at Isaac's shaky hammer pull takes my mind off sacrifice and catches my funny bone. But at the time, with his quivering thumb holding the hammer over what he said was an empty chamber, I was more than a little taken aback.

"Course," Isaac said, "no round is under the hammer," and he guided the hammer gently down with his thumb. "So, if I got me more'n five cutthroats to shoot, I'm gonna have to reload."

The engine sighs in relief, and we almost freewheel as the Trailway tops the grade and starts down the other side. The Joshua trees have been replaced by sand, sand, and in the distance, sand. Shimmering lakes turn into more sand when we get close. Dust devils spin like tops across the flat desert surface. My seatmate looks up. "Sixty, maybe seventy miles of this and we'll be stopping in Las Vegas," she says, and returns to her reading.

"What is in Las Vegas?"

She looks up and casts another critical look at the unchanging landscape. "A couple of bars, a few casinos, a place or two to get a bite to eat and go to the bathroom. If we don't get there pretty soon, the driver's going to have to stop and let me out. I'm liable to need some relief 'afore we come to Las Vegas."

She nods her head towards the rear of the bus. "That soldier in the back will have to walk a block or two when we get there. The café where the bus stops doesn't feed coloreds."

I hadn't seen many colored people before I joined the Navy, except for Indians and a few Mexicans. I never gave much thought to their lot. But I must be changing some, because those words don't sit right. A man wearing a uniform means he's taking a risk; he ought to be able to eat anywhere he chooses. Besides, he's not colored; at least, not Negro. He's probably Indian, a Ute or Paiute, maybe, or one of those Bannocks Isaac mentioned. He's probably going home. Or maybe he's not going home at all. Maybe he's a Navajo from Arizona or a Cherokee from Oklahoma headed for his next duty. Maybe he's not Indian at all, but Mexican. Whatever, he's a soldier and ought to be able to eat wherever he chooses.

Before Las Vegas, the old woman brings the bus to a halt by threatening an in-the-bus flood if the driver doesn't pull over to the side of the road while she disappears into a gully. Emptying her bladder must have loosened her tongue, because she keeps me occupied with her life story after she climbs back into her seat. I know what she's doing: warming me up for a little honest proselytizing. I am saved by Las Vegas. The sign on the café window where we stop reads "WHITES ONLY."

I watch the soldier. He steps out of the bus, sees the sign, and lights up a cigarette. The driver, embarrassed, waits until the passengers disappear into the café. I wait, too. I've decided to take a social stand, a new phenomenon for me, unless you count that standoff with those sassy country kids back at Danny Ishisaka's place. I'm hungry but I'm not eating in there.

"You need the bathroom," the driver says to the soldier, "you can use this one. You'll have to go to the backdoor. You want to eat something, there's a burger joint a block and a half down the street. They got a restroom, too. We're pulling out in fifty minutes."

The soldier nods, takes a drag off his cigarette, and walks up the street.

The driver looks at me. "This shit ain't right."

By now, I've lit up my own Chesterfield. I inhale and blow a stream of smoke and watch it float past the lone neon sign into the desert air. "No, it isn't. I think I'm going to eat down the street."

As it turns out, the soldier doesn't want company, but the hot beef sandwich and mashed potatoes, both drowned in greasy, brown gravy fill my stomach, and the walk loosens me up a bit. Too soon, the Trailway doors hiss open, and we climb aboard.

The bus rolls into the evening. Despite leans, lurches, and down and up shifts, I sleep.

Between stops at St. George and Cedar City, we manage to take on enough passengers to nearly fill the bus. The sun is a couple of hours from peaking over the Wasatch Range that parallels our path north when we let the old woman off in Nephi. At Salt Lake City, we lay over for an hour and a half before we pick up a new driver and a fresh crop of riders. I am the sole survivor from the original California passengers.

Gratefully, the bus is nearer empty than full. I have a seat to myself. I spend the time watching northern Utah, then southern Idaho pass by my window. Outside of Twin Falls, the rolling sage brush and a narrow bridge spanning a narrow chasm carved by the Snake River reminds me home waits a few hours west.

The bus is running late. The schedule said we should have arrived in Boise twenty minutes ago, and we've just passed Mountain Home. Nevertheless, Mom, Dad, and Grant with his Nancy are no doubt waiting at the station. It won't be long. Home.

Thursday, June 3, 1943
Family

The raucous crowing of roosters rouses the whole county, announces the sun an hour or two before it's due.

On the back porch, I pull on coveralls impregnated with every dairyman's bouquet: a mixture of spilt milk gone sour, detritus of hay and straw, splashes of bleach and strong soap, all accented by cow manure clinging to the soles of black rubber boots parked on the back steps.

As if I'd never been to sea, never suffered the brutal wages of combat, never languished in a hospital, never loped through orange groves astride a pinto mare, or kissed a California redhead on the shore of Mockingbird Lake; as if all my recent yesterdays matched those of my youth, in the dark predawn, I take to watering and feeding an assortment of barnyard animals.

Later, side by side, Grant and I fall in with Dad and Bradley Payton, a fifteen-year-old who helps with the morning and evening chores. He looks like his older brother, and his younger brother, and his three older sisters. Their dad is Lehi Payton, a fellow farmer and bishop of the local Mormon community.

The Jerseys feed on hay and an allotment of grain while we hook up the milking machines. After the machines do the bulk of the work, we hand-strip each cow's teats and coax out the last ounces of rich cream before we turn the cows out to pasture. In the milk house, we strain the milk through hospital-clean filters and separate the cream. Then we scrub the floors and clean the buckets and the separator. When we're finished, we wheel the steel cans of milk out to the side of the road where the creamery truck will soon pick them up; all of this before sitting down to Mom's breakfast.

Breakfast consists of hot coffee, bacon, eggs, and flapjacks, but, as in all the breakfasts of my youth, not before a blessing on the food followed by hot cereal under a blanket of cream so thick city slickers would swear it had been whipped.

After breakfast I find time to sit on the front porch. A cock pheasant struts out of the Jensen's pasture across the road. The Jensen's Holsteins water themselves at a trough next to their barn. In front of our house is Mom's garden: pubescent rows of corn, beans, peas, tomatoes and strawberries; hills decorated by infant squash, cantaloupe and cucumbers.

Red-winged blackbirds sit on the fence posts. A magpie picks at the carcass of a bull snake on the dirt road that fronts all the farms in this corner of Ada County. Our John Deere tractor, mud clinging to its cracked tires, sits out front of the shed whose whitewashed sides show signs of weathered failure.

Smells assault my nose: cows, pasture, pigs in their sty, chickens in the yard, and residue from morning's breakfast filtering out of the house from under the front door—all these remind me of my youth. My mind absorbs them, like Mom's thirsty garden loam soaks up Boise River irrigation water in late August.

I can't see the diverted river water running in the ditch that runs parallel to the road, but I can hear it smash into the gate that keeps it off of our fields until it's our turn to irrigate. The water will be almost ankle deep in the pasture then. Water snakes, thick, gray and sluggish will be everywhere. Mom will make Dad or Bradley check the garden before she weeds or gathers the corn and tomatoes. Before college, the job was mine and Grant's. We'd kill ten or fifteen snakes with a hoe. I don't think Mom and Dad knew we carted them in a wheelbarrow over to the pigs. It's true: pigs will eat anything.

A pickup, an old International whose faded red paint has seen better days, passes by. It raises minor clouds of road dirt. In another month the swirling dust will hang in the air and follow a fleeing vehicle down the road until it comes to the highway.

How I loved to ride with Grant down that dusty dirt road until we came to the school, with first through third grades on the ground floor and fourth through sixth on the upper. Dad has since sold the horses. Too bad.

Max, the three-year-old mutt that replaced Mary, the dog of my youth, wanders up to the porch and teases a back scratch with his wagging tail. He lays a beseeching chin on my knee. My mind flits to Shadrach, that other porch, and Sherrill O'Toole. Without her, do I belong here? I reach down and oblige Max.

Grant and Nancy walk past the corner of the house. They proceed down the driveway, holding hands, lost in each other's words. She tosses back her head, laughs, turns loose of his hand, and links her arm around his waist. Her head rests on his shoulder while they walk those last steps to the mailbox. She faces me, but doesn't see my wave as she deposits a letter and turns the flag up.

They walk, hand-in-hand, up the driveway. I feel like an interloper, an uninvited guest, a Peeping Tom almost, to their intimate moment. For the second time in the last few minutes, I think of Sherrill O'Toole. Does longing truly reside in the heart? If so, why the hollowness in the pit of my stomach?

They are closer now; I can hear the words, almost make them out. It's time to blow my cover.

"Well, aren't you the lovebirds?"

They both look at me, surprised. Grant puts an arm around Nancy and draws her into him while they continue to walk. "You should be so lucky." He smiles; Nancy smiles, blushes a little, and diverts her eyes from mine.

I smile back. "Yes, I should be so lucky."

Church on Sunday is no sanctuary for Grant and me, and the sermon and music prove to be anticlimactic. Families of away husbands and sons cling to us, like our safe returns somehow guarantee the well-being of their loved ones, like our presence puts the lie to the newsreels and headlines. All they see is the stripes and bars and the crisp creases. Grant looks proud and confident in his dress uniform, and my Navy whites hide from their eyes the furrowed scars on my back and shoulder.

Of our boyhood chums, only little Tom Edwards is in the congregation. I've always wondered what condition attended him, why he was so frail, so small. I never knew his mom or his dad. He lived in town with an older aunt, and she seemed perfectly normal, size-wise. But Tom, he was frail, sickly, and tiny. He was bright enough, but always a bit shy. Not without cause, given the boys' hazing and the girls' silent disdain. In junior high school, I became his only friend; my singular bit of real Christian charity as a youth.

Now, while his attention borders on hero worship, making me uncomfortable out front of the church, I recall his twelfth birthday party. Just the two of us and his aunt. We ate cake and ice cream and shot tin cans off the back fence with his Daisy air rifle while his aunt cleaned up the kitchen.

Jim Jensen careens across North Africa in one of Patton's tanks, Harold Bascom mans a tail gun in a bomber that flies from England to Germany and back on a regular basis. Bradley Payton's brother, Joe, is probably in a fox hole on some God forsaken island in the Pacific. Kay Kendall, the girl I loved in seventh grade, married Bob Undland, the pharmacist's son. Kay informs Grant and me after church that Bob is in the Navy, stationed out of Pensacola, Florida. Tom Edwards, little Tom Edwards, he lives at home with his old aunt in downtown Boise. Lucky bastard.

After church, while Mom and Nancy work on the afternoon meal, Grant and I string our boyhood bows and wander out in the cow pasture. Separation, my wounds, his wedding—they create an awkward distance between us. We talk about what tomorrow holds, about life in the Navy versus life in the Army. He asks about my wounds, says he thinks they've made me somber and hopes in time I can return to my cheerful, carefree self.

"Grant, that's not going to happen." I notch an arrow. It's a hand-made, lemonwood bow, one of two Grant built in woodshop, but my wounded shoulder cries out its silent rebellion as I pull back and let loose the arrow. We follow the arrow's flight into the afternoon blue, watch it stop its ascent and lie on a brief bed of air before it points down, plummets to the earth, and buries itself in our peaceful pasture.

We walk. "It's more than wounds of the body, more than wounds of the mind. They stole something from me out there, Grant. They stole that carefree sense that for a few years lets boys on manhood's threshold cling to the carefree notion that life, for them, is good and will go on forever. Remember how we used to point our bows straight over our heads? Half the thrill was not knowing for sure if we'd have to dodge a falling shaft lost in the sun. For me, that's not fun anymore. Those Japs at Henderson Field showed me I can't always get out of the way. It's the physical hurt and the mental damage for sure, but what hurts deepest is knowing that all the carefree stuff we did as kids—that youthful innocence—it's lost, and I'll never get that back."

I pull the arrow out of the ground, turn, face Grant, and give him one of those smiles he lamented were too rare. "Some of the changes are good, your Nancy for one, and shooting arrows out in the cow pasture feels like old times."

Grant looses an arrow of his own. We chase it down, sit on the grass, and watch the grazing cattle down by the pond at the far end of the pasture. What a stroke of luck he's here.

Grant gets serious. Tells me how deeply he feels about Nancy, how everything from her bold brown locks to her disarming Alabama drawl intrigues him. "She's not your stereotypical southern girl, you know, at least not a northerner's stereotypical southern girl. I didn't find her running around barefooted. Her dad doesn't spend his days behind a mule on the family's plot of sharecropper's land. He's a lineman for the power company and makes pretty good money. She's never gone hungry that I know of. Above all, she's beautiful, intelligent and caring, has a great sense of humor, and while her brand of Christianity is a little more strident than mine, she's tolerant but not willing to give in on her view of things. I love her to death. Can't wait to have a baby with her."

"Is that some kind of announcement?"

Grant chuckles. "No, no announcement. Not yet. At least we're not trying to."

That candid confession silences both of us. In the distance a B24 flies under a pillow of white clouds that fluffs up the horizon. The irony accosts me. Liberators flying in and out of Mountain Home Army Air Force Base, a thousand miles from war ships in San Diego Bay, and B17s flying over the tops of orange trees. No place escapes this war. Grant breaks my train of thought while we watch the plane.

"Scuttlebutt says we're moving closer to the action. I think there's something to it. Several training cadres have already been given orders for England. We're probably next. It's no secret this war won't end until Hitler is kicked back to Berlin. You don't have to be at the Pentagon to figure it out. With all the buildup in England, we're going to land in France. So far I've had it pretty easy, but who knows what's in store? Maybe more training, but closer to the action, maybe…"

Grant looks at the pasture we sit on, scratches around and pulls out an errant blade of grass. He chews on the end while we, each of us, contemplate private thoughts.

"Anyway, Nancy doesn't need any little Grants until this war is over."

A pang of jealousy strikes me; those words and my words: your Nancy for one.

We walk back towards the house. That's not fair, resenting her. I contemplate telling Grant how serious things are getting with Sherrill O'Toole, but think better of it. I don't want to explain back-to-back rejections if Sherrill follows Elaine's lead and dumps me.

In a quiet moment, I'll tell Mom. She's non-judgmental. She'll say something about how good comes out of everything bad; that finding Sherrill might be the good that comes from losing Elaine and suffering wounds. "Or," she'll say, "maybe not. Maybe the good will come after Sherrill." Her naïveté borders on inane. She has no idea of her son's fragile mental state.

Tomorrow, Grant and Nancy go back to Georgia. I'm happy for him. Me? I've got another week after Grant leaves. Maybe Dad and I can get in some cribbage.

Another week. Another week before duty calls in Papago Springs. I wonder what a prisoner welfare officer is, and why I'm supposed to be brushing up on my German while I'm on leave.

Sherrill. Sherrie O'Toole. I miss her.

I wonder, what's the scuttlebutt?

Part 4

Ich liebe dich, Sherrill O'Toole. Ich liebe dich. Wartezeit für mich.

Sunday, April 23, 1944
The Face of the Enemy

My stay at Papago Springs lasted over three weeks, long enough to come face to face with captured line officers and crewmen, mostly from the Führer's Submarine Service.

These prisoners were bitter and intensely loyal, all of them Vaterlandsfreunds: patriots. Men who looked like me but wished me ill will. Men who sent to the bottom of the sea others who looked like me—like them—all for the love of their Deutschland.

On the surface I was a prisoner welfare officer, a title concocted by Naval Intelligence to provide access to prisoners on a face-to-face basis. The title, totally unofficial, nevertheless held a smidgen of legitimacy. The United States was required by provisions of the 1929 Geneva Convention to deliver information to the International Red Cross on the status of captured enemy combatants. Indirectly, the Navy's facade provided the body and means to accomplish that purpose.

But my primary mission was spelled out in the orders I received when I first arrived at Papago Springs. I was to "interview German prisoners of war in their native language as much as practicable, the purpose thereof to expand your understanding of the German language among native speakers. Secondarily, you will stay alert for pieces of intelligence that may be useful in the war effort. To assist you in determining what may be useful, you will employ the criteria used to censor shipboard mail on your last combat assignment. Finally, you will familiarize yourself with the standards for 'humane treatment' of enemy prisoners of war as defined by the Geneva Conventions, prepare reports and funnel them through the appropriate channels. At no time are any camp personnel, Army, Navy, or civilian, to believe you have any other function than that of prisoner welfare officer. You, however, will not lose sight of your priorities: first, to immerse yourself in the German language, and second, to glean naval intelligence from the prisoners. You will also make yourself available to the local Army duty officer attached to U.S. Postal Censorship at Camp Papago Springs and all other camps you may subsequently visit. At his pleasure and direction, you will provide censorship assistance with prisoners' incoming and outgoing mail, always looking for ways to improve your translation skills and keeping an eye for intelligence that may be useful."

Master Sergeant Travers, a career soldier nursing a bad back, greeted me when I arrived in Arizona. He became my mentor, having preceded me in the rigors of reporting prisoner welfare by six weeks or so. He knew no German, but he understood the military. In his view, Navy or Army, it didn't seem to make much difference when it came to wartime bureaucracy. In retrospect, I'm sure he's right.

His unofficial mentoring proved most helpful. For example, as Travers put it, "gleaning naval intelligence was crap designed to make you feel like you're doing something important. And me? I'm supposed to guarantee prisoner welfare? That's bullshit, too. The only German I know is what I might've picked up here. So, what the few English speaking German officers tell me, that's what I write. That's fine with the Army. With this screwed up back, they had to do something with me.

"Hell," he continued. "It's plain to me you're here to learn German. No Kraut sailor shows up here until the big boys at Naval Intelligence have dined on the main course. All you are is a hound dog nosing around under the table looking for scraps while you soak up the language. You could miss the king of the spies, misspell every word in the Red Cross reports, and still pass written reviews with flying colors so long as you learn to speak German like you was born and raised in Berlin. Why learn German? Your Navy is like my Army – you'll know when they want you to know."

He's one savvy career soldier, that Travers. I made a mental note: be clear to my superiors that Travers was wise to my mission, even though I said nothing to him about it.

By the time I arrived at Papago Springs, Travers was ten days away from moving on. It was right when the influx of Italian and German prisoners of war had started. Total Axis prisoners incarcerated in the United States prior to May 1943 numbered in the low thousands. In May, twenty-two thousand arrived at the intake centers in Maryland and New York. In the ensuing months the number swelled to several hundred thousand. No small task: dealing with enemy prisoners of war when very few of the guards or administrators spoke any Italian or German. No wonder my academically acquired German, better than no German at all, was in demand.

With the British ground successes in Africa and the American campaigns in Tunisia and Algeria, German and Italian prisoners from Rommel's Afrika Corps soon overwhelmed allied capabilities to deal with them in Europe. When I showed up in June of 1943, the several hundred submariners had been outnumbered by ground troops from Africa.

I was useless in terms of dealing with Italians, but, after my first embarrassingly inept beginnings, I soon fell into my role as advocate for the captured warriors of the Third Reich.

The idioms messed me up the most. I could handle 'Aus den Augen, aus dem Sinn'. I was, after all, familiar with 'out of sight, out of mind'. But what on earth do I do with 'den Bock zum Gärtner machen', 'turn the goat into a gardener', or 'Du bist wohl vom wilden Affen gebissen', 'you have been bitten by a wild monkey'? I had neither professor nor friendly German speaking cohort to lean on. I can only imagine how my linguistic stumbles entertained the prisoners after my visits.

By the time I'd finished my sojourn with the captured German military, I had a new view of those jungle-rotted, starving, dirty Asian faces that cut me down in the South

Pacific. I saw now their appearance had nothing to do with their intent. I saw now that blond, blue-eyed, clean shaven boys who looked like me were every bit as serious in their deadly purpose and as capable, if not more so.

Isaacs's words about the Nez Perce who hunted him down came to mind: "It wasn't the Nez Perce did me harm. It was people not getting along did me harm."

And Enrique, that simple, honest fisherman, his words to those sassy adolescents that afternoon at Danny Ishisaka's, defending Lloyd Steiner's German heritage while standing on a Japanese farmer's front lawn: "Lloyd's daddy, he come from Germany. I'm pretty certain Lloyd's got cousins and uncles wearing Nazi uniforms and fighting over there."

Enrique, and the words of that most unlikely sage, my paramour's grandfather, merged with my close association with the enemy at Papago Springs and other camps. They combined in ways that, contrary to the proverb, bred not contempt, but understanding. They refreshed my outlook, overriding my sense of moral certainty.

Today? The enemy? I fear him and respect his ability to deliver his deadly intent. I no longer hate him. Now I contend only with fear; fear based on the sure knowledge of my adversaries' commitment to my destruction coupled with their efficiency at carrying it out. Hate—hate is gone. On the way out it left my mind's door open a little, an invitation for kinder, gentler feelings.

Who was it that said 'absence makes the heart grow fonder'? Surely not Shakespeare. Not Shelley. Some obscure Roman poet I think. Fonder is not the issue. I miss her! Her frequent letters continue to share upbeat happenings in California, but more and more they deal with abstractions of the mind and longings of the heart. Once a month or so, I arm myself with a sack of quarters, nickels and dimes, and feed a pay phone for a ten or fifteen-minute exchange of voices. The distance, the careful choosing of words, the spontaneous silence on the other end of the line; I know it's not just me, it's her, too. Our feelings are made tangible by the absence. The world is at war, and we have found love.

One of Sherrie's letters put yet another perspective on my vision of the enemy. In passing, she told me that Freddie Soliz, the rumored rapist and murderer, was found dead, stuffed in the trunk of his car. Some high school kids skinny dipping at Mockingbird Lake came across the car in about ten feet of water. What kind of war is this, this mayhem in Southern California's Shangri-La?

Who Rosa's killer might be occupies my mind. Is he the one who killed Freddie? A lonely soldier stationed at March Field, maybe? Perhaps a G.I. at Camps Haan or Anza? It didn't make sense for a lonely soldier to kill a guy just to get at his girl. No, this is another kind of war. Whoever did this is a sick son of a bitch. If not a brown-skinned wetback, is it a Martin Holcomb lookalike? I fear for Sherrie's safety. And in my next letter tell her so. Tell her to do no more driving and riding alone at Hacienda Del O'Toole. Tell her I love her.

In the months since Papago Springs, I have visited camps in Utah, Texas, and Oklahoma. By Christmas I was in Clinton, Mississippi, where I watched an experienced intelligence officer question a cadre of senior German officers, a cache of generals and admirals. From there, it was off to the Pentagon.

On the way to Virginia from Mississippi, I stopped by Georgia and visited with Grant and Nancy. Despite Grant's suspicions that he was bound for England, he remains stateside.

I had nothing to share with Grant and Nancy about my future. I didn't learn what it was until I reported for duty at the Pentagon, where until last week I was hidden away in the Navy Department's catacombs learning advanced techniques of interrogation.

Buried in the nuances of the enemy psyche, I was ill prepared for the telegram from Sherrie:

Gramps passed in his sleep last night Stop Please call Stop

The call to Sherrie conveyed my shock and dismay that this great man, a simple soldier with a love for horses, was gone.

Sherrie, beside herself with grief, nevertheless demonstrated great poise, at least until she began to talk about that last time the three of us sat in the backyard of Hacienda Del O'Toole.

"I'm so glad you got to know him," she said.

"And me, Sherrie."

She didn't respond; the line seemed dead.

"Sherrie?"

"I'm here. I don't know what to say. He left so suddenly."

"Sherrie! Listen to me, Sherrie." The line between us again went quiet while I struggled for words to give her succor. "It's like that sometimes, Sherrie. It was that way with the Captain. He was here, saving me, then he was gone. I know it seems that way for you. Except, he lives on. In you and in your cheerful outlook on life. He's not gone, Sherrie." My mind raced ahead of the words. Through the silence I heard her soft sobs. "Sherrie, I'd give anything to be there with you. He loved you." More soft sobs. "Sherrie, I love you. Please don't cry."

And so it went—alternating words and spells of silence and more words until the quarters were gone and there was nothing else to say, until the next day, when I called again, and the day after that, when I did what I could to dispel her grief and buoy my outlook. But the demands of war disallow time for a proper grieving. I have orders.

In tandem with selected Canadian, American, and British intelligence people, I have been attached to Operation Overlord, the invasion of France. In that grand theater, we are to wait offstage, close by the action, in England at first, France when it is safe. Our purpose: debrief captured combatants of interest, line officers mostly, staff officers when they manage to get captured; get to them while they are still stupefied by their prisoner status. The fact that most of them will be army, not navy, is immaterial; I know German.

Before I boarded the train for Chicago, then Montreal, I spent the better part of twenty dollars for one more scratchy call home and to Sherrie. I knew she would be at her parents when I called. She had told me so in our last phone conversation, and I told her to stay by the phone on Saturday evening.

In addition to the popping static, Sherrie's words came at me as if she was talking in an echo chamber, each uttered word overridden by the end of the previous one. Nevertheless, I caught her last words about praying for me and a promise to write often. Did she catch mine as the operator cut in and asked for another five dollars and forty-five cents for three more minutes?

I counted the quarters lying on top of the pay phone's coin box. Shit! I was short. "I love you, Sherrie! Wait for me."

So, here I am, on a Canadian Royal Air Force transport, traveling with my Canadian and American counterparts. In compliance with our orders, we share conversation in the enemy's language.

She'll wait for me; I know she will.

Below me, the snow bound Nova Scotia coast gives way to the black waters of the North Atlantic.

"Ich liebe dich, Sherrill O'Toole. Ich liebe dich. Wartezeit für mich."

Flecks of cloud turn into a solid wall of fog. The plane climbs. We burst into the sunlight and skim over a vast expanse of whipped cream that reaches to the horizon, reaches to England.

"I love you, Sherrill O'Toole. I love you. Wait for me."

Part 5

Here, today, regardless of tomorrow, you're part of the solution.

October, 1945
Return Home

Wait for me. Those were the words in that silent message I sent out across the North Atlantic when I left for the war in Europe some seventeen months ago.

Has she? Waited? The letters that came in bunches to England and then Paris said yes. She said as much when I called from the first pay phone I could reach when the Navy plane touched down in Norfolk, Virginia. Silent intervals hung in the air. They cost me the same quarters and dimes into the coin slot as the words themselves, but the value per ounce of quiet was like gold dust in terms of meaningful communication.

The hush time, when the line noise was created by lightning strikes in Oklahoma maybe, or some bored operator in Memphis tapping in, was when I sensed the longing that gave her words credibility. She loves me. She waits.

The fear then the hate had left me before I left the States, and in Paris I found confidence. I let it and caring fill the void. I love Sherrie, and, since that day in Paris, I've told her so. Not in so many words, but in precisely those words: I love you, Sherrill O'Toole. And she has responded in kind.

Why then uncertainty? It relates to caution, not fear. Distance, time, and working through the war on different continents, they paint the present a different color than the past. They work in tandem to change expectations and distort recollections. I'm concerned our opportunity could become yet another casualty of war, lost before we discover, as Sherrie put it on that last horseback ride to Mockingbird Lake, "something real and lasting between us." And there's the ghost of Elaine's abandonment, when I last gave away my heart's desire and suffered for it.

The war is over and I have a thirty-day furlough, pending a debriefing with Canadian military investigators about a German Navy bigwig I interrogated in England. So, I left northern Virginia and made my way to Philadelphia, Chicago, Toronto, and finally Quebec. Back in Chicago, I turned my back on my parents in Boise, and Grant and Nancy in Georgia, and boarded the Santa Fe Super Chief bound for California.

After my furlough I have four months of some kind of Naval Intelligence thing in the Pentagon before I become a civilian. By then I expect to trade in my Navy hitch for a wedding ring, or know the reasons why not. If all works well for her, for me, for us, I'll go home to Boise with a bride on my arm.

I read somewhere that the only states flatter than Illinois are Delaware and Florida. I find that hard to believe. How much flatter than perfectly flat can a state get? I don't think we varied six inches up or down until we crossed the Mississippi. That corner of Missouri and the plains of Kansas we are presently crossing could, by the lack of altitude change, be Illinois. To deal with the monotony, I dig out my latest journal and review the entries from the last year-and-a-half.

I turn to the beginning, that four months in England spent translating the words of German staff officers incarcerated in some earl's mansion in the English countryside.

Little did our captive colonels, generals, and vice admirals know that every room, every walkway, every veranda bench, tree, and garden fountain was wired for sound. They talked freely, and all the while their words were recorded for translation by the likes of me and my companions. They didn't reveal much about the current situation, but we learned a ton about the Nazi hierarchy, especially Himmler and his infamous SS. All of this will, I'm sure, be put to good use when it comes time to mete out punishment, although I've read that Himmler did himself in rather than face the Nuremberg inquisitors.

Outside my window, the Kansas rank and file, dry cornstalks, brace for winter's onslaught. How different from the green of ordered orange orchards where my heart's desire waits. How different from the rows of crosses I passed at St. Laurent, outside of Normandy, or the forests of trimmed and spiked tree trunks between the coast and Paris, Rommel's asparagus they called them, designed by him to prevent allied gliders from landing airborne warriors behind German lines.

Aside from the switch, cornstalks for crosses and barren poles, what's missing in my Kansas panorama is the shell shocked, ravished landscape we passed through on our way to Paris and the long rows of village buildings, both shops and houses, with their street-front walls all blown away.

Only days, not weeks, had passed since de Gaulle sent Leclerc's French tanks down the Champs-Élysées in a victory parade. I close my journal and let in the memories of my time in Paris.

By the first of September, 1944, I was reassigned and attached to Naval Headquarters in Paris. I spent most of my early days there translating captured German military documents that had been pre-screened and deemed of "naval importance." Other times I helped the local constabulary with the interrogation of captured Germans. Now and then, my experiences with stateside interrogation of prisoners and the translation of conversations between high ranking German officers in England would help me to ferret out an officer hiding in private's garb or civilian clothes. I had them transferred to military detention. Paris was in French hands now; officers so dressed were classified as spies by any interpretation of the 1929 Geneva Convention. I suspect, in French hands, more than a few faced firing squads. I felt no guilt. To the contrary, on those occasions I congratulated myself for a job well done, as did my superiors.

France when it was safe. That's what they told me six months earlier. Safe, I think, is relative. No question, my presence in Paris was safer than what those poor bastards were going through on the front lines. But I arrived in Paris before the clichéd ink was dry on the Kraut's surrender of the city, and German soldiers were still being rounded up. More than a few didn't take kindly to the surrender notion. They were the ones who made life dicey, what with their random sniping and taking pot shots at anyone in a uniform, French or American.

God help the German regular who surrendered to a French citizen; better to turn over his weapon to anyone in a uniform, that is, if he wanted to live. And God help the collaborators when the citizenry corralled them. Their humiliation was total and they often paid with their lives for consorting with the enemy.

The Pullman wobbles and jerks. I shift my gaze from the window and look around inside. A few passengers look up from their books and magazines. A few quit talking. The train slows. Before long we stop. A conductor works his way down the aisle. He tells us we've been pulled over on a siding to let a northbound freighter move through. Somebody gripes about the wait. "I thought this was the Super Chief. I thought the Super Chief didn't wait on anybody."

"War rules are still in effect," the conductor says. "Nobody's bothered to cancel them. Passenger trains make way for war material and trains carrying troops."

Twenty minutes later a mile-long freighter passes by. It's hard to know what is inside the freight cars, but Army Jeeps, halftracks, and light artillery pieces are lashed down on the flat cars. They are not new. I can't help but wonder what unit is being moved and why. Maybe it's a National Guard unit going home. The caboose careens down the track. I watch out my window and replay that comfortable notion in my mind: maybe they are going home. I watch until the back of the caboose is a faintly rocking image disappearing towards Missouri. The train groans, cars take up the slack in their couplings, and a cacophony of clangs moves the length of the train. We begin to move. Before long the Super Chief is up to its former speed. I watch a new battalion of Kansas corn stalks pass in review while my mind returns to Paris.

On one particular day, I was assisting with the interrogation of German sailors captured by the local police. I came onto this assignment quite by accident. I was in the office of Captain Armand Durand when the call came in from the police. He and I had become friends of sorts in the few days I had been in Paris, thanks largely to his ability to speak English. Durand was the French Army liaison with the allied forces in the new military jurisdiction established by de Gaulle in Paris. Since the prisoners were sailors and Durand's German was sketchy at best, he prevailed upon me to follow him down to the station. "It's only a few blocks out of the way back to your headquarters," he said, "and your German skills would be of great assistance."

I learned belatedly the prisoners in German Navy uniforms were actually Frenchmen who'd answered the occupying Germans' recruitment posters. My German was better than theirs, and I wouldn't want to be in their shoes now that the local gendarmes knew they were French, although Durand stayed behind to arrange their transfer to a military prison. At least, that's what he said he was doing.

Before I left the station, a rabble of French citizens moved in force down the street in front of the police station. Their chants were like the baying of wolves on the hunt, the ones I read about as a kid in Jack London's stories, and their purpose was as deadly. They had picked up the track of a traitor and were now intent on running him or her to ground.

By the time I finished with the local gendarmes, the hunt had moved down the street and around the corner. I almost missed Monica. She was hunched down on the floor in the back seat of my Jeep. Of course I didn't know her name was Monica. I wouldn't learn that and all the other stuff, like she was six or seven months pregnant, until later.

I'd already jumped in the front seat when my conscious mind caught up with the subliminal glimpse of a single tuft of her brown hair laying on the outside of the gray coat she had pulled over her head. I wheeled around and looked at her. She lay on her side with her legs drawn up fetal style, but not quite to her chest. Her head, jammed into the base of the back seat, faced the rear of the Jeep. In that cramped posture, she could only guess what I was up to.

I stared in stunned silence. I bore no sympathy for the likes of her. At the time I didn't know her German was a husband rather than a lover. I'm not sure it would have mattered. I wasn't French, but I shared their disdain for anyone who provided aid and comfort to the men who had laid waste to this land. For all I knew, her man was this very minute drawing down on me with a scoped Mauser from a church tower or a vacant apartment.

Behind me I heard the crescendo of the pack as they retraced their route. They would be here in a minute, or less. When they found her, I knew what they would do. Rough hands would haul her to the ground. Someone would produce a knife or a pair of pinking shears and her hair, along with a fair amount of her scalp, would disappear. If she resisted she would be beaten senseless. Either way, she would be put on display, beaten some more, spat upon, or worse, and paraded down the street. Gendarmes would look the other way or help. She'd probably survive, maybe not. Sleeping with the enemy was an unpardonable sin.

I'd seen it before in the last few days: the hairless, bleeding scalp, clothes dripping urine and smeared with excrement, breasts and privates exposed and in some cases bleeding, the taunts and rocks and garbage raining down on them as they rode an endless, shameful gauntlet through the streets. It was about to happen again and I was going to participate.

For me, it wasn't a decision. Although I didn't realize it until later, I was on automatic pilot, my response dictated by my past, my recent mentors, and my options. As the pack rounded the corner and approached my Jeep, their quarry's sanctuary, I stepped on the starter, revved up the engine, and drove away.

For the next hour I drove around Paris in a quandary with this scared, strange woman huddled behind me. What to do? I had to return to my base by 1400 hours, and I couldn't turn in the Jeep with her hiding in the back.

Eventually, I decided to corner Durand. I drove back to the police station and looked for his vehicle, a lend-lease Jeep with French insignias. He was still there. I parked around the corner, admonished my hidden lady in German and English to stay put, and went inside. He was flabbergasted and annoyed that I had gotten myself involved in this thing.

"Where is she now?" he asked.

"Around the corner, hunched down in the back of my Jeep. Anybody who walks by is bound to see her!"

Durand muttered some unintelligible French curse under his breath, looked around to make sure no one was close by, and whispered directions in hurried words. "Go back to her and keep the engine running. Anybody gets too close, drive off and circle back. When you see me go by, follow."

I did as he directed and before long I was tailing him through the streets of Paris.

Eventually, he spirited me and Monica behind the walls of an orphanage where the Sisters took Monica in. They were the ones who learned her story and discovered her pending motherhood.

I never did hear what became of her or her Kraut husband. But that afternoon, with a terrified fugitive huddled on the floor in the back of my Jeep, I rediscovered me, the me who was lost that February in 1943, when I lay on the edge of the tarmac in my own shit while my adversary pinned me to the ground with a bayonet.

I have revisited that afternoon in Paris almost daily since it happened. My actions flew in the face of that conviction I kept repeating in those forlorn days at the hospital in San Diego. How many times had I thought it? I know I said it to anyone who suggested otherwise. On the sidewalk, out in front of the hospital is where I told the chaplain how I felt: "What I've seen lately, doesn't seem to be all that important what you're brought up to be…"

And to Nurse Carol, "…it doesn't matter to me one way or the other if God comes out of the chapel to help."

My mind shifts to that wild ride and Isaac's gentle observation: "Me, I found out bottling stuff up put a miserable slant on the future. Messed me up something awful until Sherrie's Grandma showed me how a little hope and humor makes life joyful." Those words of Isaac's that day on the sulky resonate with the way I've come to feel since I turned my actions over to my intuitions and saved Monica from the mob in Paris.

Isaac, Enrique and Danny Ishisaka, and the unknown Nez Perce warrior who chose to rescue a helpless enemy rather than kill him—they lived out a lifetime of my coaching at home, at school, at church. They guided my foot to that Jeep's starter.

Back in California, Sherrie had talked about moral guideposts, had said that's how we differed, she and I, from Hemingway's Catherine and Frederic. After that afternoon in Paris, I saw she was right. I knew then Sherrie was waiting for hate and blind fear to move over and give me a clear view of my other options. I left hate and most of my fear in the States, but blind fear; I left it on the cobbled street with the vengeful Parisian mob.

After the Monica incident, my letters to Sherrie carried a new confidence about my feelings for her. Like sweeping radar detects the appearance of enemy aircraft, Sherrie's innate ability to read between the lines sensed the change. She responded with tender words of love, of caring, and reiterated promises to wait. That was all I could hope for—all I could ask for.

"God's in the chapel," the Chaplain had said on the sidewalk that day two years ago. "It would be pure shame to let good Christian upbringing go to waste."

Out my window, the sun, a blood red orb, rests on the far lip of a field of wheat stubble. The short brown stalks are reinforcements for the monotony of the last half day's endless army of corn.

I hear the engine's whistle, lean against the window, and look ahead. A lone green GMC pickup waits at the crossing. For some reason it reminds me of Enrique and his stewardship of Danny Ishisaka's farm, and Enrique reminds me of Isaac watching, helpless, while his rescuer prayed somewhere in the heart of the Bitterroot Mountains.

The sun teeters on the brink of the horizon. It's ironic, I think, that three quarters of a century ago Isaac watched that same sun sink behind towering peaks. And now—now he is no more; he has gone to a better place. I wonder, what sun there sets on the horizon?

Thoughts of Isaac bring up Sherrie's letter, the last one before I left Paris. "Mom still hasn't cleaned out Gramps' room," Sherrie wrote. "Sometimes, when I miss him so terribly, I go into his room and lie on his bed. I can sense his presence there—smell the Old Spice residue on his pillow mixed with the clean smell of the Ivory soap he always scrubbed with at the end of a day. Last week, I detected something else: the faint residue of lilacs. It was Mom. Mom has used a little lilac-scented toilet water at the nape of her neck for years. Mom's been doing the same thing I have: communing with Gramps with her face buried into his pillow."

The whistle blows. Kids wave from the back of the pickup as we zoom by.

Beyond the pickup, on the western edge of the world, a wisp of vapor floats across the sinking sun. Is it my imagination that shapes the vapor? The sun slides off the edge of the Kansas plains. The warrior remains, if only in my mind's eye. Isaac's warrior: the one who wears a coyote-skin cape, the one astride his spotted horse, the one who raises his bow in a silent salute. I watch him slide into the last residue of drifting mist; he fades into the twilight.

Soon. Soon we will turn west. West to California—my Shangri La. And my tomorrows.

October 26, 1945
Shangri-La

Once I get off the train, I claim my baggage and walk up Seventh Street until I come to a phone booth outside of Krueger's pharmacy. I call Sherrie's folks. On the thirteenth ring I give up. Strange, even though they didn't know precisely when I was arriving, they knew it was on the twenty-sixth, midday or thereabout, and they knew I'd be calling. I look at the clock inside the pharmacy: a quarter after nine. My watch says seventeen minutes after twelve. I adjust the watch so it matches the pharmacy's West Coast time and wander inside. Breakfast sounds good. I sidle up to the food counter and order the weekday sixty-five cent special: two eggs, bacon, coffee, and toast.

The man behind the counter works hard at destroying my ability to eat breakfast before the eggs get cold; the questions come at me rapid fire.

"Don't get many Navy men around here. You passing through? You see time overseas? Which side? Pacific or Atlantic? You due to get out soon, or are you a career Navy type? Me? I was in the Army. Just caught the end of the big war with the Huns. Never did go overseas. Had me enough duty to know I needed to get back in school. No boys to answer the call when the Japs bombed Pearl. Don't have but two girls. One's married. The other's a senior in high school. You married?"

Finally, this question comes when neither fork nor cup are involved with my mouth.

"No, I'm not married and I have had enough of the Navy. I'm here to visit a gal I met in San Diego. Her parents own an orange ranch not too far out of town."

"The O'Tooles. You must mean Sean O'Toole and Barb."

"Do you know them?"

"Hell yes I know them! Everybody knows Sean and Barb, their daughter, too. And Barb's dad, Isaac. Isaac passed, you know."

I nod.

A customer steps up to the counter next to the cash register. After an exchange of goods, money, and pleasantries, she turns and wanders out the door.

He picks up the conversation as if no interruption had occurred. "I heard Sherrill is home for good. Not that she was ever really gone. She spent the whole war in San Diego. Can you imagine that?"

I take a sip of coffee and stare at the counter.

"Sean said Sherrill's officer is back from Europe. Said he thinks this might be the real thing. You have to be him."

His smile is genuine. I'm starting to like him. He's not much different than the pharmacists, barbers, and small business owners of my youth: a gossip, but one who knows the difference between spiteful backbiting and the spread of cheerful community news.

I put down my fork and extend my hand. "I'm Martin Holcomb."

His hand reaches across the counter. "Karl. Karl Krueger." He steps back, assesses me, and then, as if I didn't know, "I own this place. Sean and I like to hunt doves together, and every month or two he and Barb join up with Sylvia and me—Sylvia's my wife—and we do dinner. Sometimes at their place, sometimes at ours, sometimes at the Mission Inn or out at the country club. You couldn't be tying up with a better family." He looks at me and waits. When I say nothing, he covers his tracks. "That is, if tying up is what you have in mind."

He's playing with me. I take a sip of coffee before I answer.

"Right now, I'm interested in getting out there to see Sherrill and her folks. They aren't answering. I suppose I could wait them out or catch a cab. Is there a taxi service?"

"A taxi service?" Krueger scratches his chin, as if the answer required serious contemplation. "Yes, there's a taxi, but that uniform is a ticket to wherever you want to go. Just stroll out of here and walk on up to Market Street. Turn left and hang your thumb out. Someone will pick you up within minutes. You can count on it; too many around here have their own sons and husbands riding into town on their thumbs. Market becomes Magnolia. You want to get out at Jackson Street. From there it's no more than a two or three mile walk, that is, if someone else doesn't pick you up, and they will. Once you cross Victoria…"

"Once I cross Victoria I know my way." I'm thinking it's probably two miles past Victoria, which means it's closer to four miles once I start up Jackson, which is a lonely country road as I recall. "I think I'll try calling once more before I start hoofing it."

Krueger has disappeared from the counter when I return from my fruitless phone call. I find him over where the pharmaceuticals hang out. He's talking on the phone and writing. He hangs up. "Did you get a hold of them?"

"No. No answer." I hesitate. "You suppose I could leave my bags here and come back for them later? Walking is a whole lot easier when I'm not toting all this stuff."

His answer is quick. "Sure. I'll store them back here with all the medicines. No one is allowed back here but me and the missus. You can pick them up later when you have wheels. I close at seven on weeknights."

The walk up Seventh Street is longer than I thought. It takes me past the Mission Inn that Karl talked about, past the little Golden State Theatre. The bigger, grander Fox Theatre commands the far corner of Seventh and Market. I cross, turn left, step off the curb and hang out my thumb. Not ten minutes pass before a middle-aged couple in a pre-war Nash stops and invites me in. They cart me a couple of miles before they pull over and stop. "Sorry," they say, "we're turning here. Stay on Magnolia. Someone will pick you up." The third car by is a '32 Ford roadster with two high school kids. They give me a ride in the rumble seat to Jackson Street, where I hop out, wave them a thanks, and strike out on foot.

It takes me a while to walk to Victoria Avenue. The wind is picking up. The orange trees shake and tremble, and the tossing fronds that decorate the tops of the palm trees remind me of that night in San Diego, when the rain and wind-whipped eucalyptus trees preceded my discovery of the Captain. What brought that memory, buried these many months? I mull the causes, barely watching for oncoming cars as I cross over Victoria Avenue. Perhaps it was the wind. Perhaps it was walking by the Golden State Theatre. Sherrie said Rosa Lopez worked there. Perhaps her violent fate dredged up that dreadful night when the Captain died.

I focus on Sherrie and tomorrow, our tomorrow, and lean into gusts that grow stronger with each passing moment.

A car approaches and slows down. The driver gives me a careful once over as she passes by. Despite the wind, the sun is warm; I feel the sweat soaking into the back of my shirt and take off my coat. Another car approaches from behind. As it gets nearer it slows down. I give a quick turn of my head as it passes by, hoping I'll recognize the O'Toole's Packard or Sherrie's Plymouth. It's a sheriff's Chevrolet. It pulls over and stops. I make it easy on the driver, there's no doubt he wants to check me out, and stop when I reach his window.

"How you doing?" I say.

A familiar face looks out at me. Its owner is Alfred.

Since I last saw him, I've been around enough veterans of the officers' club to know an always pickled professional drunk when I see one. They know how to hide the signs to all but their drinking peers and a few non-drinking peers, the ones who have to tolerate them because the drunks really are good at what they do, or they are no good at all, but their drinking buddies are, or, more likely, their drinking buddies outrank everyone else. Whatever, I see Alfred for what he is: an accomplished drunk. Like the pro that he is, he puts on an air of friendliness, at least tries to, but the smile that hangs on long after the hello is reminiscent of the wolf's in that story about Little Red Riding Hood.

"If it isn't the sailor. Last I heard you were winning the war single-handed in Europe. You come home to your girl? She's home now you know. She told me so herself, down at the Oasis last week. She's not in the Navy anymore. She's footloose and fancy free. "

Alfred is one of those people who, despite their best efforts, can't help making themselves easy to dislike. I think about correcting him. In the United States Navy, enlisted men are sailors; I am an officer. But then, he knows that. Besides, I'd learned from Sherrie's stories that he's kind of unpredictable, and I really don't want to get in a pissing match with a souse hiding behind a sheriff's badge on a lonely county road. So I take a safer course.

"Yes, she told me about that when I talked with her on the phone before I left Washington."

That little disclosure, while it isn't strictly true, seems to level the table a bit, hopefully without irritating him much. What she really said was she'd seen Alfred in town, and he was as full of himself as always.

I forge on. "Nobody answered the phone when I called, I figured I'd hike on out here and wait. They know I'm coming sometime today. What brings you out this way?"

Alfred looks at me with a disconnected half-smile that tells me his mind is one sentence behind our current conversation. About the time I figure he isn't going to answer, he catches up.

"Not much going on down on Magnolia." He nods towards his seat. "Get in." He nods again. "I'll give you a ride."

I try one lame excuse. "Do the rules allow just anybody to ride in a department vehicle?"

Alfred's reaction is delayed and, as I expected, blasé. "Are you going to tell anyone? I'm not going to tell anyone. I doubt the O'Tooles will tell anyone. Get in."

I walk around to the passenger side and slide into the front seat. After all, it's only a mile or two. Anyway, this wind has really whipped up; probably we're in for one of those infamous Santa Ana blows that comes in off the desert from time to time.

Alfred doesn't say much; he just pushes the Chevy up the road. We get to the fork where the main road becomes dirt and curves left, while the other smaller dirt path bends right and leads to Mockingbird Lake. Alfred reaches down and pulls up a third-full bottle of beer. He tips the bottle up to his lips, takes a hefty swig, and returns it to its nest by the side of his seat. He looks at me. His countenance carries a conspiratorial attitude, as if somehow, now that I had succumbed to his nobody-knows offer of a ride, I was part of the gang, a member of the pack. "Like I said," he says, "what they don't know won't hurt them."

I let slide the fact that he hadn't said anything of the sort. He was drinking a Rainer Ale, only the third bottle of that brand I had seen since I left Idaho. The other two were empty, one down where Sherrie and I had picnicked on the shore of Mockingbird Lake, the other lying in the grass by the canal; in fact, we just passed that very spot, the one where Rosa's body was found, where I saw the black-and-red banded snake that eats rattlers. Back on that spring day, I found the appearance of the snake in an erstwhile Garden of Eden unsettling and the coincidence of the two bottles odd. Now, with the benefit of two years squeezing the truth out between German lies, the Rainer Ale arouses my suspicions.

The idea that Alfred could have something to do with Rosa and Freddie's murders percolates as we drive up the road that leads to Hacienda Del O'Toole.

Alfred turns into the long driveway.

Motive? He didn't like Freddie, that's for sure. But murder? Rape? Doesn't seem to fit. Maybe my recent experiences, along with the fact Alfred is a high order asshole, have led me down the wrong path.

Alfred pulls up in front of the O'Toole's house and parks behind Sherrie's Plymouth. He reaches for his bottle, finds it, and polishes it off.

"There you go, Sport. Don't say I never did anything for you."

Sport. I guess that's his way of letting me know I've been accepted, but only as an underling. Otherwise, if I was an alpha dog, I'd be Buck or Akela. I look at the house and back to Alfred, who is looking at me with a smile designed to accentuate a patron's tolerance of his protégé. I humor him.

"Thanks for the lift, Alfred."

I open the door and step out. The pinto stands out front of the garage. She's looking at us, her ears tilt forward in that familiar pose horses assume when their curiosity is aroused. She is saddled and has been ridden. I can tell by the sheen that sweat has given the black spots on her withers and rump. Her reins hang on the ground. In the far pasture, Abednego leans up against the near fence and watches.

Alfred turns the engine off and gets out of the car. "Hey, that's mighty strange."

"It sure is." I move past the Plymouth towards the pinto.

When the gap between us closes, she turns and starts for the back lawn at a fast walk. At the prospect of green grass, she lowers her head, and begins to graze.

Alfred, like any high functioning drunk, has come out of siesta mode and is on full alert. He works his way between the driveway and the side of the house. The pinto moves off a few feet and resumes grazing. Alfred carefully moves out on the lawn and puts himself between the horse and the orange trees. While I hold my position to cut off her escape down the driveway, he herds her through the open corral gate.

Once the gate is closed and all avenues for freedom are cut off, the pinto allows me to approach her. Talking in soft tones, I place a gentle hand on her neck, reach up with my other hand, grab the reins, and lead her back to the hitching rail in front of the stable. I look for Alfred; he is walking toward the back screen door while he studies the ground. I wrap the reins around the rail and scan the corral and the pasture beyond. When my eyes move to the tack room, I notice the stable straw strewn on the ground. The straw is wet; globs of gooey vermillion cling to it. Some straw pokes out of the dampened earth, pushed there by the heel of a boot. I pick up a few strands. The sticky red stuff is blood not yet fully congealed. The wind carries the straw across the corral when I let it go. I shift my attention to the tack room.

A long, worn handle pokes out from the tack room into the quadrant of daylight that pushes back the dark inside the doorway. Dread, buried all these months, kin to that which attended my discovery of the Captain's crutch lying in the rain, floats up from the pit of my gut and fills my mind. I step into the doorway. The handle belongs to a pitchfork. In the muted light in front of the workbench is Shadrach's body. My eyes take in the punctures where his life's blood has poured out on the floor. Horror takes my breath away. Sherrie! I rush out into the corral.

Ahead of me, Alfred approaches the steps. My eyes, like his, move to the ground, in my case the soft dirt inside the corral, and I see what I had earlier missed: in the dirt, drag marks, boot prints, and flecks of wet, each tinged with dark blood. I break into a run.

Alfred stands on the first step, opens the screen door and pokes his head in. The blast catches my ears almost at the same time Alfred falls back and rolls onto his stomach at the foot of the back steps.

I splay myself on the ground headfirst, like a runner in a frantic attempt to beat the throw to second base, and crawl the remaining distance to Alfred. He lies face down in the dirt, his legs squirming a prone, slow dance with the ground. His left arm claws at the dirt in front of his head. Beneath his right hand, which clutches the side of his face, blood pours out and spreads across the hard, dry dirt in front of the back steps.

Another shot comes from the house. Jesus! I hug the ground.

The car…a radio…a shotgun on the passenger's side…Sherrie's in there!

Again, a shot comes from inside the house. I cringe, hug the ground.

Alfred has a gun!

My fingers slide down to Alfred's waist, grope, unlatch the holster, and retrieve his revolver.

I gather myself, scramble to the house, and flatten against the outside wall. The solid feel of the pistol's grip in my hand gives me a sense of control.

The back porch forms an 'L' off the wall I'm standing against. I scan the back porch and the back corners of the house, the only two ways an assailant can come at me, all the while curling my finger around the trigger. Belatedly, I move my thumb and nudge the gun's safety to off.

Shadrach! The image of his bloody, punctured body, his old eyes dulled by death, heightens my sense of foreboding.

I force myself to wait.

A pesky, brown English sparrow flits across the lawn and lands on the picnic bench, its feathers ruffled by the persistent wind.

Alfred lies still.

Six or eight feet down the wall I'm leaning against there's a window. What if he's there—at the window—waiting to ambush me?

My mind struggles to recall the inside floor plan. The porch opens into the kitchen, the kitchen into the dining room. Past the door between the kitchen and the dining room is the door to Isaac's bedroom. My back, I conclude, is up against the outside of Isaac's bedroom.

I lean against the wall, willing myself to calm down.

Alfred lies on the ground, his right knee soaked with blood. I watch. He doesn't move. Oh Christ, no! He's bled out.

Finding enough calm to sort out clear thoughts proves hopeless. The silence, dead silence, unnerves me. Sherrie's in there! I can't just sneak off to the car and go for help!

Desperation gives way to frustration, then to anger, which moves me to action. I scramble to the corner of the porch where it joins with the wall.

The sparrow is gone; Alfred lies motionless. A deep breath, a futile attempt to control my shaking gun hand, a dash for the screen door, and I yank it open and charge through, past the entrance to the kitchen, into the far corner of the porch.

Bang!

A roar born of fear comes out of my mouth, and I spin and fire blindly at the screen door that slammed shut behind me.

My gun barrel moves towards the opening into the kitchen. I see nothing. Except for my heart, a kettledrum pounding on my inner ear, I hear nothing.

Seconds elapse, five seconds, maybe ten. The beating drum fades, becoming a faint echo. I hear—something. My mind, like the sweeping dial of a radio, searches for the source, tunes out the residual heart-thumping interference. I hear it again – a quiet sniffle followed this time by a discernible sob.

With Alfred's quivering revolver at arm's length, my edgy finger wrapped around the trigger, I crouch and move to face the entry into the kitchen. Beyond the door between the dining room and kitchen, half out of the doorway to Isaac's bedroom, lies a man's body, face-down on the floor. The fingers of his right hand are splayed over the stock of a shotgun.

I cross the kitchen and approach. Two bullet holes in his back and pink froth that has spilled out of his mouth onto the dining room floor make it clear he's dead.

I step in front of the body and confront Isaac's bedroom. Framed in the doorway, sitting on the floor, leaning against the dresser on the far wall, is Sherrie.

Anguish and shock work in tandem with the smeared lipstick, the streaks of mascara, and her bruised and bloodied countenance. They contort her face into something out of Dante's worst nightmare. She stares with one eye bludgeoned shut and the other glaring like a blind man's into nothingness. Dark, venous blood seeps out of a jagged gash above her collarbone and trickles over and around the sides of her exposed breast and onto the torn blouse at her waist. Her bloody bra lies on the floor in front of the bed. Poking out from under the bra is the curved tine of a hay hook; its mate likely hangs on the tack room wall.

In her lap, the fingers of her right hand wrap around the butt of Isaac's 1870 Remington revolver. She looks at me with her good eye and squints through the other. Except for the swollen left side of her face, her features are bone white. Her lower lip quivers, she starts to speak, then stops.

For a frozen moment, I'm paralyzed, then I'm across the floor, kneeling in front of her, afraid to touch her. Not knowing where to start, I lay Alfred's revolver on the floor and place tentative tips of shaking fingers on her undamaged right shoulder.

"Oh, Sherrie! Sherrie…"

She reaches up. "Shush," she whispers, and places her trembling fingers on my lips. Her good eye, a solitary, emerald Cyclops, locks onto my eyes, then looks down and discovers her uncovered breasts. She returns her gaze to me, moves her fingers off my lips and gropes for the tattered remnants of her bloody blouse. She catches a corner, pulls it up, and clutches it at the top of her throat. The muscles at the corners of her mouth relax; the genesis of a smile. She looks down at Isaac's revolver. Tears well up and run down her cheeks. Her split and bloodied lips struggle and quiver before she curls them around words she means to utter.

She lays the revolver on the floor between her stretched out legs. "Gramps said—" Her hand reaches up in shaky slow motion and wipes the pink spittle spilling from the corner of her mouth "—he hadn't shot it in forty years—didn't even know if it would fire."

November 1, 1945
Tomorrows

The stark shock of that day made sleep difficult the first few nights after it happened.

Her attacker was an opportunist, the police are now saying, and, based on their search of his rented house, the man responsible for both Rosa's and Freddie's deaths. What if he had never been hired by the irrigation company? What if he hadn't been patrolling the canal when innocent people crossed his path? My mind works on a litany of additional what-ifs. What if Sean and Barbara hadn't gone to San Bernardino to shop? What if Sherrie hadn't decided on an early morning ride before I arrived on the train? What if Alfred hadn't shown up and given me a ride? What if Barbara had put away Isaac's revolver after he died? And, what if? What if that seventy-year old pistol had refused to fire when Sherrie pulled the trigger?

I let loose of these useless questions, peel them away and discard them as if they were thick rinds on navel oranges hanging from Sean's trees. What's left are realities. I am sustained by the good fortune that snatched my darling from the evil that would destroy her. Alfred did give me a ride, and in doing so, at the cost of his life, saved Sherrie's. Most important, Sherrie will, the doctors say, suffer no long-term physical damage. What remains to be known is whether her spirit, while bent, will refuse to break.

In the last seventy-two hours, in the face of the rush to the hospital, the police investigations, and sharing with Sherrie's parents our disbelief of these events, Sean and Barbara have insisted that the nurses allow me into Sherrie's room. When I'm with her, just the two of us or together with her parents, she either sleeps or lets salty rivulets slide off her cheeks while she holds my hand or one of her parents'. When one of us tries to talk, she shushes us. "It's going to be okay," she says, and forces a smile from her fearful visage.

Her stamina. Her courage. I see them for what they are: conduits that lead to her soul, the wellspring where her charm, her grace, her quiet confidence reside. Oh! How I love her!

My regret revolves around Alfred. I'm bothered by my suspicions raised by his character, or lack of it, and his liking for Rainer Ale. I can't help wondering if, in the midst of gun shots and scrambling for cover, I could have stemmed the flow of his life's blood into the hard dirt? I forgive myself for not knowing that Sherrie, not her attacker, had fired those last two shots and killed Alfred's assassin.

The final irony for Alfred: he had faced that same shotgun earlier, when Isaac shooed him off by shooting a hole in the bottom of the back screen door. In both incidents Alfred was buzzed. In the former, the man holding the gun only intended to sober Alfred up. In the latter, had Alfred been sober and thinking clearly, might he have hesitated before he opened the screen door? The answer, like the question, is moot. He did open the door and he took the full force of that twenty-gauge, the one Sean kept on the porch during bird season, full in the throat. Now, the community has labeled him a hero.

Sherrie lives because Alfred distracted the sick bastard who speared Shadrach with a pitchfork and hooked Sherrie out at the stable before he dragged her into the house. Without Alfred's distraction, Sherrie no doubt would have shared Rosa's fate, and I may have suffered Freddie's. I'll say nothing to muddy Alfred's hero image. I'll be going to his funeral day after tomorrow, and I'll be wearing my dress whites.

When visiting hours are over, Barbara, Sean, and I talk in the quiet of the kitchen while we sip Barbara's cure for sleepless nights: Hershey's cocoa, sugar, and vanilla whipped into hot milk.

"Maybe it would be better if she stayed at your brother's house until the memories have a chance to glaze over," Barbara says to Sean.

I look at her, at Sean, and all at once I feel like an outsider. Sean sips his chocolate, and studies the table while the tips of his fingers caress the sides of his mug. Nervous, I sip my own chocolate and wait.

Long seconds tick by. Sean looks at me.

"You've got a say in this," he says. "What's your take?"

I'm dumbfounded and unsure of how to decipher Sean's words and Barbara's obvious concurrence, as evidenced by the way she now waits with him on my response.

I stare, first at Sean, then at Barbara. She shares with Sherrie the quiet expectation of good things to come. I find myself musing about how that facial trait becomes both of them.

"Martin," Barbara says, "Sherrie has her own mind, but she has shared with us some of how she feels, and…some of how you say you feel." She reaches out and touches my wrist. "Right now, you're the center of her life."

"Barb's right," Sean says, "and you're part of what happened. Nothing's going to change that. Here, today, regardless of tomorrow, you're part of the solution. So, what's your take on what's best for her when she comes home?"

My answer comes only after I mentally acknowledge my inclusion in the O'Toole circle. "I suggest we put it to her."

Barbara nods. Sean angles his head to the ceiling while he contemplates. After a second or two, he drums his fingers on the table. "Works for me," he says. "She's not bashful about making her wishes known, and I'm sure in this case, she'll not be making an exception. Now—"

"Now, I'd like to say something." I did my best to couch my interruption in a friendly demeanor, but the interruption alone was enough to put an edge on the atmosphere. Had I been too abrupt to set a stage for gratitude? I hope not, and I choose my next words with an eye towards taking the charge out of the room's milieu.

"Not only Sherrie, but both of you and Isaac, you've all played a huge part in bringing me back from the damage I suffered at Henderson Field. What happened to Sherrie…" *Her fate: so close to mine.* "I didn't come here to say hi. I came because on top of being a raving beauty, she's the most sensible person I've ever met. Now, because of what's happened, I know she's also the bravest. Most of all, I came because I love her."

The two of them look at me in silence. Their silence, however brief, unnerves me, compelling me to fill the void with more words.

"I didn't mean to be so wordy."

"Oh, no," Barbara says. "We knew how you felt."

Sean joins in. "It seems to me you only answered what was asked. Anyway, you and Sherrie will have to work all that out. What's important is that Sherrie bounces back from what she's been through. None of us will feel right until this is behind us."

I can only nod.

* * * *

Sherrie is home. The doctors filled her full of anti-tetanus stuff and sulfa drugs. When she woke from the surgery, they made sure she wasn't suffering from a detached retina, and confirmed the damage to her face was no worse than a wannabe fighter might suffer after four or five rounds with Joe Louis. Then they released her.

I've extended my stay and will be hard pressed to make it home to Idaho before my leave is up. I'm staying in that same guest bedroom I used before I went to Europe. The last two days, Sherrie and I have taken short walks, sat at the backyard picnic table, the kitchen table, or the two-person veranda swing

Sean installed on the front porch while I was away. We don't say much, and what we do say is spaced between quiet periods spawned by Sherrie's vacant stare or my inability to find any neutral ground to talk about. Sherrie holds on to me, my hand or my arm. If I detach myself for even a second, to light a cigarette, to open the pasture gate or the back screen door, she latches hold of me before I take more than two steps.

On occasion she lets out a giant sigh designed, I'm sure, to calm the anxiety bouncing around in her insides. The sighs come once or twice sitting at the backyard picnic table, the one where the sparrow preened while Alfred bled to death scant feet away. They came once when we walked out through the corral and the pasture to the apricot trees, and again when we returned and sat on the front porch swing.

I don't know if the pools in the corners of her eyes are caused by the hurt from her wounds or the recollections of violence. For me, flat on my back in the hospital in San Diego, it was both.

She sits close to me. I can feel her thigh touch mine. I reach my arm around her and she rests the back of her head against me. We sit, quietly, together but apart, each of us caught up in our private thoughts.

There on the porch, I risk our future.

"Do you remember when first we sat here? It was a weekend." I let those words soak in, hoping the pleasant memory will ease the current angst. "My first visit to your home. You went to church and left me here to go on that wild ride with your gramps and Abednego."

Sherrie moves her head back and forth, making a nest where my collarbone meets my shoulder, wincing when her bruised face touches me, and lays her hand on my thigh.

"Afterward, when we had eaten your mom's fried chicken, we came out and sat in chairs. The swing wasn't here. Do you remember?"

I stop talking to give her a chance to acknowledge my words. She just stares out across the lawn to the orange trees, so I forge ahead.

"I remember you told me that my pain and hurt would go away in time, like it did for your gramps. The next thing I knew you were standing behind me. You bent down, slid your hands around me, hugged and kissed me, twice on the cheek. I remember how I felt. Like maybe I was wrong—taking on this broken world by myself. You gave me hope—let me see for the first time since Guadalcanal that maybe I didn't have to stand alone, like the Captain, until I surrendered to the mind's tormentors.

"I suppose I never told you, but while I was eavesdropping on those German generals in England, I read Hemingway's *A Farewell to Arms*. I thought it might help me appreciate your vision of a tomorrow that might feature us. He was sure mixed up, Lieutenant Henry. He couldn't separate the random events of an amoral world—malaria and syphilis striking one of his soldier buddies—from acts conceived and nurtured in depraved men's minds—the war and the mayhem it caused. At one point, desperate because Catherine was dying, he prayed. Desperation, that's all his praying was. In Henry's eyes, God's reality was moot, since He obviously didn't give a damn. I can relate to that notion. I even felt that way myself once."

I pull Sherrie closer to me. I can feel her breath on my neck.

"Loneliness, it seems to me, stems from bitterness, and bitterness resides in the why. Why did He put us in a place where so much pain and misery comes our way? I haven't figured that out. I do know this – however appealing the image of wolves lying down with lambs, it's not to be in this world. Random pain occurs—evil exists. I've experienced both at a personal level, and now—and I guess that's why I'm talking about it—so have you."

When I stop talking, she looks at me. Says nothing. Waits until I decide to continue.

"At UI, maybe while you were studying Hemingway at USC, I read about Edmund Burke, an eighteenth-century English statesman. What he said about evil goes to the heart of what you and I have been through. Maybe Henry should have read Burke. He might have seen things differently. I have thought about Burke and his words a lot in the past few months. I don't remember the exact words, but they were something like: evil triumphs when good men do nothing."

I pull her even closer.

A gentle zephyr curls around the side of the house and anoints us with an essence of orange borne on a hint of desert chaparral from beyond the pass that leads to Palm Desert and Indio. Sherrie reaches across my lap, lifts my hand, bends her head, and brushes her split, scabbed lips across the tops of my fingers. Her simple act sucks the air out of my lungs and brings tears to my eyes. She is listening! An eon or two passes before I can breathe; before I can talk. When the words come, my eyes continue their communion with the landscape stretching out from the porch where we sit.

"Can I tell you something? Coming out here, crossing the plains in Kansas, I saw Issac's warrior. You know, the one he saw in the Bitterroots? Isaac thought it was pain induced hallucination, until that old Indian told Isaac about the warrior who saved him. Remember that? And while the warrior prayed and Isaac lay on the ground all busted up, the warrior-father appeared in a vision to the warrior-son, and Isaac saw him too. I saw that warrior, the father, there on the Kansas plains, sitting astride his spotted pony like Isaac told us that afternoon in the backyard. I remember Isaac saying those Nez Perce were sent to Kansas and Oklahoma. I want to believe the warrior I saw came from the recollection married with my imagination and the sun's rays sliding through the clouds at sunset. Then all of this happens, and what saves you is Isaac's revolver, the one taken off a dead Nez Perce in Montana in another century. The same Nez Perce, it turns out, who shared a vision of his father with Isaac. It's all connected somehow."

We sit, together, in silence, on the porch.

"Seeing that warrior makes me uncomfortable, just like it did Isaac. It flies in the face of our Christian upbringing, but Indian visions are a lot less unchristian, it seems to me, than what you have been through, a lot less unchristian than men waging war instead of peace. Isaac said God showed himself to men in ways they could understand. Maybe I didn't understand. Maybe He figured that warrior on his spotted horse might speed things up for me so I could be here, whole, for you. Maybe that's why He, God, put that wisp of warrior on the Kansas horizon. Crazy, huh?"

Sherrie wipes away tears with the tips of her fingers and pushes her head back into my shoulder. Before things get out of hand, I keep talking.

"I may only be twenty-five, but I've grown. Being cut down in one's prime does that to a fellow."

A rush of adrenaline forces my mind to race ahead in pursuit of my accelerating heartbeat. I inhale, hoping for enough air to let me utter the words, the ones I'd rehearsed in my head a thousand times in the last few days.

"Love, my love for you is like sunlight—invisible. And they work together. While one peels away layers of dark nights, the other sheds despair. Together they hold the promise of bright tomorrows. Do you know…?"

My pounding heart overloads my brain. In this unplanned interim, what was to be a question becomes a declaration.

"I need you. If you will have me I'm going to make you my wife, and we will walk hand in hand in the face of whatever the natural world or Man's design delivers. If that's not your desire, your heart's desire, then I'll drift. Not a pleasant prospect, but one I will survive, something I wasn't sure of after Guadalcanal, before you."

She stares at the orange trees beyond the rose garden, beyond the lawn. I have no idea what emotions are working inside her. I thought I knew before I started down this path, but now I can't tell.

Her head, nestled into my shoulder like it is, has put my arm to sleep. I want desperately to take my arm from around her long enough to restore blood flow and let the tingling go away, but I wait. My imagination dredges up worst case scenarios.

She looks at me. "Martin…my dearest Martin." Tears and that perpetual hint of a smile—they overcome the garish remnants of her battering. "I love you so." She takes my free hand, the one resting on my knee, raises it, and brushes the top of my fingers with her bruised lips. "I'm going to mend while you go home and visit your mom and your dad. Tell them the news—" She kisses the palm of my hand and presses it lightly against her cheek "—that we are to marry. Then go finish your Navy thing. When you return to me, hand in hand, just as you said, together, we'll face our tomorrows."

EPILOGUE
October 6, 2006

When Megan's mom came bouncing into the house with an armload of groceries, Megan put the box of journals and the case into the bedroom and forced herself away from the urge to lie on the bed and finish reading.

After dinner, after helping to clear the supper dishes, after a quiet walk out among the orange trees with her dad, after her parents had gone to bed, she retrieved her cache from the bedroom, fetched a bottle of chilled Riesling from the refrigerator, and moved onto the living room couch. She poured a glass of wine and wrapped herself around her grandfather's compelling story.

Hours later she turned the last page, closed the journal, leaned back on the soft twill of the family couch, and contemplated the ending. Not an ending really, but a beginning to another story, one that Megan didn't need to read, one that had gone on for half a century or more, one she had helped live over the last twenty-six years. Megan looked at the pendulum clock hanging on the wall.

My gosh, she thought, *it's tomorrow already!*

She took another sip of wine, leaned back and let it slide down her throat while she reflected on her discoveries of the last few hours. She knew she'd have to read all this again and take notes, perhaps even use a highlighter. Almost before she finished the highlighter notion, she modified it. She decided to copy the journals and highlight the copies, instead. Belatedly, she noticed the Riesling had long since lost its chill.

No matter, I'm tired.

She drained the wine and set the glass on the edge of the end table next to the couch. She looked at the case, and realized she wasn't ready for sleep just yet. Her grandfather knew this family epic would intrigue her. And according to his lawyer, the story was not complete without the contents of the mystery case.

Megan fumbled around in her purse until she found the envelope George Thomas had given her. Inside was the combination. She fished it out and opened the case.

She struggled to recognize the scent that floated off the blue felt cloth that hid from her view the case's contents. It wasn't unpleasant, nor was it unfamiliar; she just couldn't connect it to any recent item or event. Her mind registered the source of the aroma as soon as her fingers touched the cloth: oil, machine oil, the kind her dad used to touch up Mom's sewing machine or his shotgun. The cloth wasn't soaked in it, but carried just enough in the fibers to emit an essence reminiscent of earlier times.

Gently she laid back the first fold in the cloth. Lying in a field of blue were five cartridges, two of them empty, three with lead bullets poking out of the casings. On one of the spent cartridges, a tinge of green oxidation clung to the ridge where the lip on the rim of the cartridge met the casing. The sheen on all of them was dulled by time's residue.

She tried to pick up all five cartridges, but found her hand was too small, so she settled for the two empty ones in her left hand and the three live rounds in her right. She sensed the difference in weights, and let her mind speculate on what damage those two thumb-sized bullets must have done, and what her grandmother and then her grandfather must have faced when her assailant lay dead on the floor.

She saw the cartridges and what she knew lay beneath the remaining fold of cloth as more than the talisman she'd wondered about in her girlhood, the one that would have melded her grandparents' dreams into a common destiny. They were that, and they were a stamp of authenticity, a signature to three generations of Americana portrayed on the pages of the journals bequeathed to her by her grandfather.

She laid back a corner of the cloth and beheld the handle with its diagonal gash. The gash was even darker than the handle's seasoned walnut-brown hue. Maybe the oil had seeped into the scratch when her grandfather wiped it down with the oily cloth he used on the metal parts.

How had the scratch gotten there? Had the Nez Perce scratched it struggling with his people's enemies? Or had it happened that day in the bedroom at Hacienda Del O'Toole? Or?

Perhaps I'll figure that out as I complete the story.

Megan pulled back the rest of the blue felt cloth, and cast her eyes upon Isaac's gun.

About The Author

After retiring from dual careers in business and education, Dan Strawn now lives in Vancouver, Washington, with his wife, Sandi.

His work has appeared in various editions of Idaho Magazine and in Trail Blazer Magazine. His essay about Moscow, Idaho, was a finalist entry in the University of Oregon's 2005, Northwest Perspectives Essay Contest. His essay, *About Being Out of Date*, is included in Clark Community College's soon to be released *Elderberry Wine*, a compilation of student writings.

Lame Bird's Legacy, his originally self-published novel about the 1877 Nez Perce War, was favorably reviewed in the December, 2008 issue of Idaho Magazine. The book has now been edited and will be re-released.

His second novel, *Isaac's Gun – An American Tale*, relates an intriguing tale of healing, romance, and murder that bounces between war in late 1877 Idaho and World War II in California.

The Return of Black Wolf, his current work in progress, deals with the shared fate of Nez Perce Indians and wolves in eastern Oregon. The story moves from pre-history to modern times and carries strong, yet even-handed, spiritual and ethical components.

His 2009 book, *A Body of Work*, was intended primarily as a memoir for his family, but he has been pleasantly surprised at the unsolicited copies that have sold on Amazon and Barnes & Noble.

Strawn works with the Nez Perce National Historic Park as an interpreter of the Nez Perce experience at Park sites and at both elementary and high schools.

On occasion he teaches for the mature learning division of Clark Community College in Vancouver, Washington.

CPSIA information can be obtained at www.ICGtesting.com
Printed in the USA
BVOW040926220911

271839BV00001B/1/P